Nightwolves On The Prowl

By

Clarrissa Lee Moon

World Castle Publishing
http://www.worldcastlepublishing.com

Book Two of Memoirs of the Nightwolves Series

World Castle Publishing
Pensacola, FL
Copyright © 2011 by Clarrissa Lee Moon
ISBN: 9781937085117
Second Edition Smashwords January 2011
Third Edition: World Castle Publishing June 1, 2011
http://www.worldcastlepublishing.com

Cover Artist: Fantasia Frog Designs
Editor: Lea Ellen Borg
Printed in USA

Note from the author

I realize that the names of the dark Gods in this book, and in future books, are completely fictitious, yet I used the correct names for the Gods and Goddesses of the Light. Orochi is actually a Japanese demon, not a dark God, so using his name won't matter. Those who are in the know, will know why it is so. For those that don't, read the books on Magick and you'll understand why.

I used the spelling for Magick with a 'k' to differentiate the magic (no 'k') being used by magicians and stage artists, from those who actually practice real magick (and run with WILL on the astral planes). Though there are some stage magicians whom I wonder if they should have the 'k' included, or not. Some are just that good, to be hiding in plain sight. However, like them, this book was made to entertain you and I hope you enjoy all of my new exciting worlds and travel with me often as more are created.

I'd like to thank my boys, Jerimiah, Cody and Cameron for letting me use the computer for hours on end. I want to thank Jerimiah, personally, for being the one who came up with most of the chapter title names. I want to personally thank Cody for keeping me fed when I would forget. And, I want to thank Cameron, for reading all of my stories and giving me feedback and ideas when I would write myself into a corner. Having the three of you as my sons has been a blessing and a pleasure. Thanks also, to Laurie and Kenny for getting me the research I needed for more authenticity in my stories. And finally to Liz, who busted butt in editing my books! Good work guys. Keep on astral running. Ride hard, ride free!

I'd like to thank my favorite Rock band, Nickleback, and my favorite Heavy Metal rock band, Godsmack, for rocking me through my writing. Keep rocking! Also, a thanks to my two favorite Rap bands, ICP and Twiztid. The love scenes were inspired by a CD mix I made with my various favorite "Mood" music. Oh, yeah, it worked. HA!

(The Typos Below are Deliberate)

Just one More note: i have Three very special people i hope read the whole series. You know who you all are. if you do, hey, i am here, still Alive, bring me in from The cold. Sushi and Margaritas until the End Of time On our own island in Nature's paradise.

Table of Contents

Clarrissa Lee Moon

Nightwolves on the Prowl

by Clarrissa Lee Moon

Catrina's Prologue

Finding your soulmate is a great gift. No gift of the Gods, however, comes without a price and when you are a child of the Gods, the price can be even steeper. In order for my mates and I to find each other, we had to stay celibate. The Gods also tacked on a save the world quest.

Thanks to a prophecy that is told in many of today's religions, by the end of 2012, four and a half billion people or more could die. Great plagues, famine and wars will take their toll. "The end of days", which is really not the end of mankind as most people think, but a change of life as we know it.

The reason for this is twofold: one scientific and one metaphysical. The scientific side is this: A major shift in the Earth's gravitational pull has been happening slowly for the past ten or so years. Surprisingly, not a lot of people know this, but it is a scientific fact. December 21, 2012 will see the full end of the "Shift" in the polarity of Earth. Even its' axis will be tilted more than it is now. Minor Shifts have happened, to some degree, every 5,000 years or so. Some shorter and some longer time spanned between the shifts. With these shifts, depending on the severity, they can cause earthquakes, tsunamis, flooding, Earth temperature changes and many other weather deviations. Some believe that in 2012, we will see a shift on a magnitude that hasn't been seen in thousands of years. At one time, our Earth's surface was one solid piece of land. Then, after the first 'Great Shift', the tectonic plates moved so far, that many smaller continents were made. The Ice Age happened and the Neanderthals perished.

For the metaphysical side: Myths and legends record that during this time, all the magickal races (dragons, vampires, werewolves and the like), were sent to other various dimensions through portals and astral doorways, which can only be opened or closed during a major polarity shift. Hence, the reason they are myths and legends in today's cultural histories. This was done to protect man from races that were stronger, faster, smarter and much more lethal in magickal uses than man, who had no way of protecting themselves against them. Man, too, eventually would have been wiped out, as the Neanderthals were. The Gods and Goddesses decided to separate the pure magickal races and let ingenuity and science rule man for a time. Not all magick was lost to Earth, but the greater magicks and the beings that can wield it were removed. Science has ruled heavily, but with science, too, there is a price. Pollution, skepticism, and a disregard for nature and natural cycles, as well as the imbalance of feminine and male roles in most cultures and newer religions got the attention of The Gods once again. Now, They want the door opened, to hopefully bring back balance between the female and male aspects, as well as a healthy respect for the Earth and The Gods themselves. Therefore, a great change is coming and most are completely unaware. And, with great change, always comes a great price.

The Gods and Goddesses of many of the older religious pantheons of Earth got together and decided to have children that would be mated to other pantheons, to combine and amplify power like in the days of old on Earth. The merging of two powerful houses' of Lords in marriage would have influence over a more vast area. By putting us in human physical bodies that were birthed by human women, it gave Them a channel of power here on Earth for a more effective use - to help bring down the death toll, ease those left through the new changes here on Earth and to protect them from the more aggressive magickal races that are coming back. I am one of those children; the first born daughter of the Triple Goddess and Her Consort, from an ancient Celtic pantheon. There are six of us - three daughters and three sons, all placed into separate physical mothers at conception. Only my youngest brother and I share the same physical father - a High Dark Adept, who also happens to be a Mafia Don. Lucky us. Searching for my soulmates, using astral magicks, opened a whole can of worms on my astral spiritual heritage; more than I was ready for, in many ways. It could be part of the reason why it took fifteen long years to find my mates on the physical plane.

The prequel to this story (which may be written sometime in the future) and book one, will tell the tale of how I had learned to use my powers and astral project out of my body. Using this method of astral projection for finding my soulmates, I met Antonio, one of my mates, briefly, for about three seconds. I tried again sometime later and made it to Demitri's mansion, Antonio's eldest brother. Their middle brother, Andre, had felt me coming; curious, he followed me home using the same technique. I fell in love with all three of them and when made to decide which one, I said all or nothing. They chose all. We found out later, that's the way it was supposed to be and made peace with it. I had also met my brothers and sisters (who had different physical parents then me), but we have the same spiritual Mother and Father. During this time, my evil physical father, a High Dark Adept, tried many times to keep us apart and even tried to kill me a few times. Then, another new enemy joined the fray. The outcome was me being cursed and my powers brought down to minimum levels. Many of my psychic powers were blocked and without those powers, I could not find the physical location of my mates (though we now lived in the same town). We had gotten that far, before I was cursed. Even blocked, I would not stand down, and many magickal battles ensued, leading up to a battle with the dark God Orochi. We won, and that lifted my curse; but, lost because we died. The Goddess brought us back and "Blessed" us by modifying our physical bodies. I, then finally got to meet my mates. They brought my brothers and sisters to their home and I got to meet them physically as well. We were then wed by my youngest brother, Gerard. Unfortunately, fifteen years of darkness had left its' toll on me and I froze on my wedding night. This story is what happened after that. And I thought the hard part was over...sh'yeah.

These memoirs I have written, were not only written by me, but by the other Nightwolves. I think of them as the true heroes of this tale, months before The Great Shift happened. I can't really claim to be a hero, since I was born and made for this job. To me, a real hero is one who chooses the path of great danger even though they may be the most ordinary of us all. It takes great courage to face the Great Shift with no extra tricks up ones sleeve, so I had them write their own memories from their view point and I put them together within this story, here and there, as best I could. This story is for them, as it should be, for the truly great heroes of our time.

Chapter One

Spell of Seduction

Japan was as exotic and interesting as I had always dreamed it would be. The best part of visiting this country was that I didn't have to pay for it. Even though I was mated to three of the richest, handsomest men a girl could hope for, my time as a runaway at age twelve, then as a single parent of three boys, had made me overly aware of expenses. Throwing money out for exotic vacations would try my budgeting phobia to the end of its endurance. I wouldn't have been able to do it.

It was a good thing this wasn't really a vacation either, but a mission General Pierce had hired me and my mates for; to go with his Special Forces team and a squad of marines.

My mates, family and I, are a Magickal Mercenary team that work for General Pierce, who runs a black op Special Forces operation out of Truax Field, otherwise known as Navy Air Station in Corpus Christi, Texas.

General Pierce had noticed a lot of strange things going on, during what were supposed to be normal, run of the mill operations. He had told his friend and head of a Special Forces team, Captain Vincent O'Hara, to keep an eye open for anything unusual. Captain O'Hara did, and found me 'helping out' during an attempted hijacking of an American plane. Once O'Hara had concluded that I wasn't a terrorist and was one of the good guys (albeit, I was different from the norm), he called General Pierce and told him what he knew about me. General Pierce then came out to see me and we struck a deal to merge my team of unique 'people' with his Special Forces team.

Once General Pierce hired us, we clued him in on why things have gotten 'weird' out in the field. The closer December 21, 2012 came, the more earthquakes and other weather deviations would happen on Earth because of a drastic polarity shift. Those who knew what was going on, called this 'The Great Shift'. What most didn't know, was that portals from other dimensions were also opening up, mostly when an earthquake happened. Through these portals came the Greater Magickal Races that had been pushed out of our plane of existence by the Gods and Goddesses during the last "Great Shift", so humans could then inhabit the Earth in safety; letting their ingenuity and science rule them, instead of being enslaved and used for a happy meal. The Greater Magickal Races had become too much of a threat to the continuance of man and had been deported, so to speak. That could explain why humans had such a fear of anything out of the ordinary and burned it at the stake throughout history.

Once we convinced General Pierce and Captain O'Hara of the some of the extraordinary events happening, they allowed us to do our job of trying to fulfill our reason for being born on this Earth's plane: to try to make treaties with the Greater Magickal Races if we could, to help bring down the death toll from the natural disasters happening, and to protect mankind from the more aggressive Greater Magickal Races that didn't want to play nice and would try to rule the world that they had been deported from so long ago.

General Pierce's team would take on the mundane problems of terrorist and the like. These days, we were finding out that the two jobs were heavily interconnected most times.

The mission to Japan was a scouting operation of an area where an earthquake had happened a few weeks ago. With the equipment one of my mates, Antonio, and a Special Forces soldier, Wizard, had put together, we found an open portal from one dimension to our Earth plane in Japan. We had put this particular mission on the back burner, since we had five other high magnitude earthquakes happen within a six week period. Those portals that had opened caused reports of deaths that didn't look quite right for deaths from an earthquake disaster. Each of the Greater Magickal Races we had so far encountered during those missions hadn't been open about a treaty with the humans. We then had to get strongly physical with these races, sending their scouts back through the portal, sometimes in pieces, and close the door from their world to ours. This was a temporary solution due to the fact these portals were only opening early; once the Great Shift was completed, those portals would open again simultaneously. We were hoping when this happened, we would be able to either come to a more satisfactory conclusion or a deadly permanent one.

We had received no reports of unexplained deaths from Japan's portal, nor was there any great damage to Japan, even though they had a record-sized earthquake. They had gotten lucky. My mates and I got picked for this mission, along with O'Hara's team and a squad led by Sergeant Pearson. He was not one of my favorite Squad leaders, because he had a wild hair up his ass about us being 'evil', due to him having had a strong Christian religious upbringing. He didn't think we should be making treaties with any of these races, nor should General Pierce have anything to do with 'our kind'. If burning witches and vamps at the stake was in vogue again, he would be quite the happy camper. I happened to be both of those, due to The Goddess 'Blessing' me and my mates, turning us into super vamps, 2.0 style. Luckily for us, Sergeant Pearson's attitude wasn't the norm for most of the Alpha 53rd Recon of Marines attached to the General's black op. Most of them liked us and thought of us as family after going through so many missions with us. Only a few bad apples were in the platoon and lucky me drew one for this trip to Japan. I wasn't going to let him spoil this for me. Japan was beautiful with its cherry blossom trees and old world Japanese style architect. Personal space didn't mean much to these people, but I had learned to slide my way around the masses of people in the streets of Hyuga, Japan.

I was watching the rickshaws and traffic go by, while Antonio held the small version of the device he and Wizard had put together to detect an open portal. I didn't mind playing tourist while they did the hard work, but I was still conscience of watching our backs for anything unusual. We were all wearing our 'street clothes' not wanting to alert the local Japanese authorities of our military presence here. Though, true, my mates and I weren't military, per se, but mercenaries after a fashion. We still had to keep a low profile if at all possible. O'Hara was walking ahead of me, scanning from left to right. I would bet money he was actually looking for suspicious things or people, while I was doing the touristy looky-loo and looking for anything out of the ordinary.

O'Hara, at 6'3 and 225 lbs of pure muscle, was otherwise known as The Rock and was used to the exotic sights. His call sign, The Rock, wasn't because he was a mean war machine, but because of this eyebrow thing he does. He had brown hair in the traditional buzz cut and light brown eyes to pull it off. He has been the leader of this particular Special Forces squad for over five years which was considered *the* top Special Forces team today.

O'Hara may be used to waking up in a new country every day, but going around the world doing 'mission impossibles' and seeing exotic things was still new to me; so I soaked up as much of the sights as I could.

One of my mates, Antonio, was also world savvy due to having several corporations around the globe and branch offices for a variety of businesses everywhere. Japan had quite a few of Antonio's and his brothers, Demitri and Andre's, corporate interests. My mates ranged from 6'1 to 6'3, with dark brown hair and deep brown eyes. They each looked like the Highlander, but even better than Duncan McCloud did. Demitri loved to wear his hair long for me because of the whole highlander thing. Demitri knew he could keep me breathless by just walking into a room with his hair pulled back into a tail and flashing that sexy grin of his at me. His brothers would go back and forth with their hair. Some months, they wore it long, then, out of the blue, they'd come home with short hair, driving me nuts. I think that's why they did it most times. I always wore my hair long for them, even if they whacked theirs off from time to time. They would all have a fit if I didn't keep my hair long. Damn males.

I had never been out of the good 'ole USA, except for a few places in Canada, before becoming a part of this team (at least not physically speaking). Astrally speaking, I had been to places most normal people would faint over knowing they existed on astral planes. So, physically walking down a lane in a town in Japan, with all these different smells, colors and cultural habits, was thoroughly exciting to me. I noticed a few of the younger marines with us doing the same thing, so I didn't feel as bad.

The signs on doorways and shops, as well as the streets signs, had me in wonder. They looked so foreign and unique; I was having fun just trying to imagine what the signs really said. I thought I really ought to start learning foreign languages if this kept up. I knew a little of a few other languages, but not enough to get by like Antonio, who knew twelve different languages fluently. This was nothing new to him, and he barely looked up from the scope to see anything around him, being totally blasé about it all.

I wanted to kick him.

He looked up sharply and turned to me. Whoops, I forgot about the bond between us; he could feel anything I felt and I hadn't shielded from him.

He gave me a confused look that said 'What did I do?', and I just shook my head at him and mouthed the words 'I'm sorry'.

He gave me his 'We'll talk later' look and went right back to the scope.

Figures - give him a new gadget and it takes all of his attention. Typical of Antonio, being the science and computer nerd he was. There were days I had to drag him out by the balls, literally sometimes, because he got so caught up in some new technical thing and would forget to even eat. I would then remind him of what he was forgetting to pay attention to and he would readjust his attention to include me and the rest of the world; at least until the next new idea hit his brain or came out on the market. Then we went through the whole ritual again. I was getting used to it though and found it an endearing quality of his. At 6'3, and nicely built from spending time in the gym and with his brothers practicing martial arts, he was as mouth-watering as his brothers were. With dark brown hair, brown eyes and a smile that could melt my heart and get my body excited at the same time, it was hard to stay mad at him, no matter what he did.

The portal echo tracking system, I called PETS for short (much to Antonio's dismay), was zeroing in on our target at the edge of town. We walked to a small park that had a Zen-like quality to it and in between two cherry blossom trees (Sakura trees they are called here), was the energy of a portal. No one, or no thing, I should say, was around it. There were a few people in the park, either sitting on a bench enjoying the mild clear weather or walking along the stone path that wandered through the park in long slowly curving paths. Green grass and many flower beds dotted the park. It was a place to come to relax and just be with nature, in all its carefully tended glory.

I had noticed that every portal or vortex we came across was always stationed in between two things. Like two rocks or two trees. Sometimes two pillars, but always in between two things that were roughly the same. The theory I had for it (and so far no one could refute my speculation), was that two of something represented what we called a 'betwixt and between' space. An edge of an ocean, the hallway of a home or a doorway can also represent a 'betwixt and between' space. A space where the Veil can be thin and beings of other realms can walk through into our world. Midsummer and Samhain, (pronounced Sow-win), were two of our Holy days when the Veil between our world and the other realms were the thinnest, allowing for visits of astral beings and spirits to come here to this Earth plane. With the Great Shift happening, portals were popping up in places where a natural disaster happens, and with the laws of magick and physics desperately needing a place for a portal, it was using twins of some object to appear.

I scanned the whole park within my view and only a few people were in our vicinity. They were looking at us with curiosity, due to the fact of having so many Americans in their park most likely wasn't a normal every day event for them. With my mate, my sister, Cassie, and I, plus O'Hara's Specials Forces team and a marine squad, we numbered fifteen as a unit. Only Cassie could pass for being half American and half Japanese; otherwise, we all definitely stood out. She stood out a bit with her being small, but lethal, in her own right. She had long black shiny hair that hung to her ass, as mine did, and dark brown eyes that threatened to engulf her small face. I was a bit of an odd duck too, even within my own group, having dressed as I always did with a black leather jacket, blue jeans and a black Harley T-shirt. I had blue eyes and long brown hair that flashed different shades due to the unusual natural highlights I had. Antonio had dressed down to match me, with his black jeans and a plain black tee shirt. The others were looking more normal, with khaki pants and polo shirts. Cassie wore a dress that had a slightly oriental style to it. The thing that really drew attention to us, though, were the black bags we all had in our hands, filled with our military uniforms, tactical vests and an arsenal that we snuck through at the base here in Okinawa, Japan. Highly illegal if we were caught, but that's what black ops were all about.

O'Hara gave me a look, after seeing that Antonio had narrowed down our search to these two trees, and waited for me to make the next move. I handed my bag to Antonio, since I was able to sneak most of my blades within my leather jacket, pants pocket and black boots. I felt relatively sure I could take on anything coming through the portal.

Cassie shadowed me on one side and Antonio got the other. I wanted more room and waved them back to give me about five feet of space. They complied with my hand signal and backed off a bit so I could scout the portal. I walked slowly and cautiously up the portal, feeling the energy coming off of it in waves.

It's a most unusual feeling and quite different from a vortex. A vortex will suck power and energy from the environment around it, whether it would be death, strong feelings, or souls and magick. Portals are more self sustaining. Once they are opened, they only gave off a high tingly feeling that felt soothing and cool at the same time, like an energetic cool pool of water.

If I was looking at it with a normal human eye, I wouldn't see anything except a normal vision of the surrounding area. But, once I changed that vision, using my third eye and vamp sight, the scenery between the trees changed. Within the space of the two Sakura trees was a drastic change from the Japanese environment around me. A desert scene was beyond the portal with sand dunes.

Lots and lots of dunes, but on one side there was a small Oasis where I could see lush trees and plants in one small spot, about a quarter to a half of a mile wide. The sand and dunes themselves were unusual looking, with a sparkling shine coming from them, since it was daylight on the other side as well.

I edged closer to the portal and tried to see around the edges in case some horde of demons, werewolves or some such creatures were ready to attack. There was nothing there but more glittering sand and dunes as far as the eye could see. In the next realm, the skies were clear and blue. No harpies or gargoyles filled the sky.

I looked around at the people still wandering in the park and there was no fear, no left over shock of death marring the peaceful atmosphere of this realms tranquility. Whatever was on the other side, either hasn't made a move yet (not knowing the portal was open), or they could be gathering their forces for a major offensive.

All other portals thus far, had been very hostile and the left over psychic residue of death always marred the immediate area of the portal on our side. That wasn't the case here.

I backed up to where Antonio and Cassie were. "I want to go through the portal to the Oasis about two clicks away from this point."

"What for?" Antonio asked.

I looked up at him, saying, "We need to make sure there are no hostiles for one, and for two, I am feeling a 'pull' there."

Cassie tilted her head, asking, "What kind of 'pull'?" They both looked at me.

"I don't know really, but it's like I need to go there. It's just an instinct really, I think." I couldn't clarify my feelings anymore than that for them.

O'Hara joined our discussion, "Any hostiles?"

I shook my head, "No, but I want to go through to the Oasis in there."

O'Hara narrowed his light brown eyes, peering through the middle of the two trees. "There's an Oasis? I don't see anything."

I gave him a half grin, "You wouldn't, not yet anyways. Once you learn how to open and see through your third eye, you will." I turned back to Antonio and Cassie. "So, how about me going in?"

"Not alone," they both said at the same time.

I jotted my chin to the rest of our unit. "These guys will need magickal backup while I am gone, just in case."

Antonio sighed, "Fine, I'll stay, but Cassie goes on the other side with you and you take three of O'Hara's men as backup."

I smiled at him, "Good idea, Cassie can wait on the other side of the door and O'Hara and two men he picks goes with me as bodyguards," teasing him with a slightly sarcastic voice.

"That's not what I meant. I know you can take..." Antonio started to defend himself. I smacked him lightly on the shoulder. "Ease up, hon. I was only yanking your chain." He clicked his tongue at me and then gave me a half grin. I had to turn back to business before Antonio's smile got me distracted.

I looked at O'Hara, and asked, "What do you think of the plan?"

"I'd feel better if Romeo guarded on the other side with Cassie and we take Wizard with us plus four of the marines. Babyface can stay here in charge of the rest of the team and Antonio stays here for technical and magickal support. That way, we both have tech support, just in case it's needed," O'Hara suggested. His plan was better than mine.

I was used to working with smaller groups and thinking of plans with minimum aide. "Good idea, though I doubt they have any tech stuff on the other side. I didn't feel any radio waves coming through, but they could have a city too far away for me to pick up from here."

Antonio added, "Make sure you take Shamus with you, as well. With him being cloaked, it could give you a magickal edge if needed."

Shamus was my astral familiar, the first who ever offered to serve me on the astral planes. Once I had his physical representation, a pewter figure of a wizard with a crystal ball, he also had power on the physical plane, as well.

"Even better. I agree, Shamus could be a great ace in the hole." I reached out with my telepathy and felt along the bond connecting Shamus to me. *'Hey Shamus, I need you, but stay invisible and cloaked. We are going through a portal and I want you to back me up.'*

'I come,' was all he said. Soon after, I felt his essence in the air around me. O'Hara started looking around a bit nervously. "Don't worry; he won't materialize until I tell him to."

O'Hara sighed a bit, "Good, I still get creeped out when your familiars do that." O'Hara faked a shudder.

'Tell the Captain I could always creep him out more,' Shamus growled warningly in my head.

"He heard that," I gave a half smile to O'Hara with a warning look.

He laughed, "He's too easy. Let me get everyone on the same page and we'll change into our gear once we're through the portal. That way, we won't scare these nice people." He moved away to the rest of the men, giving out orders and letting them know what we had planned.

'See, he was just teasing. I think he really likes you,' I reassured my familiar. He can be so touchy in his old age.

All he did was, *'Harrumphed',* in my mind; otherwise he stayed silent, listening to everyone around us.

We got everyone settled into our respective groups and my team made for the doorway in the middle of the Sakura trees. Stepping through the portal was odd; one step you're on grass, then, the next, you're standing in sparkling sand.

Romeo (Sergeant Theodore Watson, one of O'Hara's Special Forces men) and Cassie stood on either side of the portal to mark our exit out of this dimension. Otherwise, without me or my sister, these soldiers could get stuck on this world with not being able to psychically feel for the doorway.

I had taken the bag I had handed Antonio earlier that had my more lethal weapons in them and took off my jacket. I strapped the belt and holsters onto my shoulders which held my Browning nine mil. guns, one for each side holster. It was the only type of gun that I could comfortably hold in my hand, since I had a small grip.

I put my leather jacket back on, deciding against putting on my own uniform; what we called a Gaileyah. It looked a lot like a Ninja uniform - all black with a cowl to cover the face except the eyes, but we added belts of weapons to our uniform and a tactical vest.

Our tactile vests were also different from the norm, being lined with a thin sheet of silver and lead. Not much for stopping bullets, but great for stanching most magickal low level spells and knives.

I took out my guns to protect the rest of the men while they changed into their own gear. I was sure Cassie had done the same thing as I. We looked away to give them privacy, since this place didn't seem to have a locker room, as they did on the base back home.

How thoughtless of this world, I joked to myself. I could hear Romeo snicker. Being the hound dog he was, tall and lanky with down home good 'ole boy looks, he wouldn't mind showing off. I smiled to myself and kept watch, scanning the horizon for any incoming hostiles.

Once everyone had geared up, O'Hara walked over to me with his SOCOM in hand. It seemed to be the weapon of choice for his Special Forces team as a side arm. They liked the P-90 for their fully automatic weapon when things tended to get hot. The rest of the Marine squad had a variety of gun types in their hands, everything from nine mils. to Mac10's.

I cautioned everyone, but was mostly warning this marine squad, since we had never worked together before. "So far, we haven't had any hostile action on either side of that portal. If we do run into anything, and I mean *anything*, or anyone out of the ordinary, do not shoot first and ask questions later. We are here to try to get someone from here at a peace table without gun fire. I know some things can look very scary and very threatening, but do not shoot unless Rock or I give the order. Is that clear?" I switched to O'Hara's call sign, Rock, as was the habit on a mission. Now it felt like a mission, and not a sightseeing tour, but the men didn't look any steadier. Some of the men looked totally freaked out, seeing nothing but twinkling sand dunes around them. I could see they were off balance from going to one world into another. It could make them trigger happy. I didn't want to start anything here if it could be avoided. Our luck, so far, in getting a peaceful response from any of the Greater Magical races we've come across on other missions hadn't been too successful.

I didn't get the resounding 'yuuup' I was waiting for. "Is that clear?" Rock barked out, reinforcing my order. I wished he hadn't done that. It was hard enough gaining the men's respect, being a mercenary and a female one at that, without having to have to have a Special Forces counterpart commander to back me up; making it look like I couldn't hold my own leadership.

Rock had just realized the mistake he had never made before on any other mission and gave me an apologetic look. I shrugged it off. Maybe he, too, was unsettled about being in another dimension, as well. Cassie and I were veterans at this sort of thing astrally, so we were just rolling along with it. However, the excitement of physically stepping onto another world *was* really cool.

I turned to Cassie and Romeo. "Cassie contacts me here," tapping my temple, "if anything happens we need to know about."

Rock had already tested the Comms in their helmets, as well as their walkie talkies, to no avail. Telepathy would be our only way of communicating.

"Romeo, if Cassie can't do it, for whatever reason, fire one shot in the air and we'll come running." They both gave me a yup and a salute, even if Romeo's had a touch of cockiness to his. I still appreciated the support.

I walked a few feet away and with the toe of my boot, I drew a sixteen inch circle into the sand looking at the glittering pebbles within it. Like bits of glass, but not just glass. It was really pretty though, as I empowered the circle I had just made. When I said, 'we'll come running', I meant the rest of the team would come running. I would translocate here instantly to back them up; but I needed a clear focus to visualize my way from one place to another.

With all this sand, one dune looked very much like the other. In doing a translocation around here without something to make this place stand out, I could wind up on any of number of dunes in the area. Even worse, I could wind up *in* a dune itself and die.

"Don't touch this circle, I may need it." I ordered more to Romeo than to Cassie, as she would know exactly why I did it. Romeo was used to me doing odd things that didn't make sense to him at first, until he saw me use it.

Both of them nodded their understanding and I turned back to the rest of the team. Rock gave me a quizzical look, but didn't say anything at the moment.

"Ready?" I asked him. He nodded and moved to take point. I stopped him, saying, "If we run into someone or something that has magick, it would be better if I was in front."

"Why don't we both take point? I can shoot while you zap," he offered.

I stood beside him and it did look a tad symbolic, both leaders standing side by side, facing the unknown together with our men at our backs. I smiled in agreement and walked in step with him in the direction of the Oasis.

About a mile out, as we were walking, he asked, "Why the circle back there?"

Motioning to the dunes all around us, I said, "The scenery looks too much alike all around here. I needed that place to be a tad different to translocate to if they need me back there quickly."

He got it and nodded. "Can you take more than yourself instantly?"

I knew why he asked that question, but looking at his 6'3 frame and 225 lbs of weight, I shook my head. "Too much weight. Guns, yes. A baby, mostly likely. Something more than fifty pounds - no. I would be hurt, as well as whoever is traveling with me."

His eyebrow rose, "Hurt how?"

I gave him a gimlet stare. "Pieces missing, or at best, one big pulsing slab of meat," I told him graphically.

His face grimaced at the mental visual I painted for him. "Not good."

Agreeing with him, "Nope, not good. If there were more of us, my siblings, mates and such, we could combine our power and make it happen. But me alone, no way could I pull it off."

"More than three needed?" He shaded his eyes for a moment, staring intently at the horizon. I was happy I had extra energy from Antonio, between the sex and blood we had had last night; otherwise I would be dead tired in all this sunlight. The dark sunglasses helped too, in keeping the sun's rays out of my sensitive eyes. I got curious as to what he was looking at.

I answered him in a distracted voice while looking, "Yes, we would need more than three." Then, I saw what he had glimpsed at. A dark clad rider with a purple head wrap on, coming towards us fast, on a white horse.

"Hey, Lucy, I'm home," I said in a bad imitation of Ricky Ricardo.

"I Love Lucy," Rock responded. "How do you want to work this?"

"Give me about 10 feet and watch my back. Keep the nervous ones back there from shooting too soon. I'll go look nice and harmless and try to get a dialog going that doesn't involve violence." I was excited and cautious. Always cautious.

His mouth went tight, but he went along with the plan and motioned for me to keep going. To the men behind us, he gave strict orders on what to do, and most importantly, what *not* to do, in trying to establish friendly relations for further peaceful negotiations.

I felt for them, really. 'Peaceful negotiations' were not a job Special Forces or Marine Recons were geared to do. They were made for kicking ass, taking names and calling it a day with a beer when they killed everything in sight. They did their job very well with the other five portals. But, I was personally glad the shooting and biting hadn't started…yet.

I walked ahead of them all, with my hands away from my sides and palms out in as nonthreatening pose as I could make, and waited for the rider to keep coming. Feeling a bit like a sitting duck, I took the precaution of adding to my metaphysical shields, though they wouldn't stop a physical bullet or sword slash. If this guy had magick, it would most likely bounce off and let me know we had a hostile situation. Hopefully, I would have time to draw my weapons and have at it or return fire with my own magick.

I watched rider and horse galloping directly to us and the sight caught my breath. His horse moved like the wind and almost as smooth. The closer they got, the more I could see the horse's chest muscles flex with every trot it took. I loved horses, and watching this one run was watching poetry in motion. His rider rode with the horse as one and together they were a breathtaking symphony of movement.

I shook my head to get it back where it needed to be and not on the horse and his rider. As they neared my position, they slowed down, easing into a slow trot. Even with my sunglasses, I could see the shimmer of iridescent colors no horse on our Earth would ever have.

Saying this horse was white was an understatement. The sun reflected off the hide in a pearly cascade of iridescent colors. Even its' mane was sparkling in the sun. No way could this horse ever be confused with an Earth horse. Its coloring alone was unique, besides the seventeen hands of pure muscle that ran from one end of the horse to its hindquarters.

Looking into the horses eyes, I saw that they were purple. Again, no color an Earth side horse would have. The dark lavender shade showed that the horse had intelligence far above the norm for a regular horse. I was in awe of this beautiful animal and wondered what kind of rider the man had to be to have a partner like this horse.

I finally noticed my mouth was open, gaping at them both and quickly shut it before I embarrassed myself further. Horse and rider stopped a few feet from me. Close enough to speak, but not close enough for those wicked looking black hooves to be a threat to me. I appreciated the slight gesture.

The rider bowed his head. "Kon'nichiwa, sore wa meiyo ga watashi-tachi no nakama o mitaso tame ni."

I didn't understand a single word, but it sounded like the same cadence and speech patterns of the Japanese people in our world.

"Hello, despite all the weapons, we are trying to come in peace," I answered him in a light tone of voice. He tilted his head at me like he was trying to understand me. The next thing I knew, I heard him in my head. He was telepathic!

'*You don't speak the language my cousins and I have listened to through the portal,*' his mind-voice making it sound more like a statement than a question.

I answered him anyway. '*No, I am not a native of that country beyond the portal.*'

My eyes kept roving from him to his horse and back again to the mans eyes. The only thing I could see of his features were these deep cerulean blue eyes, that were hard, like chips of blue ice. With his head gear on and his Arabic looking clothes, I couldn't tell anything so far, other than he was humanoid, like us. He also wore two razor-sharp looking scimitars on his hips. I still couldn't get over the coloring of his horse and it kept mesmerizing me, which could be dangerous in this kind of situation.

'*Shadin 'le says your coloring is beautiful, too,*' his mind voice taking a lower, softer tone. My hair coloring, true, was unusual even for our world - brown, but with shades of chestnuts and reddish highlights in the sun that would flash to gold if I tilted my head just right.

'*Your horse is telepathic?*' I was amazed.

'*Shadin 'le can communicate to me, since he chose me to ride him. He can hear others and feel emotions. He is a most powerful warhorse with magick enough in his own right,*' he answered.

I looked at the horse closely, with more than my physical eyes. Shadin 'le's aura shown with a golden glow and a thread of magick was going from him to me. My lips pressed tight as I turned my inner sight to the rider and saw another spindle of power going from him to me, as well, but also tied to the horse. Shadin 'le was the anchor for a spell meant for me. The threads of blue, white and gold were so subtle, so fine; I had never seen a spell woven so artfully.

Now I knew why I had felt a pull to this world. I noted how many other mistakes I had made since stepping foot into this dimension. I didn't put on my Gaileyah and I didn't put my long hair into a braid to keep it out of the way, if I had to fight. I would never normally forget to take such simple precautions such as these when entering a totally unknown territory with the potential for being hostile. It was a damned spell.

'*Why did you spell me?*' my mind-tone going flat and unfriendly-feeling.

He drew back slightly from the anger he felt from me. '*To draw our mate here to us. Your world was too large to search for you physically. My cousins and I, along with Shadin 'le, crafted a spell to bring you here.*'

My eyes went wide with shock. '*I am already bound to my mates from my world. I can't be your mate. You must have made an error in casting.*'

He felt angry himself now and dismounted lightly from Shadin 'le, despite looking like he weighed about 235 lbs. I dropped my left foot back and readied myself for a fight.

He noticed the motion and stopped abruptly. *'I would not hurt you, Meshallima; be at ease.'*

"Cat?" I heard a voice with a warning tone behind me. Rock knew my body language too well, and saw I was getting ready for a fight.

The rider looked beyond me, asking, *'He is your protector?'* his eyes snapping blue flame.

'He is a fellow warrior. We work together as equal leaders,' my tone of mind-voice still not friendly towards him.

'They have no strong magick. How can they be true warriors?' Even in my head, I could feel his total disregard to the threat our team posed.

'I am all they need in magick; they have my back in all other areas,' I hissed in warning.

He looked sharply at me, then bowed his head. *'True, you are formidable in your own right as our Meshallima should be.'* He adopted the nonthreatening pose I had shown to him before. *'May I see your bonding cords?'*

I eased my stance a bit. *'Why do you need to see my bonds?'* To Rock, I said over my shoulder, "Hold, no threat yet." He must have trusted my judgment, because I felt them ease down behind me.

'Your shields are strong. I cannot see past your shields to your energy centers to find if the bonds are true or not.' He walked slowly towards me.

Walked? Seven hells, this man moved like a jungle cat. His footsteps barely disturbed the sands underneath his feet for all his 6'4 frame. I could see the calluses on his palms and fingers from working out regularly with his blades. His arms bulged with muscles. I couldn't see his bare chest, but he

31

definitely filled out his outfit nicely. I shook my head again to clear it. I was damn near panting and that wasn't like me.

'*What are you?*' Being inter-dimensionally politically correct be damned; everything about him was magickally enhanced. The way he moved, his scent as he got close enough for me to catch a smell mixed of sandalwood, cedar and musk, to the warhorse he rode with such ease, was slowly intoxicating me again. I had to stay mad just to keep my head in the game. Strong emotions seemed to be the only thing that kept his magick from overwhelming me; and he wasn't even overtly trying anything, yet. Now he wanted me to drop my shields? No fucking way.

'*I am one of three Dai' Khan's of this world. My other two cousins are also Dai' Khan's of two other provinces. Together we rule this world.*'

Three was a powerful number, even in this world, it seemed. Three is a holy trinity. The Christian God had three - with God, Jesus and the Holy Spirit. My own Goddess had three aspect beings called The Triple Goddess with Mother, Maiden and Crone making up Her Holy Being. The rule of three, obviously had leeway here, as well. That could be good for me if I had to lash out with magick.

'*What is a Dai' Khan?*' Though I had a vague idea it meant a king or at least a prince. I found out I wasn't too far off the mark.

'*What you would call a sorcerer-ruler. Only the strongest can rule here. We are the best at magicks in our lands and the best blades. We've earned our right to rule with strength, magick and blood.*' His inner tone of voice was strong and sure of himself, so I didn't doubt him.

'*How did you know me, to spell me like this?*' I was curious to know.

'We didn't know you personally, but the spell we sent out would find our mate and bring her to us. We knew when the spell went out and didn't come back right away that we would have our mate soon from that world. We stayed to wait at Jeno lah' leah,' pointing to the Oasis behind him. 'Pond of life. You have arrived.'

That meant the spell wasn't a specific one, but a general one, which tended to be weaker than a spell cast for an exact person. If a general spell casted was this strong, a spell sent for a direct purpose could give me a run for my money. It may even top my own magickal abilities. I may be screwed if this turned ugly and in so many ways. I noticed a part of my body wouldn't have minded that so much. I mentally slapped myself again.

'Undo the spell,' I demanded.

His eyes narrowed in response. 'May I have the name of our Meshallima?"

Names had power for those who could wield it, in any world. Giving him my name would make it easier for him to try a direct spell casting at some later point, which would be harder for me to defend against. Knowing the name of the sorcerer, however, could also give me more power to defend and even out the playing field.

So I countered, 'What's yours?'

I swore I could feel him smile underneath his head wrap.

He bowed his head, saying, 'Ja' Cullam, son of the first house of Rakul, Dai' Khan of Pladon Chino lah' din. Province River of tears. Co-Dai' Khan of Kla' din, Gods tears.'

It felt like the truth and I appreciated the translations, so I gave him his answer. 'Catrina Garcia.'

His head tilted at me, 'That is all?'

I put my hands on my hips and responded with a flippant attitude, *'I have many titles. I didn't want to bore you with them.'* He threw his head back and laughed a deep belly rumble of a laugh; even his horse snickered a whinny. Damn males.

Laughter could be understood in any language and I heard Rock say behind me, "Well it looks like she made a new friend. Pay up Wizard." The tension from the unit at my back eased up even more. Rock had bet on this first contact? It was customary for our combined teams to bet on the outcome of missions to help lessen the stress, but seven hells, even this? Again, damn males. I snorted at them all.

'The spell?' I reminded him, as his laughing slowed down.

He bowed his head and raised his left hand to me, his other hand to his horse and with a simple flick of both hands, the spell was cut.

I breathed slightly easier, as I felt the release of the spell. I looked again with my second sight and saw the threads had disappeared. I bowed my head back at him in response.

'So, Meshallima Catrina, what other titles do you have?' He tone sounded light and curious at the same time.

'First born Daughter of The Triple Goddess and Her Consort, High Priestess to The Lord and Lady, Princess of Trinidad, and Nightwolf Protector of Earth.'

He was the first, besides my siblings and mates, who had heard of all my titles. Even Rock and General Pierce didn't even know half of what I stood for. But letting this man, this Dai' Khan, know them all would give me more status here, I felt. Titles seemed to have an importance in this world, much like many countries on Earth. I would use anything here to give me an edge.

He bowed to me again. *'We are well met, Meshallima Ja'*
Catrina.' Ha! I knew it. He had given me an equal footing in
his world view with that statement. I kept my poker face on
and smothered my emotions with an air of indifference.
'Now, may I see your bonding cords?' he asked again, politely.

I looked at him archly, *'What guarantees do I have that you*
won't do any magick against me if I drop my shields?'

Even with the head wrap on, I could tell he looked
affronted. *'You are our Meshallima, a Ja' in your own right.*
Hurting you in any form would be sacrilegious.'

He could be bullshitting. He could be hiding his true
emotions better than I could.

Just to be on the safe side, I said, *'I must have your sworn*
oath that no harm in any fashion, large or small, will happen to
me, if I drop my shields.'

His eyes sharpened to mine. *'Ja' Catrina does not trust*
easily, I can see now. Fine, I swear on my throne, no harm shall
come to you in any fashion, large or small, so you may drop your
shields in safety.'

I gave him a warning look. *'Know this Ja' Callum - my*
astral spirit blood lines are Fae. If an oath is broken or a lie told to
one of my kind, ill could easily befall you without me even lifting
my hand. Do you understand?'

He nodded his head. *'Much the same for our land and*
people. A sworn oath cannot be violated.'

Slowly, I laid down my shielding. One layer at a time,
until I was bare, metaphysically speaking.

His eyes widened and he growled, *'Your bonds are blue-*
white, but your soul is damaged. Many scars, wounds are there
and some are still bleeding. How could your mates allow this to
happen to you? They do not deserve your bond.'

I allowed my anger to show. *'Never speak ill of my mates.*
Most of these happened before they were in my physical life and no
fault of theirs.'

He moved closer to me, lowering his eyes to mine. *'How long have they been in your life?'*

'A few months, physically,' I answered truthfully, still showing anger in my mind-tone.

'My cousins and I could rightfully challenge them then. Some of these wounds had to have happened within that time frame.' He sounded sure of himself.

My first instincts were to tell him he would have to go through me first, but then I thought about what kind of status that would put my mates in -making it look like I protected them, making them less than me. That wouldn't be a good thing and it wasn't true. Even I respected my mate's abilities, both physical and magickal, in being better than I was. True, they had more formal magickal training for far longer than I did, so for the time being, they were way above me. With the same training, I could possibly match or even outstrip them someday. For now, they could best me in a fair magickal duel (not that they would ever even think of doing it).

Their physical skills were more formidable. Even with hundreds of years of training, I don't think I would ever be able to best them. Men and women are different, period. They had strength and weight on me; you can't get around that. Facts are facts, and they are natural born warriors. Unless I got tricky, they would always be able to take me. But again, they would never come at me in anger, so it was never a worry.

'Some of these wounds happened in closing a negative vortex and are still healing. Again, no fault of theirs. They have to let me do my job as a Nightwolf Protector of Earth.' I walked back a few steps and snapped my fingers, reinstating my shields instantly.

"Cat?" Rock knew I had done something. Not what, exactly, but something, and he could tell by my walk that I was angry.

"Just a pissing contest of sorts, Rock. Nothing truly dangerous at this time," I apprised him of the circumstances, since he couldn't hear what we were talking about.

"I can tell you have a dialog going on. Though it's silent to us, just let me know what's going on from time to time. The suspense is aggravating, if nothing else."

I looked back at him and his eyebrow was raised. That showed me he was serious about wanting updates. I didn't blame him. If the situation were reversed, I would want the same thing. "No worries, Rock. He wants to challenge my mates to a duel for my hand."

'Your guard worries for you?' Ja' Callum asked, listening to our verbal exchange.

"He wants what?" Rock exploded in shock. I could hear Wizard (Sergeant Mark Logan) laughing in the background and offering a bet.

"Just give me a minute, Rock," I said to him. To Ja' Callum, *'He is not my "guard". He is a fellow warrior with the same level of command I have with the Nightwolves.'* I was trying to get him to understand that Rock's position couldn't be ignored or dismissed as substandard to mine.

'Command? You lead warriors and close down Large Magnitude Vortexes? They allow you to put yourself in danger? A breeding Ja' female? This can NOT be allowed', and before he could issue a challenge to my mates, I lost my temper.

I walked up to him, closed my fist (thinking of it as a brick) and slammed his jaw with it. I had finally figured out what to do about this.

The punch made his whole upper body twist and he lost his balance, not expecting the blow. He did recover fast, though. I had to give him that, as he got himself in a defensive crouch immediately afterward.

"Rock, stay out of this no matter what," I shouted and set myself for a fight.

"Nice negotiation technique." Rock gave me a half grin before turning to Wizard and saying, "Fifty on the big guy."

Ungrateful cur, I thought; didn't even think I could take the guy. "I'll double that in my favor," I shot back.

"Done." He was now taking bets with the other men in our unit. I wondered what kind of odds I was getting.

'Meshallima Ja' Catrina would challenge her truemate?' The look in his eyes made my heart twist in pain.

What the fuck? He was not my mate to ache for, even if I caused the slightest harm, even by accident. He was more my match in being a magick wielder and not human. I shouldn't even feel any guilt in fighting him, as I did when I had challenged Captain Holland to prove my physical skills.

I hardened against him. *'My mates, I fear in battle, though they would never hurt me, so let me show you what I can do.'* There, that should give my mates a standing here if I could make a good showing in this fight.

'You fight for them,' he scoffed.

"NO. I fight for myself. I am a warrior in my own right. I fear no one and nothing in any battle, but my mates are more skilled and lethal than I am," I spoke this both verbally and mentally, so Rock would know what set this off.

'I swore an oath not to harm you in any fashion, large or small. This would harm you,' he reminded me.

I volunteered an escape clause. "I release you from your oath for a physical fight. No magick. No weapons. Just physical. Agreed?"

'To harm a female is a death sentence on Kla' din. To harm a breedable female, is slow torture for many days before death is granted,' he growled.

"Good thing I am not a citizen of your world then, isn't it?" Although I was impressed with the lengths these people seem to go to protect their womenfolk. I approved. However, I needed him to fight me, so he wouldn't fight my mates without lessening my mates' standing. I was trying to protect their ego, though they weren't even here. As it was, I was looking at another spanking, I was sure. Thinking about that got my body to tighten in arousal and I shuddered in memory of the last time Antonio disciplined me.

Ja' Callum took my reaction wrong. His eyes narrowed on me and my body as if he could tell something was in the air that wasn't quite so strong as before. His stallion even waved his head and mane around, snorting to whatever it was they had both picked up. If his head wrap was off I wondered if his nostrils were flaring for a scent.

'My Meshallima needs proof of my virility. My strength,' his mind-tone low and seductive now. *'No other here has strong magick other than you. Fine, I agree to your terms. Let us dance the dance of strength, but when I win, I will claim you,'* with a tone that left no doubt to what he meant by 'claiming'. My nether regions grew swollen and wet at the thought.

Damn, the spell was gone; what the hell was wrong with me? I couldn't let him win, no matter what. My losing would cost me more than a few bucks. I was so glad my mates were on the other side of that portal or they would've have felt my physical response to this Dai' Khan.

He waited for me to make my move and I spun out two back kicks, one low and one high. Then, I dropped back into my stance. He blocked them easily. He came at me with a right hook, but I could tell he was pulling back his power, so if it had connected, I wouldn't get hurt so badly. That was his first mistake. I grabbed his wrist as it came close to my face and pulled him off balance. Spinning around, I took my other hand in a chop to his back and I didn't hold back. As the blow landed across his back, I reversed my spin and hooked his leg with mine. Using both my hands, I pushed him down to the ground with the plan of pinning him. But, as he hit the ground, he put his hands down on the ground and did a push up so strong he landed back on his feet and turned to face me in one fluid movement.

I back peddled, lashing out with my right hand in a punch to his face, which barely got his jaw. It didn't move him. His eyes narrowed at me and he advanced with punches and blows which took every skill I had to block and counter with punches of my own. He added some low kicks to my legs and I had to use my own to block those, as well. Back and forth we went across the sands. I got a feeling he was just wearing me down, using moves to make me tired and not to actually hurt me.

The fighting style he used reminded me of Krav Maga and it was one style I wasn't familiar with, even on Earth. I had many other styles under my belt, but not Krav Maga and that was one fighting style I had a feeling could have given me more of an edge in this fight. His plan was working, since I still wasn't fully healed from the EMP-like blast that came from closing the vortex. The other wounds to my soul would take even longer to heal, since I still hadn't released the pain and rage I had stored deep inside me. I fought with him, trying not to be impressed with the ease which he met my onslaught. Lust wasn't going to help me win.

I tapped into the rage instead, and tried to control the release, channeling it into my fists and legs. I actually hit him hard enough a few times to make him take notice. I got in a strong kick to his solar-plex, knocking the wind out of him for a second. Then, he backed up and looked at me deeply. He must have seen something in my eyes he didn't like because he growled and came at me like a whirlwind. In no time, he had me pinned from behind, holding me tightly against his body with my back to his chest and both my wrists grappled taunt against my own body.

He held me tightly. *'No, Meshallima, you cannot release your rage like that. It would harm your soul even more.'* He bent his face into my neck. *'Let me take your pain and replace it with love.'*

Then, before I could take another breath, we were on an astral plane together. He was still holding me, our astral bodies naked, slowly merging into an astral melding of our souls. *'Create the bond with me, so I can remove the pain and rage, Meshallima.'* I turned to him, not sure I was going to continue the fight or allow the meld, but I let my fangs drop so I could use even more of my vampire strength. His eyes widened in shock. *'No, you can't be vampyre.'* And just like that, we were back in our bodies.

I got loose from his grip and even physically my fangs had dropped, so they were showing when he was coming out of his trance. Popping back and forth from the astral so much had made me faster in snapping out of a trance like that, so I had the edge on him there. Before he could focus, I landed on him and pinned him to the ground using my vampire strength to hold him. He tried to make me move off him, then it seemed the fight had gone out of him abruptly.

I felt despair roll off of him in waves. *'Go ahead, Meshallima. I know it is in your nature to kill. I don't want to live knowing my mate can do naught but kill anyone she comes close to.'*

Even though my face was close to his neck and I could smell the sweet scent of his blood, I could hold myself in check easily enough, so I was confused at the total and utter despair I felt from him. *'Why? I don't need to feed and I have never killed with my teeth. If I can have your promise not to attack me anymore, I'll let you up and see if we can be friends.'*

Shock radiated from his entire being. *'You do not want or need to kill?'*

I snorted, *'No, I just wanted to show you I am a warrior and I fight alongside with other warriors to defend Earth from...well... really bad things that are trying to come into our world. That was why we were looking at the portal. We just wanted to make sure your world wasn't going to try to harm ours. Other than that, we try to live in peace with others, as much as possible. A peace treaty would be nice, but I won't force that issue. I firmly believe in free will. But no more fighting; you're too damn good,'* giving him his due. *'Agreed?'*

Still shocked, he answered, *'Yes, agreed.'* I slowly let him up and moved back, just in case.

Glancing back at the men, I saw that if I didn't have their respect before, I had it now.

Rock had seen that my fangs were out. "Cat, are you in need?" I could wait if I had to, but seeing the look in Ja' Callum's eyes, I thought a small demonstration would be helpful. "Yes, please." Rock walked up slowly. "He is just coming to feed me. Again, the taking of blood has to be freely given. I can't feed off of anyone without their express permission."

Rock had reached us and bared his wrist to me. "I offer my blood, warrior to warrior, with heart and soul, of my own free will. So be it."

Keeping my eyes on Ja' Callum, I said, "I accept your offering with honor, warrior. So be it."

Gently, I put my mouth to his wrist and bit down, feeding from him. All the while, I watched Ja' Callum take this all in. When I was finished, I licked the wounds closed which would heal within a day, and moved away from Rock a bit.

"He was kicking your ass," Rock said from the side of his mouth.

"I won the bet. I'll expect payment later." I refused to acknowledge the obvious.

Rock persisted. "He was mopping the floor with you and you had to pull fang."

I clicked my tongue, "I still won the bet."

"You cheated." He raised his eyebrow at me.

"Did not, he never said no fang," I protested.

His grin grew cocky, "He obviously didn't know about the fangs."

I shrugged my shoulders, "Still, not my problem. I won."

'What does your ...warrior...say?' He was still shell shocked and trying to recover his equilibrium.

'He had a bet, which I say I won. He says I cheated. I didn't,' I growled.

Ja' Callum threw his head back and roared with laughter.

Chapter Two

Allegiance of Choice

When Ja' Callum finally stopped laughing, I said, *'Thanks a lot you big oaf. Now can we get serious?'* I was exasperated with both him and Rock. Chuckling softly, Ja' Callum came up to me, took my face in his big hands, and tilted it up so he could look into my eyes. *'That is all the blood you need? You do not need to kill?'* His mind was full of wonder.

I got a confused look in my expression again. *'No, why would you think that?'*

'The Draugrall always kill. They always take the women too, to breed them, making blood children, if they do not kill them after their first blood frenzy. They have devastated our world with their greed for blood and women.' His tone in my mind had grown with anger again, but not at me.

Well, that explained a lot. The need to find a mate not in his world. The despair when finding me a vampire. The fact that such a male-dominated society has formed three male mates for each woman; whereas, in most strongly male run civilizations, men don't share very well with each other. I had noticed he had always said he and his two other cousins wanted me as a mate. I was assuming that kind of bonding was prevalent in this society, if their rulers were doing it.

"Cat, share with the class." Rock could tell we were mind-speaking again.

"He, Ja' Callum is his name by the way, is fascinated that I don't need to kill. Apparently, his world is being threatened by a tribe of vampires that do nothing but kill and take their females," I informed him.

His eyebrow rose again. "That sucks."

"I agree." I looked at Ja' Callum, aching for his world and for him.

'If you allow it Meshallima, I can learn your language quickly and you can learn mine with a spell,' Ja' Callum offered.

I thought about it and nodded, *'Permission granted.'*

He stepped closer, *'Drop your shields, Ja' Catrina.'*

I obeyed, and felt a warm flow of energy running through my brain. Golden fingers plucked in my head, taking syntaxes and verbs. He added his own to mine. On and on this went, until I had a firm grasp on his language. I felt his power pull away and I staggered a bit from the information download. I had a headache and was dizzy, but soon things were becoming clear again. He held me steady until he knew I wouldn't fall down and then let me go.

"I am sorry, Meshallima. We will not do that again until we have healed your soul completely and bonded, so I can take some of the stress off of you." His voice dropped again low and sweet, "There are many things I would show you when we have you healed." There was a look of promise in his eyes when he said this.

I shook him off, "No touchy. I am mated. Behave yourself or else we'll go on a second round."

"Hey, he can speak our language now?" Rock was amazed at hearing Ja' Callum's clear speech in English.

"Yeah, he did an information download. He learned mine. I learned his. Fair exchange. Hell of a headache though," I sighed heavily. If Andre was here, he could take it away quickly. He was the best at taking my headaches away.

Ja' Callum reached up with his hand, gently tracing my bottom lip with his thumb, "I could take your headache away, Meshallima."

"Oh shit, you're in trouble when you get home. What does 'Meshallima' mean anyways?" Rock did his eyebrow trick again.

I sighed, "It means Dear Wife." My eyes went wide, as I consciously realized what he had been calling me all this time.

Rock was chuckling, "You aren't going to be able to sit down for a week." He had found out how Antonio disciplined me one night when I scared my mates for putting myself in serious danger, with no thought of asking them for help. I cringed inside. Rock had no idea just how much hot water I was in, because that damn touch got me going again.

I pulled back, and said, "Listen, I know you think I am your mate, but I can't be. I have my three mates back on Earth and they keep me quite happy, thank you very much."

Ja' Callum stared intently at me, "They do not protect you very well. My cousins and I can do better than they."

I glared at him. "I don't need protectors, I need warriors, and my mates are that. Our world is facing annihilation. Earth needs every warrior, male and female, fighting to keep it safe. I don't have the time, or the mentality to be kept safe; wrapped in gauze from the big bad things that roam about. It would drive me out of my ever loving mind. Therefore, you had to have made a mistake in your casting and got the wrong woman. If I had to live the way you are making it sound, I would slice my own throat from boredom. I have to fight. It's how I was made."

Ja' Callum felt every emotion I put into my declaration, letting him know I meant every single word I said. Then, I snapped my shields back into place.

Rock was trying hard not to laugh.

Ja' Callum thought over what I said, then he took a deep breath. "I did not make a mistake. The spell was flawless, but I can see you have a warrior spirit. We can work on it together, Meshallima."

I groaned in frustration, trying not to shriek at him or hit him again.

"I will never leave my mates. If I lost them, I die with them. We went through too much pain, too much shit, to finally be together. You'll have to find yourself another mate."

I could feel waves of sadness rolling off of Ja' Callum. "If we do not bond with our truemate, we cannot have children. The kingdom will die. The provinces will die, if we do not find mates for them, as well. With finding you from your world, we were hoping that more could be found the same way for the rest of the populace of males. We are a dying race, otherwise."

My heart twisted for him. "There must be another? Some other world?" I was grasping at straws.

He shook his head slowly. "Ja' Catrina, you are a powerful Priestess, you know how energy vibrations of the souls work. I know you feel the pull of my soul, of my body."

I couldn't refute that. Being this near him, I couldn't stop my body from being aroused. I could control what I did about it, but I couldn't stop the natural reaction. My heart hurt and ached for him already, though I kept telling myself that it would stop once I stepped back through the portal and I was home again. Maybe I was lying to myself and that's worse than lying to another. It harms the soul even more.

A cool summer breeze floated over my skin. The Goddess' voice echoed through my spirit, *'More than one world can be saved. Your heart is big enough, child.'*

Ja' Callum's eyes grew wide and we both looked at each other.

Rock snapped, "Ok, what the hell was that?" He had obviously felt it, though he wasn't fully trained in the magickal arts, yet.

Both of us just stared at him. Then we sank to our knees and bowed our heads in honor for the visitation of The Goddess. Even Shadin 'le bowed his head and bent his knee in response.

"Well, isn't this just dandy? Both of you and even the damn horse are kneeling over it," Rock grumbled.

Ja' Callum and I both stood back up, his eyes turning to me in wonder. "That was a female Goddess, Meshallima Ja' Catrina. I have never felt the like, but from our own God, Amun-Ra. Who was that?"

I went into shock over the name of the God he was ruled by and answered without thinking, "That was my mother, A Celtic Goddess from my own world."

Ja' Callum nodded sagely. "Firstborn Daughter of The Triple Goddess and Her Consort. I remember the title you gave me, Meshallima. You are a demi-Goddess child, as well as High Priestess. An Ama' and a Ja'. I had not thought when you mentioned that title what it meant. I had wondered at the third band of color in your aura. The reasoning was not clear to me. Forgive me, Meshallima."

Most humans only had two aura bands of color dominate around them. My siblings and I had three, and it marked us as more than the 'norm'. Books on the occult explained a third aura band as unusual, but they, too, didn't know just *how* unusual.

Rock raised his eyebrow, saying, "Luuucy, you've got some 'splianing to do." His imitation of Ricky Ricardo was better than mine.

"I Love Lucy. Too easy. We already did that one coming in," I reminded him.

'Thanks a lot, Ja' Callum. Not many from my world know about me and exactly what my kindred are,' I informed him telepathically.

Responding to my method of communication, which I appreciated, he asked, *'Why aren't they informed of the blessing your world has been gifted with?'*

'A mite egotistical, don't you think?' I told him sarcastically. Noticing Rock's impatience, I turned to him. "There is a lot you and General Pierce still don't know about; you know that. It wasn't the time to know."

Rock's face was grim. "We *will* need to talk later." I knew he would put if off for now, since we were in the middle of trying to get negotiations going that didn't include me boffing this world's ruler - or rulers, I should say. Mission first, explanation later, was a warrior code.

Almost echoing Rock's words, Ja' Callum sounded firm, "We should talk now. There are many things that need discussion, but we'll have to make for *Jeno lah' leah*, before the son of Amun-Ra rises." Seeing our confusion, he elaborated, "A second sun. The heat will be too high for..."

He was having trouble translating time differences between English and his language. "We call them domars. Your rate of time may be different than ours, so a conversion is impossible to make right now. For four of our domars, it is too hot for one to be safe here in the Low Desert of Tears, Kromvah lah' din. The tears, what you most likely would call crystals, in the sand dunes will heat up."

"A second sun, Cat? What will that do to you?" Rock was concerned for my well being. I was a tad concerned too, but I had to protect those we left behind at the portal first.

"We have two soldiers guarding the exit to the portal for our return. Neither one will go back without us," I informed him.

Ja' Callum grew silent and looked towards the direction of the portal. His eyes grew concerned and snapped to me, "One is a female and powerful in magick if her shielding is any measure of her strength." His eyes narrowed, "Like you are."

I made a note to self: cloak shields when entering a new world so we don't get ousted so quickly as magick users.

I gave him a gimlet stare. "She poses no threat, as long as our men and I are not harmed. This, I swear."

His stance relaxed. "Good enough for me, Meshallima Ama Ja' Catrina"

I groaned, rolling my eyes.

He tilted his head at me and asked, "Is she mated? I cannot tell from here."

A wave of jealously roiled through me.

An emotion I had no right to feel, but answered harshly nonetheless, "Yes," I hissed, "She is mated and has many children with them."

He felt the emotion, regardless. I could tell when his look softened and crinkled at the corners of his eyes, letting me know he was smiling under his cowl. Damn the man.

"You and I are not done yet, I think," he chuckled smugly.

Rock coughed. I shot him a glare as well.

I intended to wipe that smug tone out of Ja' Callum's voice. "We'll have to go back until both suns set. I can't leave my people exposed to that kind of heat. We'll send another ambassador then, for speaking a peace treaty at that time." The faster I got out of this world the better.

He arched his eyebrow at me. "Are there guards on your side of the portal, Ja' Catrina?"

"Yes," I admitted.

He pressed further; trying to find a way to keep me here, I would bet. "Can you give oath there is nothing harmful that can come through your world to this one while you stay? That your guards on that side will keep anything from coming in?"

"Yes, why?" Why wasn't he worried about the portal in the beginning, I wondered?

"I can use the power of the Bokaris to make a temporary shelter that will keep your two guards on this side safe from the heat, but in doing so, the portal will be unguarded by the Bokaris magick until next days end."

Bokaris, meant large power crystal, in his language. I didn't remember there being any large crystals at the portal when we came through.

Rock looked at me with a question in his eyes. I shook my head, but turned my attention to Ja' Callum. "I didn't see any large stones by the doorway, Ja' Callum."

"They are there, but cloaked from sight. They will lose even that, once I meld with the Bokaris' power center and utilize them." He hadn't lied to me so far, but still, I was slow to take anyone's word for granted.

"Show me the Bokaris," I insisted.

"I don't think we would have time for a trip all the way there and back to the Jeno lah' leah before the second sun comes," he sounded doubtful.

"I don't have to be there to see it, just uncloak them from here," I told him.

His eyes widened a bit, but he looked like he'd done what I'd requested. *'Cassie, did two big crystals appear near the portal?'*

'Yes, how did you know?' she sounded amazed. *'I was just about to report the change. They are the largest crystals I have ever seen. They are deep purple, almost black; the color is so deep.'*

'The ruler of this world apparently has those stones as a tripwire alarm system. It may do other things, as well. I am really interested in those stones now and want to get more information, plus we are talking a peace treaty,' I informed her.

'Good work, sister,' her mind-tone was proud.

I snorted. *'Don't praise me yet, all is not as it seems. The main worry I have now, is that there is a second sun about to rise. It seems the desert here gets too hot for safety. The ruler here says he can make a temporary shelter to keep you and Romeo safe until the suns are set. He wants me to continue to the Oasis for further talks. Something about those stones is intriguing or I would be on my way out of here and sending in another ambassador.'*

'Why, is there a problem?' her tone concerned.

'Yes and no,' I admitted. *'Nothing life-threatening, anyway. The thing is, I have given an oath we won't let anything into this world that may be harmful. That means our unit on the other side will have to defend that portal at all costs or my word is forfeit. Can you get word to Antonio and tell me what he says about guaranteeing my word?'*

'Right away, Cat.' I felt her leave through the portal. Once on the other side, I couldn't feel her energy signal at all, so I kept one eye on Romeo, metaphysically speaking, while she was gone.

While I waited for her return, I turned some of my attention back to Ja' Callum. "How are those crystals safe guarding your world?"

If they could guard his world, they could guard ours if they had any more of those huge stones.

53

"If I told you that, you might find a way to circumvent them. Then we could be at risk here." He was right, if I had conquering on my mind. He couldn't be sure we weren't a warring people, yet.

Many on our world would be of the mind to take and conquer, if they knew about Kla' din. Without me or one of my kind, there would be no chance of allowing someone that was devious and greedy to come and muck things up here for their bottom lines. I had to convince him of our sincerity; I had an idea of what to do with those portals that would reopen in our world, keeping Earth safe from them and keeping worlds like this one safe from the greedy profiteers of Earth.

"How about a blood oath that I will never repeat the secrets of the stones to anyone you don't personally authorize, and I will never use the knowledge to harm your world unless you war with ours first?" I thought I had all the bases covered. I was wrong.

He countered, 'A mate cannot betray her bond without losing her own soul. That price would be too high. Bond with us and I will tell you all about Bokaris.'

'You'd be asking me to betray the bonds I already have. As you said, the price is too high,' I answered smugly.

He had to stop and think about that.

Cassie had returned from the portal. '*Cat, Antonio asks how long will you be?*'

I asked Ja' Callum, "She wants to know how long we need to be here?"

"Until this time next day," he said.

I told her, '*This time next day, Cassie.*'

'*I will let him know.*' She had left again.

Ja' Callum nodded towards the direction of the portal. "Does she ask those on the other side if they will guard the door?" Cassie and I were using the private telepathic band. No one else would be able to hear us.

"Yes, I need to make sure I can hold my oath to you before we go to Jeno lah' leah," wondering how Antonio was taking the news I would be here a while.

"Your mates are on that side?" he was digging for more information.

"One is, why?" I said truthfully.

Ja' Callum's voice started to growl on its own. "He allows this danger to you. He has no idea what kind of threats you may face here and yet he allows you to face them alone."

Rock, again was having a hard time in not laughing at my predicament. Normally, he was every inch the hardened warrior with a cold stare that would make smaller men quail in fear, but now he seemed to be finding this situation hilarious.

I ignored Rock for now. "One, if he didn't allow it, I would do it anyway. Two, he has confidence in my abilities to handle myself and call for help if I get in over my head. One word and he'll be here in mere minutes if need be. Never underestimate my mates in their power. They are more formidable than I am," I growled.

Ja' Callum sounded disbelieving. "And if I closed the Bokaris? How would they come and be at your side if I were a threat to you?'

"Our bond. There is more than one way into this world and with our bond they would find this place, then they would find me." I let the threat of what they would do to find me, hang in the air.

Ja' Callum's eyes narrowed again. "I shall have to meet these mates of yours, then."

Damn the man. It's what I was trying to avoid. I know my mates. If they perceive a threat from someone else trying to get in my pants, they will fight, and damn the consequences. Wars have started over this type of thing before in our own history. Helen of Troy I was *so* not. But, he had a point; a mate was worth even the cost of ones soul. If Ja' Callum had a way to keep a portal guarded and even closed, as he had inferred, we needed this knowledge and not at a sword point. Knowledge freely given was more powerful than that which was taken by force; but being sneaky would work for me as well, as an idea blossomed in my mind.

Cassie had returned yet again. "He says fine, he will help you hold your word, but be careful and he sends his love."

I smiled, knowing Antonio was mostly likely already at work throwing up avoidance spells to the area and then shielding spells. Anyone making it through those, he would know to shoot first and ask questions later. No mundane human would be able to get through his spells of protection.

I turned to Ja' Callum, to ask, "Now, about that shelter? My people will need it if we stay here. That is if you can actually provide such a thing in this hot desert?"

I didn't really distrust in his abilities, but by casting doubt on them, I pricked his pride, hoping he would make a mistake in being cautious.

Rock raised his eyebrow at me again, letting me know what he thought of my negotiation skills. Pricking the pride of the ruler you are trying for peace with wasn't the way to go. I knew that, but I couldn't seem to help myself.

From his walk, I could tell I had pushed his button. He seemed to be mentally reaching out for the power of the crystals at the gate. I tried to watch the process as he used his magick, but he was able to block me. I smiled at myself though; he didn't know about Shamus yet and my wizard would know what I wanted. Rock was still giving me a sideways look as if he could tell I was up to something. He let it go because digging for an answer now would alert Ja' Callum.

With a sudden thrust of power, I felt a shift at the gate. I mentally heard Cassie's exclamation and asked for details.

'*Sister, a tent with a water fountain and a perpetual misting system has appeared. It is very nice inside the tent itself. The stones have changed color drastically. They are almost pure white, as if all the energy inside them had been drained off. The power surge was tremendous. Are you sure you are able to handle this one alone?*'

She didn't doubt my talent, but what Ja' Callum had done was impressive and outstripped even my skills.

I reassured her I would be fine since I had an oath of protection. She took me at my word and cut off communications again with a word of caution in watching my back.

Ja' Callum turned to look at me with an air of superiority. I bowed my head to him for my sister's sake and Romeo, if nothing else. "My sister said to thank you for the consideration. Nice job."

"Sister?" he sounded shocked. Not understanding his surprise, I gave him a quizzical look. "Another Ama' and a female Ja' has visited our world?" His voice heavy with awe, he strode over to cup my face again. "Thrice this world has been blessed in a single day with you as a potential mate coming here in answer to many years of prayer to Amun-Ra. He has answered those prayers three times. Three times answered, three times blessed at the edge of our extinction, He has answered our call." He bent close to my face and most likely would have tried to kiss my lips if he wasn't wearing a cowl, but he got close enough that I could almost imagine the scent of honey on his breath. "Whatever it takes to win your bond, we will do it, never doubt that now, Meshallima. Only a fool turns away a gift from Amun-Ra or lets them go so easily." His deep blue eyes glittered with determination and his voice hardened with a ruthless growl, "I am not a fool."

"Oh, shit." Rock had overheard Ja' Callum's declaration and knew how my mates would most likely respond. 'Oh, shit', didn't even cover it. My ass was aching already from the imagined pain I would receive. If I could sit down in a month without wincing, I would consider myself lucky. And the peace treaty? I didn't even want to consider those ramifications.

I gave the only answer I could. "I would die without my mates."

"I realize that now, Meshallima. I will find a resolution that will not wound your heart. You have enough scars on it as it is. *I* wouldn't do anything to add to them." Inferring my mates had slacked on their job - again. I was getting pissed again. Pissed was good. It helped me to stop lusting after his warm body vibrating against mine; he had gotten so close to me, invading my personal space.

I moved away from him sharply. "Let's get this show on the road."

He looked confused over my verbal expression but said instead, "Your sister. She cannot be left alone with only one guard for her safety. Also, she ought to have food to add to her strength. I cannot leave a female Ja' and an Ama' with such poor protection and hospitality."

My eyebrows rose at this. "Ha! My sister can whip ass on anything coming at her. She is lethal in her own right, plus she has a whole army of warriors that can step across in a second if she needed them. As for food, she prefers sushi which is also just a hand away for her across the portal. She'll be fine. Come on, you said time was short."

"Is she vampyre as you are, Meshallima?" Ja' Callum gazed worriedly at the horizon.

"No, she has no fangs," I admitted. He actually looked torn between seeing to each females need, and then he stepped to me. "You are more vulnerable than she is then. Her shading should be adequate. It is you who will be in danger when the Son of Amun-Ra rises. It's amazing enough you can stand in the shine of Amun-Ra and not die. Let's get you to cool shading quickly."

Shadin 'le had moved near him and he mounted from the ground without even touching the horse for aide. Impressive, I thought to myself. He held his hand down to me, expecting me to take it and mount with him. Not bloody likely.

"I'll run with my men. As co-leader, my place is with them, no matter what," I sounded firm on this.

He advised, "Then run quickly, Meshallima. We are about out of time," gazing off to the side, which by our compass showed it to be Easterly. From the horizon in that direction, a glowing bright blue shine was cresting over the edge.

Rock snapped around barking his orders, "Form up. Double time to the Oasis. Move it." With it being only a click and a half away, I thought we might be able to make it with good time.

We headed out, running smoothly. I could have added even more speed using my vampire strength, but I didn't want to push the men in trying to keep up or outstrip them. I thought we did well, but the blue sun was already over the horizon and shining brightly by the time we got to the edge of the Oasis. Sweat was pouring down my neck as I slipped under the tall trees with heavy green leaves. I took stock of how tired I was. I felt like I could keel over any second and I drew on my reserves just to hold myself upright, hiding that very fact.

Never show weakness in a possible hostile situation. The men behind me gasped. Even Ja' Callum looked astounded and they were all looking at me. I held my head up, not understanding what their damn problem was. I wasn't showing the wear and tear that run took out of me. I still had my sunglasses on, so what the hell?

Ja' Callum dismounted as easily as he did the first time I'd watched him and strode over to me. "You glow blue with the shine of the sun, Meshallima. The air around you sparkles with it."

Rock nodded, "I can see it with my own eyes; you are glowing blue. No one else here is, but you."

"Look behind you, Meshallima. Look at the desert now." He motioned to the sands we had just left.

Turning around, I saw the whole landscape had changed from the bright sparkling glitter of the glass or crystal pebbles that were reflected in the sand, to a deep glowing blue color, pulsing as if power was being pumped into the air from the ground. I removed my sunglass so I could take in the sight with my own bare eyes and was astounded at the view before me.

The men also were overwhelmed at the beauty the landscape gave us and were as enthralled as I was until Rock turned to look at me again. "Oh, shit!"

He actually took a step back, having never shown fear of me before.

"Your eyes," shaking his head. "I can't see your pupils anymore," he explained.

"Let me see, Meshallima." I turned my face towards him and heard an intake of breath from him as well, but not in fear. I didn't feel that from him, just a feeling of wonder.

"Your eyes glow blue with the favor of Amun-Ra, Meshallima." He walked closer to me. "Look at mine," he commanded.

His eyes too, held a glow so bright, I could barely see the dark pupils of his eyes. "It is how we tell on this world who has power, from those who don't, as infants. The stronger the glow, the stronger their power is; the more Amun-Ra favors them," his voice had dropped several octaves.

In my world too, my eyes glowed, but with a sea green color. On Trinidad, I couldn't hide their glow at all. I did better on Earth with my sunglasses on all the time to hide the color change if I had to draw power. But, here apparently, I glowed blue and I wasn't even gathering power.

I turned back to the desert, trying to see the small pebbles within the dunes.

"Those crystals in the sand then, have power?" I asked him.

"Yes, they are the tears of Amun-Ra. Gods tears that were shed when his son was killed." He came up behind me and put his arms around me. "Legend has it, that Amun-Ra fell in love with a powerful and beautiful Sorceress from the first House of Rakul, my house, many, many generations ago. She had long black hair and deep blue eyes, so dark with power they glowed on their own. Amun-Ra came down to Kadar, what the world was called then, and assumed a form she would find pleasing, to seduce her. Strong and powerful he was, with blond hair with the shade of the sun; he mated with her and together they created his first son."

He hugged me to him. I knew what he was thinking, the horn dog. "Without Amun-Ra in the sky to travel, bringing light to Kadar's fields, soon the world suffered for it, and not wanting his son to grow hungry, because the plants would no longer grow, he went back to the skies with a heavy heart. For many cycles, he watched from above, seeing his son play and grow. The boy was an energetic child, always running across the fields with laughter spilling from his lips. His mother would look on with a sweet, sad smile. Sad, because her mate, her lover, and her God wasn't there physically to share in the wonder of their growing son. As time passed, she grew lonelier and she began to look upon with favor two other suitors for her hand. Each was a powerful Sorcerer in their own right. She couldn't decide which one to marry because her true heart belonged to Amun-Ra. Soon, war broke out between the houses." Rock had stepped closer to catch all of his words, spell bound with the tale, as was I.

Ja' Callum took a deep breath and continued. "The three houses warred for many months, ending with The House of Rakul having been taken for the first and only time ever by an enemy. The opposing houses entered into house Rakul and demanded she choose. She held her son behind her and declared neither were worthy of her hand, since they made such desolation to the lands trying to strong arm her and her family into a decision. Both Sorcerers were so enraged, they killed both her and her son, spilling their blood within the house. Amun-Ra had felt their deaths. For weeks, the skies rained and were darkened in His grief. The other Gods and Goddesses surrounded Amun-Ra, trying to get Him to stem His grief before He destroyed Kadar with His tears in a flood. They brought to Him the souls of His love and their son, but because they were not full God beings, they couldn't stay on His plane of existence. Together, with the power of the combined Gods and Goddesses, they turned the soul of his son into the second sun since he was half Godling. Demi-God. His lover, however, was not, and the best They could do was to make her into the third moon, where before, we had only two moons. The third is at some distance. She was so angry with those responsible for her and her son's physical death. That is why the orbit of Amu-Ba is like this." He bent down into the dirt using a twig and made the orbits of this blue sun, the main sun and a third smaller body of a moon. The blue sun had an elongated elliptical orbit which would put it near the moon for a longer period of time, and then it would shine here on this planet. According to his sketch, the orbit was fast, which is why it was only here for a short time, sling-shooting around this planet compared to the orbit of the main sun. "They placed her moon far enough away to cause the least amount of damage to this planet and when her son comes close to her she shines blue in the night, whereas the other two moons shine white."

He stood up with a heavy sigh. "The tears Amun-Ra had shed, turned into those crystal stones you see now shining blue, reflecting the love of his son when he visits his now happy Father. That's when our traditions changed too, to allow three mates for a single female, so war like that would never break out again and blood never be spilled for a mating bond."

"What happened to those Sorcerers who killed the Lady and her son?" I wondered aloud.

"My cousin's ancestors joined forces with what was left of house Rakul and utterly destroyed the two sorcerer's houses. They are never spoken of by name, their families deeds have been stricken from our written history. Their bloodlines were eradicated, both physically and spiritually," his tone was harsh now. Ruthless.

He let me go and walked away. "The houses of my cousins then helped Rakul rebuild; restoring what was lost to us and our houses. Ever since, we've been allies. In this generation, our houses have combined the three ruling houses because our three energies match so closely. We know we could be good for a female that could seal our alliance in a mating bond until the end of time." The look in his eyes was probing.

'Cat, Romeo says I am glowing blue.' My sister's tone sounded worried in my mind.

I answered physically and mentally so all could know what my sister had said. "You're glowing blue, apparently because of the second sun. It shouldn't hurt you, but for the love of the Goddess, don't use any power if it can be helped."

Already, I could feel the pulsing power from the ground. If I tapped into it, I might fry myself out. It would be like taking in a bolt of lightning. I transferred my suspicions to my sister, so she would know why I was cautioning her so strongly.

I felt alarm shoot through Ja' Callum. "I did not think what might happen to you if you used power now. Your soul was not born here, so you have had no chance to acclimate safely." He sounded disgusted with himself. "Already, I have placed you in danger."

"Don't feel bad; I didn't realize it either, until the power started pumping through the sands. It would be best to get me away from this as much as possible and to get me in water." I was starting to hyperventilate, trying to control the energy that was flowing into me. His gazed sharpened, taking in my breathing and moved quickly picking, me up and moving deeper into the oasis.

"You will need to meet my cousins anyway. They are near the pool." He carried me like I didn't weigh more than a feather. Being off the ground did help, but with him carrying me, I lost points with the men who were following.

I slapped his shoulder. "Put me down. I can walk, you know."

"In a few minutes, Meshallima," and kept right on moving, gliding through the small forest of trees and grass. Vines hung from the trees and I heard small wildlife flapping in the leaves up above.

It was really beautiful. I realized that the oasis was bigger than I had first thought, only having seen one end of it. It was longer going east to west then it looked. The view of the north side only looked about a half a mile wide. Lengthwise, it was three or four miles in. I thought it was odd, since most oases grew in a circular pattern outward from a pool of water in the middle of it. This one didn't. It had more of a rectangle pattern and I saw why when we reached the center. There was a small lake of mineral water that I could smell and in the middle was the largest natural stone crystal I had ever seen. The stem of it was in the water, shooting up into twins of crystals, like a tuning fork, one pointing in each direction of east and west. The radius of the stone was wider than even Ja' Callum's body and four times as tall. Using my second sight, I could see waves of power coming from the crystal, adding to the life of the small forest. Everything was interconnected. Ja' Callum had finally put me down, and even through my biker-boots, I could feel the life force pulse of the area. Unlike that of the God's tears in the sand, this energy was slower and had a steady rhythm that I could feel like a slow drum beat. I had told Cassie on our telepathic wave to get into the pool Ja' Callum had made for her and it had worked. So, I took my own boots off and waded into the water.

Rock came to the edge. "Is it working, Cat?"

"Yeah, the energy here is more like a heart beat rather than the frenetic energy of the sands. This, I can handle," I assured him.

Ja' Callum asked Rock, "Why do you call her the name of a feline animal from your world?" He had obviously ran through the list of words in English and had put the two together.

"It's a short name for Catrina. Like a code name or a call sign such as we have in Special Forces. They call me Rock. This here is Wizard." Rock pointed to him within the marine group, of who were still being amazed at the sights around them.

"And the other men?" Ja' Callum nodded towards the group.

"They are Alpha 53rd Recon Marines. They are not Special Forces, so they don't have call signs. Some have nicknames, but that's about it. They do carry rank."

"Ama Ja' Catrina is leader of your Special Forces?" He was trying to work out where I fit in.

Rock replied, "Neither, actually. She is a mercenary. It's her people that she leads. I lead Special Forces and this marine squad when I'm in the field with them."

Ja' Callum looked at me. "You came to a world without your people; only your sister to guard the gate?"

"My sister is also a Merc. That's short for Mercenary. All of my blood or mated relations are Mercs." I closed my eyes, enjoying the cool feeling of the moss green water. It looked greenish from a small distance, but the water itself was clear.

Ja' Callum moved restlessly. "You still came alone, to a world that could have been life threatening."

"I am not alone. I am with them," I pointed to the group of men.

He said dismissively, "They could not keep you safe here."

Showing complete faith in the strength of the men that came with me, I said, "You'd be surprised, Ja' Callum." Then, I felt the energy of two strong beings moving towards us through the small forest.

"Rock - incoming - two marks," I said as I got out of the water. Ja' Callum watched me get with my group and stand with them, barefoot.

Ja' Callum waved me down. "They are my cousins. They come to meet you, Meshallima."

I gave him a short nod that I heard him, but I didn't move away from my unit or relax. The power of the combined force was just too much for me to relax my guard. Two men broke through the brush, riding two horses like Shadin 'le, except one was pure black and the other was a deep, dark brown. As one, they both dismounted and walked slowly to our group with Ja' Callum standing between us and them.

"Hidayah, cortimees. Beley ita metcha Meshallima la' oto sumtame'." Ja' Callum had asked his cousins to wait a moment for introductions to me and walked over to them. Their shields combined instantly and the power grid just went wider. It was so strong, I had to catch my breath. They had their hands on each others shoulders and I could tell they were doing something within their shield, but not what, exactly. Since it was contained power, I didn't let it worry me too much. For several minutes, this went on, then they parted and stood facing me.

"Meshallima Ama Ja' Catrina, I would like you to meet my cousins - Dai' Khan Ja' Monel, son of second house of Tramon and Dai' Khan Ja' Kelo son of third house of Drakar. This is our Meshallima Ama Ja' Catrina, First born Daughter of The Triple Goddess and Her Consort, High Priestess to The Lord and Lady, Princess of Trinidad, and Nightwolf Protector of Earth."

I groaned, knowing Rock had been reminded of what I was truly hoping to avoid, but with Ja' Callum dropping all of my titles again, that hope was a moot point now.

"I can't believe you remembered all of that Ja' Callum," I said, frustrated with him, wondering why he forgot *not* to say it out loud.

Both men and their horses had bent to one knee in response to the Ama. "Blessed are we, to have such a beautiful Ama Ja' Meshallima and such a gifted one. You bring honor and joy to all of our houses." Ah, Ja' Callum had done an information download with them so they now knew our language.

Rock's eyebrow was working overtime in this world as I saw it was raised again, when Ja' Callum again went to his knee, head bent in a bow as his cousins were, and adding his voice to theirs.

They were waiting and having been through this before on other astral planes and other worlds, I did the only thing I could do. Step into my role as Daughter of The Goddess and Princess of Trinidad, "Your greetings are gracious and received with joy. Arise."

Rock was going to grill me later, I just knew it. My mates also were going to be highly upset. My siblings were going to rub this in until the end of time. I would never hear the end of it. Already, I could hear the snickering Shamus was doing in my head, picking up my thought-waves on the matter. I was so screwed. And not in the good way.

Ja' Callum and his cousins rose to their feet. "Our camp is not too far away, if you would like to come, Meshallima Ama Ja' Catrina. Have you healed enough in the water of life?"

So he knew what I was doing when I stood in the waters, drawing strength and healing into my body. I was a fire sign, an Aries, and water was counter balanced to me, so it healed and cooled, whereas, fire burned and gave energy. The sands were too full of fire elements for me to regulate fast enough. Elemental powers played heavily in this world, much as it did on Trinidad. But, on my world I created it, so I was in complete balance there.

I was physically born on Earth, so I could balance myself there easily enough; this world was still alien to me and would take quite some time to get the rhythms here in tune with my astral energy. I didn't let the thought settle in my mind that the bonding with the Dai' Khans of this world would make the transition faster and easier. Instead, I gave another mental slap to myself.

"Yes, thank you. I am ready." I knew the men behind me would like to settle for a while and eat.

We all knew there was no real danger here. Not from the Dai' Khans themselves, at any rate. Well, not to the men, but my virtue was still in danger. However, that could not be taken care of with a bullet, silver or normal. Although, I was sure my mates would disagree with that right then.

As we walked, Ja' Callum filled me in with details of his cousins. "Ja' Kelo here, is Dai' Khan of Pladon Morcene lah' din, Province Lake of Tears. He rides with Mortidin 'le, Dark Tear, as I ride Shadin 'le, Snow Tear. Ja' Monel is Dai' Khan of Pladon Chino lah' Nodan, Province River of Blood. He rides with Tradin 'le, Fire Tear. We have all fought many battles together against the Draugrall."

Both of his cousins were roughly the same height and size. Huge and powerfully built. Their eyes were glowing blue, but unlike Ja' Callum's, their natural color wasn't blue. It was just that the power was overwhelming their true colors. I would have to wait until the power change wore off to see the natural state of their eyes. The color of the cowls and clothing were different from Ja' Callum as well. Ja' Monel's clothing was white with a blue cowl and Ja' Kelo's was white with a green cowl. They both had long wicked-looking scimitars.

Worried, I made mental contact with Ja' Callum, *'Do they know I am vampire?'*

Ja' Callum looked at me, his eyes smiling. *'Yes, Meshallima Ama Ja' Catrina, they know and are settled about it.'*

'Good to know. I didn't want to have to worry about getting my head cut off.' He laughed out loud, drawing Rock's attention, who wasn't fooled with my innocent look.

I felt his two cousins grinning at me as well. Sometimes it really sucked being the only female in a group.

Ja' Callum went on extolling the many things all their provinces had. If I didn't know better, I would have thought he was trying to impress me, not only with their virility, but their holdings as well; letting the little woman know that they could provide for me and do it well. Nah, I was just being paranoid.

We broke through to a small glen that had three semi permanent looking tents in the middle of it. There was a small brook that bubbled through on one side, and a pit for cooking with a spit. Near the tents was another smaller campfire with gear laid out for camping. The horses kept moving through the camp and disappeared into the greenery.

"We like to come here often for the peace. Many times, we will spend time working on our magicks together and attuning to Kla' din. It is one of many retreats we have, so we keep these tents here through all seasons." His voiced was laced with concern over how I would take the rustic accommodations.

I tried to keep my voice even. "You, yourselves, come without guards or servants?"

"The three of us are formidable warriors and more than capable of defending ourselves, being the finest fighters in all our lands. For their protection, we do not bring the servants, in case our magicks get out of hand."

I felt I had definitely pricked their pride, even though I wasn't being snide, just curious.

"Commendable; my mates are the same way. They often go hunting by themselves to commune and hunt. They are perfectly capable of taking care of themselves and their equipment on their own."

It was one of the many things I found admirable about my mates. That these three, too, had the same consciousness, spoke well of them in my opinion. I let it show in my voice. Of course, talking about my mates constantly also didn't hurt in reminding them that I was a taken woman.

Ja' Callum's stance relaxed and the smile was back in his eyes as did the other two. "We do have amenities," pointing to another smaller tent away from the camp. "No tree leaves," he said simply, but I got it.

I gave a small laugh, appreciating the fact I wouldn't have to make do with the bushes. Use the wrong leaf and you could be itching your butt for weeks and Goddess knew what kind of plants and leaves they had here.

"The pool we were just at is safe for swimming. Meanwhile, why don't we get your men something to drink and get the fire going for food?"

The three of them moved off and started getting the camp ready for guests. Rock slid over and quietly asked, "What's the plan or do you even have one this time?" He was used to working with my doing things by the seat of my pants; this time was no different.

"Wing it, I suppose. Those crystals could be the answer we are looking for if they can permanently close a hostile portal." He shook his head and moved to help start the fire. I walked over as well, and took a seat on a stone that was fashioned for sitting.

I saw water and a pink drink being passed around from Ja' Callum to the other men in my unit. He didn't pass one to me so I just opened up my black bag. Inside, I had a smaller pack that kept drinks cold, usually used for camping; but I found all kinds of uses for it on missions. This time, I had put in soda and grabbed one for myself. I popped the top open and sipped it. Ja' Callum and his cousins stopped to stare at me as I took a drink. Rock carefully watched the show unfold as I reached in for a pack of beef jerky, took one out and started eating it.

If I wasn't allowed to eat or drink because of their stupid customs, they can kiss my white rebel pagan ass. I would provide for myself, and to the seven hells with them all. I took another drink defiantly, with a glare at the three rulers, daring them to say me nay.

"Meshallima Ama Ja' Catrina can eat and drink?" Ja' Monel's tone was in awe.

I started to feel uncomfortable and defensive. "Yes, I do. I am on mission and have expended a lot of energy. If I don't eat some food, my thirst for blood will be worse."

Ja' Kelo was the first to walk to me, bend his knee and bow. The other two followed suit. "Forgive us, Meshallima Ama Ja' Catrina. The Draugrall never eat food or take drink that is not blood. It makes them ill. We assumed you would be the same. We meant no offense in not offering sustenance for you."

Oh, that was different. I had thought it was some stupid custom such as some of the Middle-East people on Earth had for *their* women. Their clothing was too damn close, and I kept making assumptions. My bad.

"Forgiven. I, too, made assumptions and took insult." Since they didn't get up right away, I added, "Arise."

Rock and Wizard both looked wide-eyed, as did the Marines. I could hear Shamus giggling in the air. Oh, if it wasn't so damn important for me to have the status here, I would make sure they knew I didn't like the bowing and scraping shit. I was a street rat, damn it. And damned proud of it, too. All else was secondary in my mind.

They arose with an air of relief, and scooted to get me the same drink they had offered the men. "We would have served you first, if we had known, Meshallima Ama Ja' Catrina. Here, take this. It is quite good." Ja' Callum offered me the pink drink in a fine crystal glass, which I found a bit funny, being out in the wilderness, but kept it to myself.

I smelled it and took a sip as cautiously as I had watched the other men do. Usually, they wait for me to test the waters, so to speak, knowing I had an acute nose and can spot poisons or drugs easily. The fact that they went ahead, when I didn't get a drink first, and did it themselves, made my soul swell in pride for these fine fighting men. No damn otherworld drink would make them quail, no siree.

Not that they were incautious. If a way could be done more safely they would, but if not, they forged ahead and kicked ass with what they had. I smiled to myself as I drank boldly. It was sweet, but not too much so. It tasted vaguely of a peach drink. I liked it and nodded my thanks at Ja' Callum. "You smile at your men; why?"

"They are good men, fearless. I am proud of them." I said quietly, so I wouldn't make the men feel uncomfortable.

Ja' Callum looked back and forth like he was trying to figure something out. "Not because you favor them?"

I shook my head.

Then the light bulb appeared in his eyes. "The drinks might not have been good for them?"

I gave him an eye roll. "Meshallima Ama Ja' Catrina must come from a very dangerous place to fear poisons in a guest's home," he said gravely.

I couldn't deny the charge. "There are many dangers on Earth. Poison pales in comparison to what we face day to day there."

He looked confused. "My cousins and I have watched through the portal for many days. What we saw there didn't appear dangerous."

"Some places are peaceful, others are not. You have a view of a better part," I explained to him.

He sighed heavily. "We erred then, in assuming the whole of your world was like what we saw. That is why we left the portal open, so you may walk freely through, after we sent out the spell of calling."

I pressed for information, "But, you can close the portal and it will stay closed? Even after the Great Shift?"

His eyes got confused again. "Great Shift?"

I tried to expand on my meaning. "Where the poles of our world shifts, the axis may shift, too. This will definitely happen on our world. There, both things will happen, but I have no idea if a shift of that magnitude will happen here on Kla' din."

He finally got my drift. "You mean the realignment. This alignment will not be as strong, as to be a worry, but even during a major realignment, the Bokaris will work. It was why they were mined and cast so many eons ago. The knowledge of how to do it is passed down from father to son."

"And you know how to do it? Cast it, I mean?" I was deep sea fishing now.

He chuckled. "Not so fast, Meshallima. There is much I would hear from you, about you, your mates and your world." He pushed up from his sitting position near me. "First, we should feed you. Amazing really. You are a wonder. You must tell us how you are able to function as no other Vampyre has ever been known to." The awe was back in his voice.

"Fine, we can trade information," I said archly.

He chuckled and walked to where his cousins were cutting chunks of meat off of some animal they had hunted earlier.

Soon, the air was full of roasting meat and men talking in ease. I sat back and watched them converse and do their manly thing of the camp fire ritual, which seemed to be a universal man-habit obsession. I smiled to myself. My mates, too, wouldn't let me near a grill or a campfire, stating "it was man thing". My boys as well, even before meeting my mates, had acted the very same way, though they were raised by me alone.

It must be a Y-chromosome DNA phenomena, I had concluded, after my boys showed the same damned infuriating trait. Either that, or I had allowed my boys to watch too much television and it ruined them. I didn't know what did it, but like many women before me, and many women will after me, I just smiled indulgently, and let this pass.

We women picked our battles with the he-men of the world. Cooking at the grill or camp fire - we can let slide. Other things, not so much; and out comes the cast iron skillet if need be.

"How do you like your meat cooked, Meshallima Ama Ja' Catrina?" Ja' Kelo came over to ask me.

I sighed, not being able to let this one slide anymore. If I heard that long ass title one more time I was going to scream. "Ja' Kelo, is there a shorter way of addressing me properly? Something that isn't quite such a mouthful?" I asked with pleading eyes, batting them slightly.

Oh, yeah, the cast iron skillet was the last resort for a smart female. I always used my eyes first. Be nice the first time, but if that don't work, then get nasty. Besides, he seemed more easy-going then the other two did. Less ramrod.

He looked askance for a moment and then I saw his eyes crinkle at the edges. "Meshama, Catrina? Is this pleasing to you?" His tone was light and happy sounding. Dear Goddess - ok, I could live with it, so long as Rock never learned the language here.

I nodded, "Much better, thank you." He reached down and pressed his face to the side of mine while caressing my hair. He sighed happily and walked off back to the camp fire.

And he was much more touchy feely then the other two, mister wondering hands, sheesh!

He came walking back, realizing he hadn't found out how I liked my meat. If his cowl was off, I would bet money he was blushing. "Meshama?" He could tell I knew why he was there, and just waited for my answer.

"Very, very rare. Almost not cooked, if that's ok?" His posture brightened up and again with the hands on my face in a slow caress, then off he walked back to the roasting spit. Oh, yeah, I would have to watch this one.

Ja' Callum was by the fire watching the tête-à-tête with great attention. I could tell he was feeling pleased with the exchange.

I would have to find a way to keep 'Mister Grabby' at arm's length without hurting anyone's feelings (and never mind the slow burn I was feeling in my stomach). I was not that hard up, damn it. I had just gotten laid last night, sheesh!

It seemed they were taking turns caring for me, just as my mates did back home, since it was Ja' Monel who brought me my food. It was a tad disconcerting seeing the similarities in treatment. He had his own plate in hand and sat next to me. He seemed more serious than the other two did; more introverted, like his responsibilities as a ruler sat on him heavier than it did the others. He sat his plate down carefully and reached for my eating utensils before I could. He cut my meat and offered it to me from his own hand.

Everything he did was slow, careful and well thought out. I didn't know what to do, so I bit the offered meat. He then handed the tools to Ja' Callum and he was next to cut meat for me for the next bite. Again, with the same ritual, and I was starting to get a bad feeling about this, but took the bite from him, as well. Ja' Kelo was the last to cut and offer me a slice of meat. I hesitated and they all waited, it seemed, with bated breath. I looked over at Rock who only shrugged his shoulders.

Wizard was no help since he was just sitting there trying not to laugh at my predicament. I slowly accepted the meat and the air of tension eased between the three rulers. Ja' Kelo handed me the utensils for eating and reached up to remove his cowl. The other two started to remove theirs, as well. I gasped and quickly bit the inside of my mouth.

They were gorgeous. Blond haired all, but slightly different shading. The suns had set, so the blue power of their eyes had dimmed to allow their true colors to show. Ja' Kelo was the blondest and his eyes were a warm emerald green that still held laughter in them. Ja' Monel's blond hair was darker and his eyes were tawny; like an amber color, they were so deep. Not a normal human color, that's for sure, but arresting, nonetheless. These guys could have easily passed for brothers, with their similar hard sculpted features, strong jaws, chiseled cheeks and aquiline nose lines. They were like the Greek God, Apollo and just as striking. Ja' Monel had a wicked looking scar that looked as if it was from a recent wound. It ran from his temple, right along his right jaw line. His lips were tight with the seriousness I had picked up from before. This man had seen way too many battles, and recently too, since the scar was still pinkish. Unconsciously, my right hand went to his jaw where the scar was, and pressed into it lightly, throwing blue healing power to it without consciously realizing what I was doing. My eyes were sad for the pain this must have cost him. His cousins gasped when there was nothing left of the wound but a thin white, healed scar, as if he had gotten it many, many years ago. He turned his face into my palm and kissed it gently. "Your heart is gentle, Meshama Catrina. The pain in my head is gone. Blessed am I, for your healing touch." He closed his eyes and rested his face back into my hand like it was a cool drink of water after so long in the sun. I felt his spirit ease slightly with peace and the hard shield I had put around my heart cracked. I couldn't stop the call of his spirit to mine. I handed the plate to Ja' Callum, and put my arms around Ja' Monel and drew him tight against me, rocking him gently. "Be at peace warrior," I whispered to him. Ja' Callum looked at us with knowing in his gaze and he spoke softly, "His province is the hardest hit of all of ours. The Draugrall desire the stones of blood and Ja' Monel's lands hold the mines for them. There are very few women left in his province and people are taken more regularly there than anywhere else."

"Stones of blood?" Rock asked.

Ja' Callum turned to look at him, saying, "Red crystal-like stones."

"Probably ruby or ruby-like, Rock," I filled in with my guess. I brought up Ja' Monel's face to mine and really looked into his eyes.

I could see he had dreams like I did. Bad to ugly every night; never a moment of peace, even in sleep. I could recognize this, because, I too, had bad nights almost every night. Though, lately they had been easing up a bit, thanks to the patience and love of my mates.

I could take away the dreams from him, but the mind needs the release or it could go crazy. Bad dreams they may be, but it was how the mind coped. This one night, however, I could give him a beautiful dream with no harm to his psyche.

I bent to his forehead where his brow chakra was and as I kissed him there, I sent a bubble of power with a wish for the most relaxing carefree dream he could ever want and released him.

"You glow blue, Meshama, when you draw power, even though the blue sun is down," Ja' Kelo said in awe.

"She reflects the love of Amun-Ra," Ja' Callum agreed with him.

Ja' Monel's eyes were still serious, but glowed amber at me. "Thank you for your gifts. And thank you for accepting our courtship."

Huh? I looked to Ja' Callum for clarification and he handed me back my plate of food. "You took food from our hands. It's ritual for starting the bond properly. Even now, I would wager you feel our feelings better or you wouldn't have responded so deeply to Ja' Monel's spiritual plight. We have been worried about him, but with you here now easing his soul, we should be able to save him."

Whoa! Whoa! Whoa! I did what? Ja' Monel's spirit is in danger? Wait a minute, what did that have to do with me? Oh, fuck a duck!

I got up. I walked over to Rock. I handed him my plate.

He took one look at the expression on my face and said, "Oh, shit."

I walked out of the encampment.

I kept walking until I found the pool I had stepped into before. I let my head fall back and screamed at the top of my lungs. I ranted and raved until I had gotten all the bitching out of my system. I marched up and down the edge of the pool, fuming and pounding the sands around it. Then, I stripped out of my clothes, leaving them on a large rock. I jumped into the water and swam until I was tired. I swam back to shore only to see the three of them waiting for me by my clothes. Each had a sad, serious expression on his face and I walked over to them not minding my nakedness. If my kids weren't home, I always walked around naked from the pool to the house.

As I neared the rock, Ja' Callum said with a heavy voice, "Would being bonded to us be so terrible?"

I thought about it for a minute. "No, actually it wouldn't." I told him truthfully. And because I couldn't stand the pain rolling off from Ja' Monel, I hugged him tight.

I turned and caressed Ja' Kelo's face, just to take the sadness away from their eyes. Then I started putting my clothes back on.

Ja' Callum stopped me, touching my stomach and the stretch mark scars that were there in tiny, thin, white lines. "You have had children?"

"Yes, I have three boys at home," I told him.

"With your mates?" The sadness was coming back into his voice.

I shook my head, "No, by others before our bond was made."

"You can have children outside of a mating bond?"

"Yes, though they aren't full blooded, they are still very strong."

He pressed his palm to my lower stomach and reached inside with power. "You can still have children, even now?"

I couldn't take my eyes off his hand as it touched my abdomen. "Yes, though we aren't sure if they'll have fangs or not."

"If they did have fangs though, they would be like you, yes?" He gently caressed my stomach.

"More than likely." I was starting to feel like a brood mare, with me naked and them touching my womb.

They all looked amazed again. Then Mister Grabby made a move, nuzzling into my neck and trying to touch me between my legs. I was so shocked, I almost didn't move fast enough. I grabbed his hand, moving him away and stepped to the side from him completely. I held his hand with mine, smacking it like I was scolding him as I would a child.

"If I have to remind you again, no touchy, I am going to get extremely physical and you won't like it," I growled at him.

Ja' Callum roared with laughter. "Haven't you learned yet to let a woman open like a flower? You can't make her bloom before her time; she needs to be seduced. Especially this one."

"But, she feels so hot, so wet, even now. She needs a man between her legs to ease her," Ja' Kelo said disbelievingly.

"I feel her need as well, but this isn't the time for loving her body," his eyes slid down to my nether regions with a deep sigh of regret. "Not without the permission of her mates. We had already discussed this, Ja' Kelo, and you agreed."

"How you can stand there and not want to touch her, is beyond me. I can smell her arousal and feel her need," Ja' Kelo's voice was deepening in passion.

He'd be the kind of lover who could take you all night long and…wait, did I hear, "My mates? What do they have to do with this?" I couldn't focus clearly with them standing so close.

Ignoring my question, Ja' Callum said, "Of course I want her. My manhood is hard for her already, although she has not touched me. But we agreed to the plan, and we will stay with it. It's the only way with her."

Ja' Kelo looked frustrated. "Then, can we not just give her pleasure, so she does not stand in need so badly?" I almost groaned aloud with the thought of their mouths on me and sank to my knees. Ja' Monel picked me up and held me against his body, my back to his chest and I could feel his erection against my buttocks. I groaned again, almost grinding myself against him just to feel it more.

"We should not have touched her so close to her womanhood; she is throbbing now, feeling all of us desiring her. Between our needs and hers, we are building a harmonic of passion between us."

"At least, she does desire us. I can feel what she would like me to do to her," Ja' Monel groaned against my ear, which only made things worse. I was damn near screaming with need now.

Ja' Kelo begged, "Let me ease her with my hand; that should be innocent enough. Her mates might understand."

I couldn't understand what he was saying, but anything that would satisfy this need, I would take. His hand - his mouth - anything.

"You are lying to yourself, to have her any way you can get her now, Ja' Kelo. We have to help her with her honor and send her back to her mates untouched by us until they say we can. Control yourself." Ja' Callum turned to Ja' Monel. "Can you hold her and not touch her sexually?"

I felt the strength and determination ripple through him. "For her, I can do it. I will hold her honor." I was angry and wanted him to want me just as badly. I tried to rub my ass against him, but he drew himself back from me. I moaned in frustration.

"Meshama, Catrina, look at me, lamar. See me." His eyes were deep blue and hypnotic with power. "Your need is too great now to ignore - pleasure yourself. Help us hold your honor and take care of your arousal while we guard you."

I was panting with need and couldn't stop. He had given me permission. Slowly, my hand lowered to my womanhood, sinking my fingers inside myself and then rubbing my clit. "That's it, lamar, feel yourself, love yourself. We are here." Ja Callum's eyes grew bigger and bluer. He was using power on me and I didn't care right then. I took my other hand and played with my nipple while the other pleasured my clitoris. I was wet and so close already.

"You are beautiful, lamar. Do it. Let your release come," he whispered softly.

I rubbed my swollen clit faster, alternating between moving inside myself and rubbing, getting wetter all the time.

"Lamar, lover, please come for us. Imagine us filling your punany with our shafts, giving you our seed." And that was all it took. I came, screaming and shaking in Ja' Monel arms.

I heard all three groan, as if they too, came with me, even though I wasn't touching any of them. I felt wetness at my back and knew then that Ja' Monel did, and probably the others, as well. The power here so close to the water was driving all of us in passion. Wave after wave washed over me, until I was finally spent. I wasn't the only one the wave had taken for a ride.

"Loving her physically, is going to be more blessed than the heavens," Ja' Callum was panting along with the others.

Chapter Three

The Ties that Bind

Once I was able to think again, Ja' Monel let me go. I silently put my clothes on. Embarrassment didn't even begin to cover this. I didn't look at them. I didn't acknowledge them. I just stood there looking at the water, thinking of how much this was going to hurt my mates.

Ja' Callum broke the silence. "Meshama, I beg of you, don't be angry with us."

I turned, shocked. "How can I be angry with you? You saved my honor; for that I thank you all."

I felt relief flood through all three of them. Oh fuck. Their feelings and emotions were becoming clearer by the second. I stood away from them and created a circle of protection around me. They backed up. I dropped my own personal shields and opened my chakras, then connected them. I lifted out of my body and looked at my solar plex chakra with my astral eyes. There, near the top of my solar plex chakra, right below my mates' bonds, were three new smaller half-formed bonds. I was in such deep shit now. In my astral body, I turned and looked at them, not believing it; but, sure enough, the new half-formed bonds went straight to them. They were watching me. Not my body that was standing a bit away from my astral subtle body; but at me, my spirit self. They could see me now. They could also see the bonds going from me to them.

"Your spirit is even more beautiful than your physical form, Meshama," Ja' Kelo said with wonder.

Ja' Monel eyes grew sad for me though. "Look closer Ja' Kelo. See the damage to her soul? See all the scars? So much pain, Meshama. What happened?"

"What happened?" I laughed insanely. "The price I had to pay for my mates' bonds."

I left my body standing in the circle and drifted over to them in my spirit form. "The price I had to pay to keep my children safe." I grew angrier with every step I took in my spirit form. "The price I had to pay to survive the streets as a child." I evaporated into the air and became the part of the environment. "What price will I have to pay for you?" my spirit voice, which resounded through the area around them, demanded to know.

They dropped to their knees, bowing. I rarely ever tapped into my Goddess powers because they frightened even me.

I was always terrified I would accidently destroy something in my anger, so I had closed that part off from me, but not tonight. Tonight, I was feeling my Godhead and I was angry. If I lost total control, I could tear this world apart and there would be no fixing it.

Shamus shimmered into existence. "Is this really what you want to do? Who are you really angry with?"

It made me stop and listen to him. He repeated, "Who are you really angry with, Catrina?"

When I could think somewhat again, I answered, "Myself."

"Is this display going to help that?" Another astral being shimmered into existence; a huge timber wolf, my spirit guide, Shashone. "Will this do your soul any good, Catrina? Will this help you grow?"

Shamus must have called him or brought him along without telling me. But, it turned out to be a good thing to do; I was thinking again and not just reacting.

I gave the truth. "No, this will not. This will harm me."

Shashone sat down on his hind quarters and nodded sagely at me. "We can't stop you. You have free will. But think of what you do; who will be harmed; what emotion you will feel when you're done."

Shamus was getting cranky. "Think, before you react. If you must, you will; but it had better be worth it, don't you think? Or are you even thinking?"

I wasn't thinking, was I? I shimmered back into my astral form. This world, or even these people, weren't the cause of my pain. Ja' Monel had asked the wrong question at the wrong time, but that wasn't his fault. He didn't know any better. He didn't know what my triggers were and when not to ask me things.

Being in astral form, I was susceptible to strong emotions and I had never learned to really control those yet. Unless the pain and rage was dealt with, I may never learn to control the more volatile of my emotions in astral form.

"Thank you, my friends. I am sorry I lost control." I felt such guilt for letting the pain get away from me.

Demitri had warned me to deal with it soon, before something really bad happened. He wasn't wrong. There just never seemed to be enough time for me to have a 'safe' break down.

I looked back over to the sorcerers. I drifted over through the circle and into my body. I replaced my shields and blocked my Goddess powers again, so I wouldn't accidently tap into them.

Breaking the circle, I took a deep breath and walked over to them. "Arise." They rose, looking at me with a mixture of fear and guilt.

"We did not mean to cause you more pain, Meshama," Ja' Callum started.

"Stop," I ordered. Instead, I bent knee to them. "Forgive me for losing control on your world."

My astral familiars came to stand beside me, flanking on each side. "Forgive me for taking my anger out on you, when you all have been nothing but honorable. The fault is completely mine. I accept full responsibility for my actions and will pay your price for restitution or punishment if I have broken any laws here." With that, I bowed my head to them and waited for a verdict.

"Meshama, no," both Ja' Monel and Ja' Callum said in shock.

Ja' Callum lifted me to my feet. "An Ama should never bow to one who is not Godling."

I glared at him. "Yes, she should, if she messes up. Being an Ama doesn't make me any better than anyone else. Just more dangerous. Especially if I don't keep the bonds of morality and decency on me. It's like a loaded gun with no safety."

Ja' Callum looked confused at the reference. "Oh, how about a scimitar with no sheath and you run real fast?" I said. He got that one with a grimace on his face.

"See, bad thing, right?" He nodded. "That's me, if I don't hold myself to a higher standard than most, you understand?"

Ja' Callum cupped my face. "But, you didn't do any harm, so there is no law broken. Accepted?"

I wasn't happy with it, but let it go. "Accepted."

"Who are these spirits with you, Meshama?" Ja' Kelo couldn't contain his curiosity any longer.

"My friends, Shamus and Shashone. Shamus is my General for my astral familiars and Shashone is my spirit guide. He tries to keep me honest. It's his job." I turned to my familiars and introduced them to the rulers of Kla' din.

"Meshama, you keep amazing me every domar," Ja' Callum said.

I snorted, "Don't be impressed. More than half of my powers, I can't use safely, so it's useless to me."

He clucked his tongue, "That may be true today, but tomorrow brings more possibilities. Do not treat lightly your gifts, or dismiss them so easily."

"Don't bother, I have been telling her that for years; she doesn't listen," my crabby Shamus spoke before I could.

"Why don't you go play with your bones?" I snapped at him, playfully.

The Dai' Khan's didn't know how to take this expression any better than before.

"I would like to go around and check things out, if it's ok with them?" Shamus nodded to the Dai' Khans.

"I, too, would like to feel this world. Much strange energy is here. It is worth exploring if I may?" Both of them now looked towards the Dai' Khans.

A bit off-balanced, they recovered quickly, as Ja' Callum communed with his cousins. "Feel free to explore. We would hope that you'll like it here and convince her to stay awhile."

Shamus barked a laugh. "Good luck with that, Casanova. She has a strong sense of duty and things are about to go bust on Earth. She has to stay there until it's over and do her job, *if* she survives it." With that, he popped out and Shashone nodded his thanks and followed after him.

"What does he mean by that, Meshama?" Ja' Monel asked.

"What is a Casanova?" Ja' Callum followed.

I sighed. "Things on Earth are getting bad. Portals are opening up with greater frequency and hostiles are coming through. The Great Shift is only a short time away and once that happens, all hell is going to break loose there. It's my duty and that of the rest of the Nightwolves to see that death and destruction is kept to a minimum. Also, we need to either make treaties or keep the hostiles out with weapons and magick if need be." I summed up everything going on there. They might as well know, since once the hostiles were done with Earth, their world could be next.

I knew I wouldn't have to spell it out for them when Ja' Callum got his 'death to all enemies' face on. Total ruthlessness. I had to love it.

"You could die doing this thing?" he growled.

"Yes, I could." I had already died once, but I wasn't going to tell him about it. He looked about ready to blow a fuse as it was.

He grabbed my hands. "Meshama, let us come to your world, not only to help, but we must speak with your mates."

"They won't be happy campers," I warned him. This was my price for losing my control, though I knew he didn't mean it that way. The universe, however, has a way of balancing things out.

"If you mean they will be upset, we are expecting that. If we could get them to agree though, would you welcome our bonds?" He looked so intently into my eyes, so determined, as if he would blow through worlds to have me. He was probably strong enough to do it too, just as my mates were. I was flattered. I couldn't lie about that. I also knew I wanted them or the beginning of the bonds wouldn't have already started. If I was honest with myself, I did want them. I just loathed hurting my mates over it.

I sighed, "Yes, I would accept the bonds, if you can get my mates to agree." He looked so happy; he almost kissed me, but stopped himself in time. The other two were also grinning. It was good to see Ja' Monel smile. I had a feeling he didn't often have a reason to.

They had swum in the pool to get clean and with a wave of their hands, their clothes were cleaned as well. I was jealous. I wish I knew how to do that. While we walked back to the camp, I filled them in on Earth's situation - the hostiles we had already battled and won against and the things we needed to do next. They were astounded by what we had already done and asked many questions, which I answered if I had the knowledge. Trying to explain cars to people who didn't even have radio was really difficult, let alone the technology that could make even a mundane dangerous to our kind.

When we got into camp, Rock wasn't looking happy. "Took you long enough. I was about to send a two man team to see where you went off to."

"Sorry Rock, I had a lot to assimilate, though. Things are cool now." I gave him my best bullshit grin.

"Good, did you get a treaty fixed yet?" Great; he bought it.

"In a way, yes, for the most part." I wasn't too sure how to answer that one.

"What's the condition?" He was sharp; I had to give him that.

I met his eyes levelly and told him, "They need to meet my mates and have a sit-down with them."

He stared at me a long time to see if I was joking. When he saw I was totally serious, he started laughing...hard.

Wizard came over, and inquired, "What's up?" His blond surfer dude good looks were waiting to join in the fun. Oh, I was so not going to hear the end of this for a long, long time.

Rock told him the joyful news and when they both could catch their breath, they started laying odds on a series of outcomes. Most ended up with me not sitting for a year and the sorcerers dead.

"So, Cat, what's your bet?" Wizard asked me, grinning ear from ear.

"Fifty says I can't sit for a week. No, make that two. Bad fight between the men, no death," I concluded.

"You're in and bet is noted." He was actually writing this one down and going to the rest of the team to get their bets, as well.

Ja' Callum had let us go on for a while, then he said, "What do you mean you can't sit for a week or more?"

Which, of course, set Rock and Wizard off again. It was so hard to keep a secret within the Nightwolves. The whole damn gang is going to know about this before I even make it back to the Nightwolves Lair.

Before Rock or Wizard could give him a totally graphic side of it, I said, "It means, Ja' Callum, I will be spanked so hard my butt is going to hurt for seven days or more."

Of course, the things that go along with the spanking, I didn't mind so much at all. I shuddered again remembering the last time.

He looked shocked, then did a double take when he felt my desire start up again.

He put two and two together and looked really hard at me. "This is allowed and you enjoy it?" Rock and Wizard started in with the hilarity again.

I grabbed Ja' Callum by the arm and pulled him into a tent. I had to stop and take a look when I walked in. It was a sweet set up with a soft bed, pillows and silky-looking sheets. Very nice.

His two cousins had followed us in and Ja' Monel looked furious. "They spank you like a child," he roared.

The roaring got my attention off of the décor. "Yes, they do, if I deserve it." Then, I got a saucy grin. "But, I spank, too, if they piss me off. It's a fair trade."

They didn't know what to say to that. Ja' Kelo's eyes were wide, most likely trying out the images in his mind, the horn dog.

"Or, I put them on the couch if they really make me mad," I added.

"What is the couch?" Ja' Callum looked like it sounded like a torture device or something.

"If one of them gets me mad enough, he sleeps on the couch. No sex. NO bed with me. Get it?"

From the side glances they were giving each other, it still came out sounding like a torture device to them. Typical males.

That night, the Dai' Khans let the men use one tent, while they used another and insisted I take the last tent for myself. I didn't argue. Sleeping with a bunch of men in one small tent, I could do without. The snoring alone could drive me insane. Rock had me on third shift for guard duty, though the Dai' Khans were slightly offended that we felt the need, until I explained to him we do that wherever we went, just in case. Just like we didn't give up our weapons -

ever. It was a rule we had to follow. They could understand that and let it go without anymore insult to them over it.

Oh, my mates were going to be pissed when I got home. I had braided my hair before going to bed, so I wouldn't have to fuss with it when I awoke for my turn. I lay down on the floor, instead of the bed, so I wouldn't sleep too deeply. The bed looked like it was heaven and I wasn't riding any dream clouds tonight. I had taken my swords out of my black bag and laid them down next to me. It was what saved my life that night.

I was sleeping peacefully enough, until I heard Shamus yell, "Wake up. Attack!" Then, I heard the tearing of the wall of the tent in one long quick slash. I jumped to my feet with my swords in my hands when this black shadow had landed on the bed, throwing things around, looking for whoever was supposed to be in the bed. While it was busy doing that, I slashed at it with the sword in my right hand. Whatever it was shrieked and a burning smell had begun. Shamus threw a witch ball made of light at it and it blinded it for a moment.

I brought down a cross-slash with my second sword against the side of its torso. Again, another shriek came from the thing. The creature turned to me to see what was hurting it. Glowing blood-red eyes looked out from a humanoid face with fangs that made mine look cute.

It scented me and actually licked its lips and started to come at me with his hands extended. "You're the one we came for," it hissed.

I stepped back, surprised at the declaration. He kept coming at me with those fingernails looking like razor sharp claws. He used them like knives, as he clawed at me. I twisted away, not wanting to see if the tips were poisoned or not. Shamus kept throwing energy balls at it, while I took turns cutting its sides, trying to get its neck.

I could hear yells and orders being shouted from outside. I needed to get out of here quick, because it sounded like there were more outside. I let my fangs extend and hissed at him, which threw him off guard enough that I finally cut through part of his neck.

"Good job. Get it again," Shamus gloated.

It didn't go all the way through, but enough to make this blood sucker go down to his knees, so I could finish the job easier. Once I cut the head off completely from the body, I ran outside with Shamus following and took in the scene. Rock and a marine were back to back with each other, firing their guns at incoming black shadows. I saw two writhing creatures on the ground, moaning over the bullet wounds they received. Thank the Goddess, Rock had brought the silver ammo and obviously loaded their guns with it once they knew the Dai' Khans had vamps on this world.

I went to chop off the heads of those that were down. Shamus went to Rock's team to blind the vamps with light balls. I ran into the tent the men had been sleeping in. Wizard was fighting a vamp off that had his teeth in his neck. I didn't hesitate and brought down my blades into the creatures back, getting its attention. It let go of Wizard and stood up to come at me. I did my fang hissing act again, but it was too pissed to care. It leapt with its hands and claws extended. I sliced down on its wrist, doing some serious damage. I whirled into it, cutting with a downward stroke so I could hamstring its legs. It dropped to its knees and I took off its head with one blow. Wizard was gasping, but breathing, with blood pouring down the side of his neck.

"Shamus, get in here," I shouted. He popped into the tent. "Take care of Wizard. I need to see if anyone else needs back up." Shamus nodded at me, bending over Wizard as I ran out of the tent.

I came to a dead stop when I saw the Dai' Khans standing back to back in a triangle, fighting off four vamps. They were using their powers combined, to move as fast as the vampyres did, which explained why they didn't have enough focus leftover to throw witch balls or fire balls at these fanged creeps. Watching these guys go at it with their silver scimitars was like watching the finest dance of blades I had ever seen. Again, their movements were enhanced with magick.

Their blades just whirled and slashed in such quick succession that the vamps where being hacked into pieces. Vamp sushi, I thought to myself and then gave out a giggle. Damn, I was losing it. Two other marines were firing into the bodies of a couple of vamps that were feeding on a third marine.

"Hold fire," I yelled, as I jumped over one vampyre, kicking it in the head and slashing at another. Their blood frenzy was so intense, the silver bullets weren't doing a whole lot here. But, with me kicking it, that got the vamp pissed as hell, which was good enough for me. I took it on with my swords, slashing in and out. It would dodge and try to rip back at me with its claws. I circled back and while slashing at the one in front of me, I kicked at the other one to get him pissed, too. It worked - sort of. It raised its head enough for one of the marines to empty a whole clip into its brain and that was the end of that one.

I gave the one in front of me my full attention then. This blood sucker was a big one and wasn't going down easily. It also was slightly different from the others, as it actually wore jewelry. A large red stone was hanging from his chest and glowing in the campfire light. Every time I hurt it, that damned stone would glow bright red and he would be at me again like he wasn't hurt at all anymore.

Shamus yelled, "The stone, Cat. The stone is power for it." I finally got it, when I slashed the hell out of Mr. Super Vamp and he got back up to come after me again as if I'd done nothing to it.

Sometime during the fight I heard, "Meshama, no." Then, I heard Rock yell, "Back off. You'll distract her," but I didn't look to see what the problem was. This vamp was too powerful and getting on my last nerve.

I hacked at him again and then kicked him in the chest. While it was bent slightly, I whirled in on reverse and slashed it across its back, then got in front of it again. That damn stone glowed and it got back up looking refreshed. I had had enough. With my left sword, I brushed aside both of his claw like hands and with the tip of my other sword, I hooked the chain the stone was hanging on and snapped it back. The necklace broke off of super vamp's neck and I kicked it away towards the fire. I went back to work chopping and cutting. This time, it wasn't recovering so well. I got it down on its knees and with both swords, swept like a scythe through its neck. It hung there until I hacked again, cutting the rest of it off and the thing was dead.

The silence was thick in the air after that and my breathing sounded like had pumped bellows.

"Meshama, are you all right?" Ja' Callum came over and proceeded to check me from head to toe with his hands for wounds. Ja' Monel wasn't far behind, his face grim again.

Ja' Kelo yelled to Ja' Callum, "Cousin, we have a problem."

I pushed the worried hands away and went to see what was wrong with one of our men. Corporal Malcolm was slowly losing blood from the wound in his neck; he had already lost so much.

I moved in to heal the wound. Ja' Callum watched as my hands glowed with power and the wound healed. Malcolm still wasn't out of the woods until I got his blood regenerating fast enough in his body.

I was tired, but looking for the next wounded man when Rock yelled, "Cat, in here."

Wizard was still in the tent, moaning in pain.

Shamus looked at me with sadness in his eyes. "I can't heal this wound, Cat."

Ja' Callum hissed in sympathy for Wizard. I went to lay hands on the wound myself only to get zapped back.

"What's wrong?" Rock asked.

"The wound, it's wrong," I said.

He looked worried now. "What do you mean?"

"That's what I was trying to tell her, the wound is evil. I can't touch this one. All I can do is stop the progression," Shamus explained.

I looked closer at the wound with my second sight and saw black astral parasitical worms wriggling inside the wound.

Ja' Callum must have used his own second sight. "He has been infected. You won't be able to heal him, Meshama, until the wound is cleansed."

I nodded in understanding. Some of Earth's legends talked about this sort of vampire bite. "Get me some clear water." Ja' Kelo ran out to get me what I wanted.

I patted Wizard's shoulder. "Hey guy, hang in there ok? I will get you all fixed up."

Wizard moaned, "It burns, Cat."

"I know, bro, I know. But, not for long. I ain't going to bullshit you though; this will hurt like a mother."

Ja' Kelo walked back in with a cup of water and handed it to me. I placed my hand over it and invoked the blessing, "Dear Lord and Lady, please bless this creature of water and consecrate it to Your power. As I will, so mote it be." I poured white light energy into the water.

Then, I asked Ja' Callum and Rock to hold him down and poured the now blessed water over the wound. Wizard yelled loudly. The wound bubbled, like I had poured hydrogen peroxide into it.

"I am sorry. I am so sorry. I hate hurting you, but we have to clean the wound." I hated that I was hurting him like this, but I knew it had to be done or else he would turn into one of those creatures.

He was panting with the pain. "Go for it, sis."

I poured more on, knowing it was feeling like acid to him, as he tried hard not to scream.

I looked again at the wound and saw that it was cleaner. "Good, we got to it real quick. Shamus held it off well. Almost there, one more time buddy. Hang in there," I said, as I tipped more of the water into the wound.

He was able to hold in the scream this time, only moaning now from the pain. I looked again and saw that I could actually heal the wound completely this time. I let the healing flow into the wound.

He still groaned from it, but the wound closed and I didn't get zapped.

Shamus was grinning at me. "Good job, Cat. And since you killed the one who had bitten him, he shouldn't be able to be called."

Rock looked alarmed. "Called? Like a slave? I thought that was a vamp myth, Cat. 'Movie crap', you said, if I recall right?"

I looked up at him from my crouch near Wizard. "Yes, for *my* kind of vamp, Rock, it's movie crap. There are many, many types of vamps, however - all with their own codes, legends, and rules that control their ways. Some kinds of vamps can enslave you from just a bite and some do not. It all depends on what kind of vamp tribe it comes from. This type apparently can enslave from a bite."

"Meshama, there are other vampyre tribes? Some that are not infectious with their bites?" Ja' Kelo asked, sounding astonished with the news.

"Many kinds of vamps, some are good guys. Most are not," I admitted.

Ja' Callum wanted to know, "And your vampyre turning came from one of these good tribes?" Rock and Wizard both looked really interested, since they had never found out how exactly I, or my mates, became vampires 'super style'.

I pinched the bridge of my nose and sighed heavily. "I wasn't bitten by any vampire tribe, good or bad."

Ja' Monel asked before anyone else could, "Then how, Meshama, are you vampyre?"

I gazed up at Shamus. "Don't look at me; it's not my call, Princess." Oh, that old coot - when we get home...

"Yeah, and while you're at it, what's with the princess thing that gets dropped every now and again, hmmm?" Rock asked a tad sarcastically, his eyebrow doing double time now.

"Yeah, enquiring minds want to know," Wizard quipped.

I sat down and slumped my shoulders. "Lost Boys," I told Wizard. I had no clue as to what to answer, or how much, on the rest of it. Rubbing my face with my hands, I groaned in frustration. "This fucking sucks. I hate this shit."

"Meshama?" Ja' Callum squatted down with me, rubbing my shoulders.

"Ok, short, short version. You know our world is facing a crisis situation with the Great Shift happening in 2012, December. The Gods and Goddesses of old, decided to put the spiritual children they had into the bodies of pregnant human women so we may grow in physical form, due to a ban on doing it the old-fashioned style like in legends. For instance, Zeus' many half mortal children that were cursed by his wife, Hera. We were born and then mated to other pantheons of Gods and Goddesses so the power would be more spread out on Earth to help save it and heal what gets messed up. I had to find my soulmates to make the connection between the Egyptian pantheon and the Celtic one. Sort of like an arranged marriage, but we really are meant for each other, since we were created that way. In searching for my mates, we fought a dark God and all of us died, even though we won. We were brought back and were 'blessed' with super vamp powers, so we could be more effective in dealing with the Greater Magickal Races. Ergo, you see the vamps outside that I kicked ass on with nothing but swords. Now, if you all don't believe me, I could really give a shit." With that announcement, I stood up to walk out of the tent before I could hear a remark that would piss me off. Not a good thing, after a battle, since my blood was still pumping.

"Wait, you still didn't explain the princess thing or the, 'your world,' statement you made once." Rock was fishing for all the goodies in Cat's bag.

"Ha, this one won't be so hard to swallow. I have my own world called Trinidad, which I created myself, just like this world you are now on. You know you aren't on Earth anymore, so now it won't be so hard to believe there are actually other worlds out there. Being half a Goddess, I made Trinidad and the more time and power I put into it, the more it will stabilize on a physical plane. At the moment, it is mostly half and half. You'd have to know physics and psychic energy to get the meaning of that. Just know that if we went to Trinidad now, it would seem just about as solid as this world does. Because I created it, I am the princess there. Anything else?"

"Meshama has her own world?" Ja' Callum sounded flabbergasted.

Ja' Kelo asked, "Can you take us there, Meshama? I would love to see your world."

I stopped to think about that and then it hit me. "Yes," I said brightly, "I could, when the second sun rises. It would provide me with enough energy to create a portal from this world to Trinidad! We could just walk there!"

"Bah, "Shamus snorted, "I was wondering how long it would take you to realize that."

I rounded on him. "You knew? Why didn't you tell me, Shamus?"

"Some things you need to figure out on your own, Princess," he intoned sagely, but in a mocking tone of voice.

"You are my General, not my spirit guide you, you... oh, I can't think of anything that would fit you right now." I stomped out of the tent. I heard him giggling at my exit, the old coot.

Nonetheless, the men weren't going to let me get out of any more conversation this time. "Oh, Cat, not so fast," Rock said, making it sound like an order.

I spun around. "What? I told you everything. Ok, most things. What now? I have to clean my weapons. We have to burn those vamp bodies and we need to find out how and why they attacked here in the first place. Or, did that escape everyone else's attention, but mine?" I added archly. That stopped the deluge of questions I had seen coming. Ha!

I cleaned the nasty vamp blood off of my weapons. The stuff stank like rotten fruit with maggots. We made a pit outside of the camp for burning the bodies and made Corporal Malcolm as comfortable as we could, since he was going to take some time replenishing his blood loss. Wizard pushed himself in helping out, and by the time we had settled around the smaller campfire, he looked about ready to keel over. I caught Shamus' eyes and gave him a mental request to give Wizard some energy on the sly. He did as I asked, and soon, Wizard perked up a bit, though he didn't consciously know why.

Shamus hovered near me for a while. We had drinks and got some food cooking, which made my mouth water at the smells. I had expended a lot of energy, and sure, blood would have done nicely, but I wasn't about to ask anyone for a sip after the small dust-up we'd with this world's tribe of nasty vampyres.

I started the discussion. "So, Ja' Callum, is this kind of fight usual for this place? From the way you were talking earlier, this place sounded pretty safe."

His face hardened at the imagined slight. "No, Meshama, this has never happened here before. My apologies."

I gentled my tone of voice. "I didn't mean to throw insult. I only meant to point out a fact that since I took you at your word in believing this place to be a safe refuge, this attack had to be prompted by an unusual event."

He relaxed his expression to one that seemed to be appeased and bowed towards me.

"The vampyre that tore his way into my tent said to me, before I whacked his head off, 'You are the one we came for,'" I told the group at large.

"Whoa, you sure have a way with men, Cat," Wizard said jokingly.

I ignored him with a half grin. "The question now is, how did they know I was here?"

Surprisingly, Shamus was the one who offered a possible answer. "I think I know that one. When you had your little ...uhmm... temper tantrum, you set off an astral signature of extreme power. Much like a solar flare, but imagine it on the astral plane. They may have a way to watch over this world from an astral perspective and saw the flare."

I turned to look at Ja' Callum. "The vampyres are not native to this world?"

"No, Meshama Catrina, they use astral doorways to come in from their world to ours. They have done this for millennia now. We can close and guard portals, but as you know, from being a Ja', astral doorways can open anywhere, anytime. We've no way to stop that." He sounded tired. It looked to me like he was suffering from information overload. "You won't be safe here anymore, Meshama Catrina. They know you are here now and they covet you. They have never stopped once they set their sights on a goal. Women who have power above the average, they covet the most."

"The fact that they sent a Master vampyre so far from an astral doorway, putting him at risk, shows how much they want you," Ja' Monel took up from Ja' Callum. "Masters are protected heavily and never before had been put at risk. I am impressed you took one out by yourself, Meshama. It speaks well of your own warrior abilities." He tilted his head to me in respect.

I got a warm fuzzy. Oh, damn it, not now with the mushy stuff, Cat, I told myself.

Ja' Kelo added sadly, "They usually stay near the doorway they open up, so as to guard the way for when their kin return from a hunt."

"And to have a safe escape route if the fight comes too close, sacrificing their brethren in the process," Ja' Callum said further, with disgust lacing his voice.

I pressed for details. "So they have strong magick." To be able to open an astral doorway from one world to another takes great magick. Not everyone can do it, not even within my own family. Not without one hell of a power boost.

"Only the Masters, and only with the blood stone for a focus. It adds a charge to their magick. That's why they usually safeguard their masters. Not all Draugralls can wield any magick. It's why they go after females that are the strongest in magickal power. They hope to breed more magick wielders among them," Ja' Callum explained.

Ja' Monel added, "That's why my province is hit the hardest. My lands are rich with blood stone." It explained his battle weariness. I was willing to bet his province, too, has been picked clean of any magick carrying females.

"So, the Bokaris are useless for keeping the Draugrall out, I would bet. Astral doorways can be anywhere. They aren't stationary or permanent," I mused out loud.

Ja' Callum nodded. "You are right, Meshama. The only warning we usually have, is when the three moons are in the night sky together. That is when they usually come into our world. They are early in their attack. A three moon rising is only one night every 33 days. We are not due for another until 14 more days."

So, this was my fault. "What about your provinces? Can you tell if they were hit there, as well?"

"We did get an alarm from our chimes, but the guard we had left behind took care of the matter. We only lost a few people this time."

So, the attack wasn't planned out well enough for a successful major hit. It was more like a volley to distract from the real goal, of finding the direction of the power that was here. Then, they opened another doorway closer to the camp. To get to me.

Rock asked, "What's a chime?"

Ja' Callum reached inside his vest and pulled out a five inch long crystal. "This is what we use to communicate with those who have no spirit tie to us or who may not have the ability for telepathy."

"Ha, a magickal telephone, Rock. That's cool, Ja' Callum," I smiled at him.

He smiled at me with a tad of confusion. "Your world does not use these?"

"No, we have telephones. Well, we used to, but now we have cell phones and I hate it. They can cause physical illnesses which the damn companies don't tell the public about the EMR waves, or they don't work half the time because you're out of range. My personal favorite, is getting a bill for seven hundred bucks when they swore they would only charge forty five dollars, the Greedy Profiteering Corporate Gluttons," I snorted, disgusted with most of the companies back on Earth.

"They swear oath, then break it? This is allowed?" Ja' Callum looked incredulous.

"Most people are like sheep on Earth, Ja' Callum. Not enough people get mad and demand that the companies do faithful business anymore. People trust the government to watch out for that kind of thing, but it doesn't. The government is worse than the damn greedy corporations most of the time. Our world has many problems. America's apathy is just one of them, and it's also the most dangerous."

"Can't you do something as Ama and Ja'?" Ja' Kelo asked me.

"No, I hold no authority there, nor would I want to. I just protect the place as best I can, same as Rock, and hope people get wise fast enough before the next step in civilization's cycle is taken," I sighed.

I knew it wouldn't happen unless the Great Shift made warriors come out of the woodwork. If not, and if people still were sheep, the next step in the cycle will happen. It was what the black covens and such were hoping for. It would make for easy pickings.

Rock nodded. "Slavery and bondage - we're not too far from it now."

I glanced at him, knowing he would never say those words aloud on Earth. Most, just try to get along and go with the flow, following orders and hoping for the best. It's all any one person could do. To stem the cycle, on Earth, of the rise and fall of all of the civilizations throughout history, it would take a mass population outrage. Every major civilization has gone through the cycle. Slavery and bondage, revolution, growth and peace, apathy then back to slavery and bondage. America was in its apathy stage, and at such a bad time with the Great Shift coming.

"It sounds like you have danger within, as well as without, Meshama. It is hard to fight a battle on two fronts and win," Ja' Callum lectured me with serious eyes.

I turned to him. "I know that, but I have given an oath to protect. I can't back away now and let America fall. If America falls and the Great Shift happens to its' most devastating capacity, those who are black practitioners will move in and enslave the rest of the whole world. The dark Gods will come back and rule. All will be lost. Sooner or later, that darkness could spread to other worlds." I was determined not to let that happen and it showed on my face.

"We will help as much as we can, Meshama. But, we do have to put the safety and growth of our own world first." Ja' Monel's face was grim, again.

"As well you should," I gave an approving nod. "We'll take what help you can offer and give back what we can. Luckily, astral magick is my forte, but I need to understand how, exactly, they come over here in the first place."

I pulled out the necklace the Master Vampyre had had on and held it to the light. The main sun had been climbing for a while, so I used it to see inside the crystal. It appeared to be like the jewel of a huge ruby - the biggest sized ruby I had ever seen, since it covered the palm of my hand.

"Careful, Cat, we have no idea what the power of that stone could do to you since you are vampire yourself," Shamus warned.

"I wasn't planning on tapping into its power. I am just trying to determine what kind of stone it is," I said, as I twirled it in the sunbeam.

Shamus gave me his opinion. "Ruby, or a close cousin to it. It doesn't have garnet qualities. The metal around it seems gold. High quality, too. Those markings and emblems around it are not like any sigils I have ever seen. Shall I go to the Akashic Record Library and see what I can find?"

I shook my head. "We will send Simon. I need you here with me when the second sun rises."

Simon was another wizard in my vanguard. I had seven of them; all very powerful in their particular magicks.

"You're not going to do what I think you're going to do?" Shamus was getting grumpy again.

I answered him nonchalantly, "With their permission, yes."

Curious, Ja' Callum asked, "Meshama, what is your plan?"

"If you allow me, I will open a portal from my world of Trinidad to here. You want to come to Earth to speak to my mates, but I would loath to leave your world unguarded if there was another attack while you were gone. I can leave a contingent here to watch over your provinces. They can send a messenger to tell us if there is a problem while the main force will fight to protect your people until we can get here."

"What kind of warriors do you have, Meshama?" he sounded interested now.

"Dragons! I'd like to see the face of a vampyre who has to face a dragon in battle. I give you my word that my force will not do anything other than protect your world while we are gone. They can be sent right back, once you return, and I will give an oath on that, as well."

Ja' Kelo's face was inquisitive. "What is a dragon, Meshama?"

"Dragons, Cat? You have got to be shitting me," Rock broke in the conversation.

Wizard started laughing again. "Whoa, twilight zone, here we come again."

"Nope, and there is more. You'll see - if I am allowed to create the portal here." I looked at this world's rulers for permission.

They did look uneasy, but nodded their permission after a tight discussion which they blocked me out of. I didn't mind; I would have done the same.

"Trust has to begin somewhere, Meshama. We would like to meet these dragons first before they are placed as guards for this world."

I smiled at them. "Absolutely. They'll love to meet you guys,   as   well."

"Yo, Cat, dragons?" Rock asked again.

"Seeing is believing, Rock. Just be patient for a bit," I waved him down. Turning back to Ja' Callum, I asked, "Where can I open a portal?"

"What about the edge of where we entered the Jeno lah' leah? I will have my people bring Bokaris to put on the face of it, just so we know when someone comes from your portal. We won't block it unless there is a problem."

"Fair enough." I looked all around the camp. "Where are your horses? And why weren't they here for the fight last night?"

Ja' Monel answered, "They left last night for their herds. Each of them is the Leader for their herd. Mating season has just started for them. They will not be back until their females are out of heat."

Ja' Callum nodded. "That is why we worked the spell when we did, with their mating cycle so close, using that energy to help bind the spell to you."

Ahh, I understood now. That's why the spell was anchored to Shadin 'le. The spell used his sexual energy to empower it, drawing me to the portal. It would take an enormous amount of energy to span from their world to Earth's. Mating heat from horses is very powerful. Animals, even on Earth, have been used for empowering spells since the dawn of time.

"When you come back here for a long visit, we'll go to my province," Ja' Kelo said. "It has many herds of the

Shaballums. What you call horses." His eyes brightened, "Maybe a female will bond to you, Meshama."

My eyes widened with shock. "Come again?"

"Shaballums only have riders that have bonded to them. They will not be ridden any other way," Ja' Callum explained. "If a Shaballum bonds to you, it is for life."

"Oh." It sounded a lot like having a familiar to me. "Well, that sounds cool, but my familiars on Trinidad take a lot of my time. The responsibility for another familiar here might be too much for me to handle."

"Not to worry, Meshama. Shaballums are very independent. They only come when there is a need for them. Sometimes the need is only known to them," Ja' Callum said ruefully, "but otherwise they prefer being with their own herds."

"I would love to see more of them, but it will have to wait for another time." I stood up and brushed myself off. "Men, shall we get going? The second sun should rise soon. I can feel it coming."

"Will you be able to handle the power load, Meshama?" Ja' Monel looked worried for me.

"I'll need a ground," I admitted. "Would you all be my anchor?" It will take all of them to keep me from blowing apart and since they were natives here, they would know best how to control the power flow.

"It would be an honor, Meshama," Ja' Callum answered for all three.

We marched out of the camp after collecting our gear and wounded man. Once I got the wounded soldier to Trinidad, I had people there who could fix him in a jiffy. I was too low on energy at the moment to do it myself, but knew that once I began to open a portal here, that would change drastically. I needed Shamus' power to help keep me steady inside while I did the opening, so he wouldn't be able to help the soldier right now, either. I had already warned my sister I may a bit late, since I had an 'extra' errand to run.

I didn't tell her about opening a portal, since I had the feeling she would try to stop me. My siblings tended to be a bit over protective, ever since the mission in Pakistan.

We made good time and we waited for the rising of the second sun. I warned everyone there of my rules. "Listen up guys. This world has many things - beings that are very large and scary looking. But, they are no threat to you, unless I am under attack, so please don't shoot or do magicks against my people, since they are under my protection on my world."

"Of course, Meshama," Ja' Callum bowed his head in my direction.

Rock just nodded and glanced at all of his men, making sure everyone understood. Wizard looked highly curious and wide-eyed over the new events.

I made everyone back away and turned to the three rulers. "I'll make my hook into you now, if that's all right?"

"We are ready, Meshama," Ja Monel said.

I breathed in deeply and relaxed. Once I was focused enough, I took our partial astral bonds and wove a white thread through them, anchoring my power base. Their shield had blended into mine and we were within a four layered shield together which more than quadrupled our power base as one. I could feel Shamus inside, holding two of my spirit levels together, since the connections between my Ba and Ka were still healing from the EMP-like psychic blast. As the second sun rose, and the ground filled with power, I put a very small line of a power cord into the ground. I willed the energy up and into me. The rulers were busy stabilizing the energy flow, making it even for me to manipulate.

Erratic power fluxes could rip me apart inside and with Kla' din's rulers connected to me, the same could happen to them. I gathered power until I could hold no more and trained my intent on what I wanted to happen. With total focus, total control, I zeroed in on my world and recited the words of connection and opening. Looking at it from a scientific view point, I was basically creating a wormhole from this world to mine; just a lot more complicated and dangerous to both worlds if done wrong.

There was a rip, then a tear, in the fabric of the world I was in. I willed it into a circular shape, big enough to fly a huge airliner through and bonded the edges smooth using power. I then WILLED it with a spell to keep it open unless I said a code word. If I thought there was any threat from this world to mine, all I had to do was utter one single word and the hole would close immediately.

I felt shock from the rulers, when they saw how large I made the hole, but the reason would become clear when the dragons came through. Some could make their size smaller, but some couldn't, and a smaller hole wouldn't have done them any good.

I released the left-over power and undid my anchor to them. I took a moment to ground and said, "Don't fear Dai' Khans, the reason for this will be clear once we step through. I walked up to the portal and waved them to follow me. "Be welcomed to Trinidad." I stepped through to my world for the first time in years; the first time, physically, ever.

Chapter Four

A Trinidad Home Coming

I waited patiently on the other side of the portal for the men to come through. They started to come through in groups since the hole was big enough, and they took a look around in wonder, at the green hills and tall green pines where the forest began a half a mile away. I picked this meadow because we rarely used it, letting nature have its way. The fields were filled with flowers that bloomed brightly. Colors of yellow and purple dotted the grassy ground for miles. Mostly, lilacs and pansies with some dandelions mixed in here and there. At the edge of the field was patchouli under the protection of the leaves of the great trees that edged the huge meadow.

Rock looked around and took in the sights, as did the Dai' Khans of Kla' din. This was a historical first for Trinidad to have visitors from two other planets at the same time. I looked around proudly at my world, feeling like a mother showing off a new baby.

"I thought you said it wasn't completely solid yet Cat?" Rock asked, stamping the ground.

"I am here now in physical form, so therefore, it will be completely physical as well. It's a metaphysical thing. Once I am gone again, it will stay more solid. The more often I do this, the more it will be solid and stay this way." I breathed in the fresh air and sent out hellos to everyone within calling distance of me.

"It is beautiful and full of life, Meshama. We are honored to be here," Ja' Monel said. His smile was back and I was happy to see it.

Ja' Kelo and Ja' Callum just kept looking around, watching birds fly through the skies and listening to the ocean surf off in the distance.

"Ok, now please stay relaxed. This is really the fastest way we have here to get you all to the castle of Trinidad. We'll have to ride big, huge dragons, but they are dear friends of mine."

I called out to Cornelia and asked her to bring a small wing of dragons with her to carry people for me.

'I come,' she answered.

I looked up at the skyline in the direction of the castle and watched for the black dot to appear.

When I saw it coming, I warned everyone, "Look, there is my friend. She comes." I had never seen her move so fast through the air before. She sped towards us like a bullet, in her hurry to get to me.

I heard gasps around me, but I couldn't take my eyes off of my dragon friend. She was huge, long and lean. She was black from her snout to the tip of her tail, with large wings already pulling in and back-winging to slow her descent to the ground, as close as she could get to me. She blew out fire from her nose, letting me know how excited she was and ambled over, the ground shaking under her great weight.

"Um, Cat," Rock sounded nervous.

"Don't worry, she just wants a hug." And I ran to meet her, catching her around her large neck as much as I could and holding her close. She purred at the contact and smoke puffed out of her nostrils.

"Hello, dear friend. I have missed you so much." My throat clogged up as I fought hard not to start crying. I had missed my people so much and *my* world.

Soft gurgles of dragon laughter rumbled through her throat. She shrunk down to the size of a large horse so I could hug her better. More gasps and a long 'whoa' erupted behind me.

Wiping aside the few tears I couldn't stop, I took a deep breath to introduce her to the men. "Everyone, this is my dragon friend Cornelia, First Dragon of the First clan of Dragons of Trinidad. I am her rider, when I am home."

The Dai' Khans bowed their heads; the soldiers didn't quite know what to do. Some just nodded their heads. Rock was brave enough to say hello.

"Cornelia, these are the Dai' Khans of Kla' din, the world we just came from. Ja' Callum, Ja' Monel and Ja' Kelo. They are sorcerer-rulers of their world. These men are Captain Vincent O'Hara, Sergeant Mark Logan of Special Forces on Earth. Their call signs are Rock and Wizard and we usually use the call signs on a mission. The men behind them are Alpha 53rd Recon Marines, real bad asses in their own right, also of Earth. One of them is wounded, so we need a gentle dragon to carry him."

She snuffed, but in my mind she answered telepathically, *'I will have my young daughter come carry the wounded one. She flies smoothly and is even tempered.'* She ambled closer to the Dai' Khans, slowly lowering her snout to their chests. She started with Ja' Callum, who looked at me with a question in his eyes.

"She wants to catch your scent to say hello," I told him.

She proceeded to sniff each man one by one. *'No evil here, Princess. I will call the others.'* She was as paranoid over the safety of Trinidad as I was.

I told the men, "She welcomes all here with respect. She calls other dragons to carry us to my castle."

'How long will you stay with us, Princess?' She sounded wistful.

I answered out loud, "Not long, I am afraid. Only a few short hours." Her head slumped down for a moment in sadness and then raised back up again. She knew my duty.

Ja' Monel caught the exchange. "She talks to you?"

"Yes, she is telepathic. All of my people are," I explained to Ja' Monel.

The Dai' Khans eyes grew wide over that declaration.

"Oh, shit," one of the marines blurted out, before he could stop himself. I scanned the skies and twenty five dragons were coming down through the skyline to land in the field with Cornelia.

I laughed, "Sheesh, Cornelia we didn't need that many."

'They miss you too, and couldn't wait back at the dragon caves, since you won't be here long enough to visit them there,' she answered, with no rebuff in her mind-tone.

The dragon caves were near the castle within the mountain. Trinidad's castle rested at the foot of Dragon Mount.

As they landed, I greeted them all by name, walking among them, touching one on the neck, rubbing a snout here and there. One took a playful nip and I batted him away. Grange was always rowdy. He was big, green and sleek with two long twisting golden horns. He was showing off for our visitors.

"Rock, you should ride Grange here, if you're feeling adventurous?" I teased him.

"Normally, things don't confront me, Cat, but this... I'll ride something nice and quiet if you have one of those?" He looked hopeful.

118

I laughed again, and told the men to go ahead and choose their mount. I showed them where to hold on once they were on, and how to tuck their heads into the dragon's neck for takeoff. No dragon will move until he or she feels their rider was tucked into their neck properly.

With Cornelia's and Ja' Callum's help, we got Corporal Malcolm onto her daughter.

"You might want to WILL straps on him, Princess. He feels very weak to me," Cornelia cautioned.

I looked at the man sitting on Jovan and with my mind, I WILLED riding straps on him and around the dragon's body so he wouldn't fall off in flight. When everyone looked settled and ready to go, I gave the signal for lift off.

Cornelia grew big enough to carry me and be flight worthy. Once she was large enough, she heaved into the air. I had Cornelia sweep around, so I could see if everyone got off the ground all right. They did well, as warriors and soldiers tend to do; adapt and overcome in any situation. We headed off to the West for the castle of Trinidad.

It was only a fifteen minute ride going at a normal pace. If the dragons didn't have us on them, they could have shot like bullets through the skies and been there in mere minutes. Cornelia took us right to the front gate of my castle. It had seven tall towers, with the main tower being my personal quarters that Shamus shared with me when I was there.

Each tower was occupied with a wizard who stood guard duty when my world is under threat, or using the labs for their experiments, which sometimes caused explosions. I didn't care what damage they did, so long as they repaired what was damaged and no one was hurt. For the truly dangerous experiments, they were taken to a small desert island five hundred miles away.

If one looked out to the East, they would see the coastline and hear the surf pounding the sands and rocks below. There was a long whitish path that led from this point all the way down to the sea. Before entering the castle proper, there were steel gates with twisted molded metal that spelled out 'Trinidad' in an arch. There was a straight path to the castle with lawns and trees on either side, with long flower beds that the fairies loved to play in.

I waited for everyone to dismount and waved to the dragons, thanking them for the ride. Cornelia made herself small again, so she could walk with me into the courtyard of my castle. Once I stepped through the gates, the air was filled with fairies of every color and description; all waving and shouting in their tiny voices.

"Hello, Princess."

"Welcome home, Princess."

"Who are the men, Princess?"

The greetings went on and on. I just waited for the deluge to slow down, waving at them and shouting back hello's to them. My winged cats came out wanting their turn at the greetings, as well as the Chinese Unicorns and Pegasus'. I had regular unicorns, Cornish unicorns, gnomes, pixies, small elves and many other tribes of beings filling the courtyard to its capacity and beyond. I might have to start thinking of enlarging the place if this kept up.

The looks on the men's faces were priceless. They were rubber necking to beat the band, trying to assimilate everything they were hearing and seeing.

"Wow, Cat, it's like a fantasy world come true here. They all belong to you?" Wizard couldn't keep his eyes off the Pegasus'. It seemed he liked them the best.

"Yes, most were born and raised here. The Elders of their tribes came to me for protection or asked to serve me years ago, so I had to create this world for them. This way, they would have a home for their young. Could you imagine having all this in an apartment on Earth?"

He shook his head.

"Well, most people wouldn't be able to see them, but being astrally gifted, it made things tricky for me. And crowded. So, violà, Trinidad." I waved all around.

"Come on, let's get this soldier inside and settled. One of my other wizards will see to him quickly." I urged everyone along.

We finally got up the steps and into the ballroom of the castle. I led them to a smaller room where we had couches and tables all around and put the tired soldier down on one of the couches.

I looked up into the crowd. "Oh, there you are, Skylord. Can you come help him? I am worn out from creating the portal."

Skylord was a very tall man with ebony skin. Although he was bald, he still wore the traditional wizards head gear with jewels encrusted along the seams, as well as the wizard robes. Even his three inch black leather belt was embossed with jewels.

I had always thought it was a wizard union requirement or something. I had yet to see any of them just wear jeans and a tee shirt.

"Right away, Your Highness," he responded, with his deep rumble of a voice, moving silently to see to the wounded soldier.

Looking at the men, I said, "If I introduced you to everyone here, we could be at it for days. Let me just get some refreshments going for you." I waved them to take seat anywhere they pleased and scanned the masses again. "If we could have some coffee, tea and some fruit drinks. Also, some sandwiches and snack trays... I would appreciate it."

I didn't bother asking for a specific person or being to do it. I knew someone would hop to it and we would be served quickly. They liked the fact that I had visitors and would take advantage of showing off.

"Oh, Princess, you've comes home. The Trixie misses you, she does. Please say you are here for long, long time. No more go off to bad world and leaves us, please say it is so." She was fluttering around my head so excitedly, she couldn't stay still long enough for me to catch her eyes.

"I am afraid I can't stay Trixie. I am sorry. And Earth isn't bad; it's just a hard world."

"Bad, if it makes you sad, and it does. The Trixie knows it does. Makes you cry, it's bad there. Stays here, we will makes you happy," she implored.

"You all always make me happy to be home. But, if I don't stop the bad guys on Earth, their troubles could soon be ours. I told you this years ago, Trixie," I slightly admonished her.

"I knows it, I knows it, but Princess, so much has happened here. Look. Look."

And many small beings popped into the room. Tiny mothers with even smaller babies. All looking pleased to show me their young.

I oohed and awhed, telling each mother her babe or babes was beautiful. "Wow, have you all been busy while I was gone?" I was a tad jealous because I ached badly for another small babe of my own. I loved being a mother. Some of these fairies and pixies had twins; I was promised in a dream that I would have twins with my mates the next time I got pregnant.

She looked upset. "Yes, many, many babes. Many, many not names yets, Princess. Must have names to belong, you knows this."

I could see that I've been slacking on my duties here. "I am sorry, Trixie. I will leave an astral self behind for as long as it takes to name every new babe here. She'll write it down in the book of names in my quarters, so I will know what was done." I took a deep breath and pushed a part of my soul out - an astral subtle body, who can stay and do what needs to be done, then come back and reintegrate with me later.

"Not as goods as all of yous here, but it will do, Princess," she said sadly.

"Someday, soon, I will be able to come home. We'll party for months when that happens, all right?" I promised her.

She brightened up. "Oooh, a party, the Trixie loves a party. I still remembers the last one. Cravens falls in the pool. He was so cutes. Cutesy baby. Cutesy baby." Her tinkling laughter filled the room.

No one could resist smiling at the sound. Even I had to smile, though I remembered the last time I was here was when Craven was barely two years old. It had been that long since I had been able to visit my world, astrally. Being here physically, for the first time, I would not let sad thoughts mar this happy event.

Drinks and food came, all were served. Ja' Callum tasted his drink said, "This is good, Meshama. We appreciate your hospitality. Your world is full of wonder."

Ja' Monel nodded in agreement. "There are so many beings here we have never read about, even in our oldest records."

"Yeah. You made a believer out of me, Cat, but getting the General to believe all this, and not have me in for a psych evaluation, is going to be the trick," Rock grinned at me.

"Isn't there a portal on Earth you could take the General through to show him, Cat?" Wizard asked.

"No, not yet," I shook my head. "I haven't found a source of power large enough to create one. I was looking for a node big enough to try it, but we always seem to be so busy there."

Rock looked confused. "A node?"

"Yes, a pool of ley-line energy. You should have read up on this in your books I gave you to study for the arts," I scolded him again.

Skylord was done with the wounded soldier and came over to me. "You need blood Princess. You can feed while you are here in physical form and it will actually do you good," and he bared his wrist to me.

He recited the ritual words and I bit into his vein. I licked the wound closed when I was finished, finally feeling much better.

Ja' Callum looked disappointed and said, "You could have asked us for blood, Meshama. We would have fed you. It is our duty now to see to your needs."

Skylord's black eyebrows went up into his forehead.

"Don't ask," I grumbled.

He placed his hand under my chin and tilted my head up to catch my eyes. "If you break oath, you could lose us, Princess. Lose even Trinidad," Skylord reminded me.

"I haven't broken oath, the bonds are still clean. It's something I will deal with when I return to Earth."

"Good. I knew we could count on you." Walking away, I could hear him say under his breath, "This ought to be interesting."

124

I turned back to Ja' Callum. "If I drink from you before you have that sit down with my mates, that could be bad."

Ja' Callum understood and nodded his head, appeased with the explanation.

"My astral part will take care of everything that needs to be done here. Meanwhile, we still have Kla' din to protect and Earth to defend against the black covens and hostile portals." I turned back to the Dai' Khans. "Now you have met my dragons. With a wizard to guide them, they are unstoppable and not susceptible to vampyre bites. Is this now acceptable to place them in your world while you visit Earth?"

They did the inner telepathy meeting again and it was Ja' Monel who spoke for them. "Yes, with your oath that they are only there to protect, not to take over." He gave a half grin, "Just to be safe, Meshama."

I nodded. "I agree, it's always good to be cautious, no matter what."

Wizard jumped up. "Why don't you have your dragons fight with us on missions?"

I narrowed my eyes at him. "Could you imagine what people on Earth would do to my dragons? They would hunt them again. Just look to our legends for validity on that. I won't risk them unless it is absolutely necessary. Besides, you have our whole Coven in your pocket. We are bad-ass enough without dragon might. It would be overkill in most cases, anyway."

He looked glum, remembering the legends of old, and knights hunting the dragons. No wonder they were so eager to go, in the last Great Shift. They were one of the few Greater Magickal Races that were *glad* to go without a fuss. It was safer elsewhere for their continuous well being. They were still deciding if they would ever come back during this shift and I couldn't blame them. Though not all dragons were as mine; some were really vicious. I hope *those* evil tempered beast never returned to Earth, but for very different reasons.

"Skylord, why don't you ask which wizard would like to go to Kla' din and guide a contingent of dragons in defense. Whoever goes might want to take a few fairies for messengers. Get volunteers; it is not without risk. They have a nasty tribe of vampyre called The Draugrall. Their bite can be infectious. They are also using astral doorways to pop into their world for ruby-like stones and females."

"I'll see to it, Princess." He left the room to gather the volunteers.

"Are there no regular-type of people here, Cat?" Rock asked.

I smiled at him, shaking my head. "No, only family members have been allowed to come here, so far."

Ja' Callum again tilted his head. "Then, we are doubly honored to be here, Meshama."

Trixie started to buzz around Rock's head. "Did you gets them warrior? Did you gets whats The Trixie lefts to yous?"

Rock looked completely baffled and turned to me for help.

I asked her, "What are you talking about Trixie?'

She snapped her wings, showing her agitation. "The flowers. The yellows. The Trixie was being nice, nice to the warrior."

Then Rock's eyes lit up in recognition. "You mean the yellow flowers on my desk? Those were from you? Yes, I got them, thank you." His eyes narrowed, "Are you the one moving my stuff around in my office?"

She flitted happily. "The Trixie did it, the Trixie did it. You don't have things in place right, soldier-warrior. Desk is not how the Princess would say 'feung shway'. Or is it 'feng shey'?" She snapped her wings again. "I don't care whats it calls it, it was wrong, wrong energy."

I started giggling, trying to smoother it. Then I couldn't resist and burst out laughing, holding my stomach. "She likes you, Rock. She has a crush on you. She is moving your furniture."

Wizard started laughing too. "You wanna' bet, Cat?"

Even the Dai' Khans got what was going on and laughed with us. Trixie didn't quite figure out we were laughing at her and I didn't clue her in. She was sweet, but get her mad and look out - pixing time. And, she could be dangerous for all her smallness, being half the size of a full grown fairy.

Rock cleared his throat. "Well, yeah, thanks for the flowers Trixie, but can you please not move things around on my desk? It makes it harder for me to get my work done."

She floated in front of him then nodded her little head. "Fine, fine, the Trixie wonts move your furnitures in your office. Wheres is your home? The Trixie can fix. You cants be at the base alls the time warrior. You must haves home nests, yes?" She flitted to his hair and started petting it, making it shiny with pixie dust. I covered my mouth with my hand. Rock's eyes begged me to help. He must have known not to piss a pixie off.

"Trixie, honey, he hasn't had time for finding a home nest. We are still trying to settle in Corpus Christi. For now, just let him get his work done, ok?" I said sweetly to her.

She giggled at the shiny she made in his hair. "The Trixie understands. The Trixie could goes looks for a homes nest for him, so he can goes be warrior with yous."

I got my serious face on, for Rock's sake. "Trixie, you know you can't show yourself on Earth, so how would you

127

go get a home nest for Rock? You would have to talk to people and they can be mean sometimes, not understanding someone who is…is…well, different and unique; special and pretty like you are."

She preened under the pleasant words I was using. All true too, but no way could I let her loose on Earth side. Before the day was out, she would wind up pixing the whole damn city in a fit of temper.

I continued to help bail out Rock, seeing his look of alarm. "Besides, I am sure the Captain can find his own home nest, by himself, when he is ready. Right now, he thinks of nothing but his work and job as a soldier, which is exactly what he should be doing."

She moved away from Rock, snapping her wings again. "Oh, pooh, wars and fightings, he'll never gets a homes nest."

I nodded sagely. "It might not be for a long, long time. But if he doesn't fight, he won't have a world to get himself a home nest on, so he is stuck for the time being."

She was agitated, stomping her little feet in the air. "The Trixie wills not give ups." She popped out of the room.

"Thank you, Cat," Rock blew a sigh a relief, brushing the pixie dust out of his hair.

I clucked my tongue, "Don't thank me; she is not done yet, my friend. Good luck with this."

Snorting with laughter, Wizard asked, "How could you guys even get together, you hound dog? Fifty says she gets mad and dumps him."

I laughed. "With enough power, she could make herself to be our size. Never underestimate a pixie. And getting mad and just dumping him would be the best we could hope for, then. A jilted pixie can make things fall off." I arched my eyes at Rock.

He turned a bit green and looked at Wizard. "Don't you dare encourage her, Wizard." Wizard just gave an evil laugh.

Skylord had come back into the room, letting me know things were ready to go and Stormlord would go with us. He was a tall lanky wizard that could make the rains come in a deluge with just a snap of his fingers. Together, they had rounded up over sixty dragons for the protection of Kla' din. The Dai' Khans had told me that once we were on their world again, they would warn the Dai'kins and the guards they would leave in charge.

I had also suggested they keep their cowls off of their faces when entering Earth world, since it looked too close to the turbans the enemy we fought all the time wore. They understood the necessity of trying to fit into another culture and of ways to make things easier.

I didn't even ask them to give up their scimitars, though I did make them bags they could carry them in, so the nice people on the other side didn't freak out. They thought this was a good compromise and agreed to it when they found out we would be doing the same thing.

As we walked back outside through the courtyard, Trixie came zooming out. "The Trixie goes with you. Say it is so. The mean Shamus wonts lets me goes. You have fairies coming along, yous needs the Trixie too," her lip was pouting.

"Trixie, sweetie, you need to help my astral self that I am leaving behind. Who but you, could show part of me what I have been slacking on. You could get her finished so much faster with your help." OK, I was laying it on thick, but I shuddered at the thought of her following into a world that vampyres attacked in. "Besides, the fairies aren't coming with me. They'll be staying in Kla' din unless a message needs to come here or go to Earth."

This appeased her and she nodded sadly. "True, true, the other sides of princess lady could use The Trixie for faster works." She then perked up. "I'll brings the princess lady selfs to yous when shes is done." With that decree, she flitted off before I could talk her out of it. Tricky Trixie!

Stormlord chuckled. "That pixy is a handful. She's got her cap set and she won't be denied."

Rock started looking a bit green again. I laughed as I climbed upon Cornelia. "Buck up, soldier. You have faced worse than an enamored pixy."

He gave me his eyebrow trick and climbed atop a dragon, settling himself in for takeoff. Everyone got on much quicker this time and we jolted into the skies of Trinidad once more.

We flew straight through the portal on dragon backs, since it was wide enough for their wingspans, and headed to the other portal that would lead to Earth. The suns had set some time ago. Antonio would not be pleased with my lateness. As we neared the other portal, the dragons landed as close to the gate as we could get. The energy of this world was enough for the dragons to stay quite solid and the look on Romeo's face was hilarious. My sister, too, looked a bit taken aback, but composed herself faster than Romeo did. His hand was tight on his SOCOM.

I walked up to her and gave her a hug in greeting, then turning around, I addressed the Dai' Khans. "This is my sister, Ama Ja' Cassie," giving her the title they would have given her themselves.

Her eyebrows rose into her hair line over the introduction and tapped into my head on our private path.

'*Sister, what have you done now?*' as she watched the Dai' Khans kneel and bow in respect.

Laughing, "Screwed the pooch, I'm afraid," I said aloud. I might as well get as much enjoyment out of this as I could. The hard part hadn't even begun. On a private path I told her, '*Tell them arise or we could be here all day.*'

"Arise and greetings to the Dai' Khans of this world. It is an honor to meet with you," she said graciously. She had always been better at this sort of thing than I was.

"An honor for us to meet the sister of our Meshallima Ama Ja' Catrina. This world has been blessed many times since your arrival," Ja' Callum answered her.

'*Oh, sister, you've really got yourself into hot water this time, haven't you? How could you?*' She sounded displeased with me now, as she should be. Ignoring her for the moment, I said, "This is Sergeant Theodore Watson of Special Forces, otherwise known as Romeo."

They greeted each other, though Romeo was still flabbergasted over the dragons roaming around us.

'*Sister,*' she hissed in my head. I knew what she wanted to know.

I shrugged my shoulders. '*Shit happened. Most was out of my control. I cleaned up the best I could. Most things are now known and there is now a portal from this world to Trinidad.*'

I heard her deep intake of breath over this news. '*That was the great workings I felt happen earlier today? I knew it was you, but I couldn't figure out what, exactly, you were doing.*' She sighed, '*Well, that explains the dragons.*' She shook her head. '*If you can sit ever again in this lifetime, I will be surprised.*' Oh, great. Her, too? Shit!

The Dai' Khans had done an information download to Stormlord, so he would know the geographical layout of this planet and where to place the dragons, where the vampyres would mostly likely hit, if they came at all while we were gone. I was hoping once I removed myself from this world, they would go back to their periodical raiding. Stormlord and the dragons took off with Cornelia in the lead, after giving me a dragon hug. She made me promise to take a long ride on her when I came back through the portal. I was happy to, since I wanted to see more of this world soon. If I could sit on her back by that time, that is.

We waited for the men to get back into their street clothes and loaded their black bags with their gear and weapons. I took a look around and saw I couldn't delay any longer and we walked through Earth's portal.

Chapter Five

An Earth Homecoming

As we stepped through the portal into Earth, Antonio spun around from the group of men he was talking to. He faced me, as I walked up to him with three rulers at my back from the world of Kla' din. He most likely was expecting me to run up to him, wrap my arms around his neck and give him kisses. When I got about three feet to him, I dropped to one knee and bent my head instead.

"Ca-Tri-Na?" he snapped out. He knew I was feeling guilty about something or I wouldn't have greeted him in such a manner, especially not in front of the other men.

The shocked gasps of the rulers behind me blurted out, "Meshama!"

'We need to talk, mate, but not here. At the hotel,' I told him on our private path.

"And this is?" he nodded to the men behind me.

"These men are the Dai' Khans of Kla' din. Ja' Callum, Ja' Monel and Ja' Kelo. They have matters they wish to discuss with you, peacefully," I stressed. "This is one of my mates, Amu Ja' Antonio Caberelli, as you would most likely call him on your world."

I heard the intake of breath from the rulers, knowing if I used the Amu title, that would mean Antonio and my other mates were like I was, demi-Gods. I was hoping this would give everyone pause before giving into violence.

Ja' Callum recovered the fastest, as he was the most even tempered of the three, and replied, "Pleased we are to meet the mate of our Meshallima Ama Ja' Catrina. She has brought many blessings to our world and we hope to be able to continue pleasant relations with you and your world."

Antonio's lips tightened in a harsh line and looked down at me. He grabbed my arm gently, but firmly and pulled me into a standing position. "Lucky for us, 'dear wife', my brothers have flown into Japan and are here now waiting for us at the hotel. Why don't we take this discussion there, shall we?"

He was infuriated, but was holding back until we could take this to a private place. He was always quick with the translations of a different language. It was like a special gift for him. Damn it.

I nodded and turned to Rock. "We have things to take care of first, but I'll get together with you later to make arrangements to get back to America as soon as possible and debrief with the General."

"Good luck," he said simply.

"Gentlemen, come with us," Antonio said pleasantly enough to the rulers, but you could hear the edge of anger in the tone of his voice.

He never let go of my arm, but he didn't hurt me doing it, either. We walked back to the hotel and I would have enjoyed the startled looks the rulers had gotten over seeing the cars speeding past and the airplanes buzzing over from time to time, since we were close to an airport, but the anger simmering in Antonio took most of my attention.

The hotel elevator was almost enough for me to start laughing anyway, when the doors closed with us inside and started moving upwards. They had no idea what to do or say about this and Ja' Kelo looked a tad green around the gills over it. Soon, the car stopped on our level and we moved out. They moved fast out of the elevator car and looked back inside it, trying to figure out what was powering the lift. I covered my mouth with my free hand and stifled my laugh.

"Gentlemen," Antonio reminded them to keep moving to our room. Antonio got the key out and opened the door, allowing me to walk myself in. Demitri was sitting in the living room suite on a large couch and Andre was near the bar getting drinks.

"Hi, Babe. Antonio tells us you did something wrong." I didn't answer him at first.

Ja' Monel started to protest, but Ja' Callum stopped him with a warning hand on his shoulder. I took off my leather jacket and started to remove all of my weapons I had hidden in various places on me from head to toe.

I placed them carefully on the table and when I had disarmed myself, I walked until I was in front of Demitri, who was now standing with a very concerned look on his face. Andre had come to join him and Antonio moved in to flank them, though his eyes were narrowed on the rulers of Kla' din, and not on me. I bent down with both knees this time and flowed forward with my arms in front of me, as prostrate as I could get.

I prepared myself for the fall out. "I deeply regret the pain this will cause you all. I think forces that are stronger than us are at work, and this couldn't be helped. Bonds have been forged between me and these men of Kla' din."

"Shit, no. You are ours. You belong to us, Catrina," Andre exploded.

He was about to attack, when I jumped up in front him. I had to pull my ace in the hole.

"Know this, mate. Any harm you do to them now, will cause me pain, as if every blow you give them hits me." I looked over to where the Dai' Khans were standing. "The same as if they were to hit you, I would feel the pain on my own body. The six of you cannot fight without causing me pain."

One of the down-sides of a mating bond, was that everything they felt, I felt, and vice versa; even hunger or a slight stub to the toe. Everyone bonded, feels it as an echo to themselves. It was one of the reasons Demitri stopped patrolling on the astral planes, because the damage he would sustain would echo to me and I would be hurting as well.

Demitri's lips went tight with anger. "Fine, we will shield then, and challenge them." Damn, I had forgotten that with enough power, one could shield from a Bondmate and then I wouldn't feel the pain.

I glared back at him. "I am strong enough now to break the shields. I want you to at least hear them out."

"They touched what was ours," he growled. "They've been inside you, Catrina. No way can we let that insult pass."

I shook my head. "No, they didn't. They haven't touched me sexually in any way - this, I swear to The Goddess."

"Then, how did the damn bonds form, Catrina?" Demitri sounded disbelieving. "Sex has to be involved."

"Not on their world, apparently. It is strong with magick." I snorted, "Seven hells, the air is thick with it for four and half hours during their afternoon time. The ground literally gets hot with magick with the rising of a second blue sun; enough magick that I was able to create a portal from their world to Trinidad."

Demitri seemed shocked. "What? You've got to be kidding."

"No, I made a portal to my own world. Then, we went there to get the dragons to guard their world while they came here to talk to you," I explained to him.

Pain ripped through my heart as an echo feeling.

Demitri was crushed. "You took them there? You thought enough of them to take them to Trinidad?" I felt his pain, his heart aching, making me hurt with him.

I closed my eyes against the pain. "I did it for several reasons. Rock and Wizard now know what we are, or at least they know about me and my sister. I don't know if they've put two and two together yet for the rest of you, but it's out there now."

"Sweet Goddess, what happened?" Andre moaned.

I said, exasperated, "Too many things. Just look in my head already, so you'll know everything and I won't have to spend half the afternoon telling you all about it."

I rarely allowed this, since having someone in my head, searching around, made me feel very invaded. Almost like a rape, but he didn't back out this time and went right on in since he had my permission. I braced myself for the invasion.

Pain again ripped through me coming from them all. "You touched yourself in front of them?" Demitri exploded.

I tried to explain, "I couldn't help it, and the harmonics were already out of control."

"Because of the lust they felt for you," he accused.

I narrowed my eyes at him. "My own lust as well. Don't put this off on just them."

Demitri grabbed my arm. "This time, it's my turn, Antonio," and he dragged me into his room. He didn't even bother closing the door; though truth be known, he often did like to be an exhibitionist with his brothers. It tripped his trigger sometimes.

"Strip," he ordered.

I took off my clothes and he pointed to the bed. "Get on your knees and grab the headboard." I did as he commanded.

I knew I had this coming, if nothing else. I looked around the room. He had gotten candles and a tray filled with all kinds of things we could have had fun with. It looked to me like he had planned for a very romantic, erotic night, and it had turned into a discipline action. No candles and rose petals for me tonight, damn it.

I heard him take his own clothes off. In the next room, I could hear arguing from among the rest of the men. It didn't stop Demitri though; he was furious.

I felt oil being poured on my bottom, which he proceeded to rub on my ass. Everywhere. I was getting more turned on than scared.

The arguing came closer and Demitri said, "This time you have gone too far. I followed astrally and watched Antonio spank you last time. You deserve that and more this time. You know it."

I felt his hand raise and then he hesitated. He had one hand between my legs, rubbing from my slit to my anus and back up again. The other hand he'd planned to whack me with just hung in the air like a threat. The rest of the men spilled into the room and the arguing stopped with the scene before them captivating their attention.

"Please don't spank Meshama," Ja' Kelo begged for me. I could feel the worry and the anger that I was being disciplined. I could also feel their desire as they looked at me naked and wet. It made my body react to their need.

I heard Demitri groan in response. "Remember, a long time ago, you said if you did anything wrong, if you hurt me, I was to spank you for it?"

I nodded my head.

"I told you then, it would never go that far. Those were my exact words. I can play 'slap and tickle' with you. I can dominate you and get off on it, but I just can't lay a hand on you in anger, no matter the provocation," and his hand came down to gently rub my buttocks instead.

I heard a sigh of relief in the background.

He said gruffly, "But, you do deserve some punishment, Catrina, and this is how I plan on taking it."

Then, slowly, deliberately, with his eyes on the rulers of Kla' din, Demitri took his cock and placed it to my core. Slowly, he pushed in, inch by inch. He never took his eyes off the Dai' Khans, as he claimed me, blatantly, in front of them. He grabbed my hips and pushed himself in to the hilt of his large dick and started to move in and out, slowly at first, then building up the tempo.

"I can spank her while you fuck her, brother," Antonio offered.

Desire pulsed through my body and I shuddered. "I may take you up on that. That made her wetter when you said it," Demitri panted.

I could hear Antonio and Andre undressing themselves and climbing onto the bed.

Andre had gotten in front of me and scooted until his dick was in my face. He held it to me, "Take me in your mouth now, Catrina."

Andre rarely got controlling in bed, but having the Dai' Khans here, trying to offer for me, made him want to do anything to establish his claim on my body, as his brother had.

Antonio looked up at them. "Watch if you want, but we are taking her right now." And with that, his hand slapped down on my ass. He stared at them, daring them to do something about it.

I groaned in pleasure. I tried to have enough control to establish a private path with the three rulers. *'Stay, watch. You'll have to seduce them, as well as me, if you're serious about wanting me. Feel Demitri's excitement with you here looking on. This is one of his sexual triggers.'*

'You don't mind what they are doing to you with the spanking?' The thought came from Ja' Callum, but they were *all* wondering.

Right then, Antonio's hand came down again and I moaned in pleasure. *'Does that answer your question?'*

I made sure they could feel what this was doing to me. I felt their heat in response and that got me even wetter. Demitri moaned when my muscles tightened down around his cock even more, making him speed up his thrusts. Antonio was rubbing my clit, while I took Andre in my mouth and sucked him off.

Every now and again, Antonio's hand would come down on my ass and Demitri would fuck me harder because of my response. I licked and sucked at Andre cock until I felt he was about to come in my mouth. Again, Antonio's hand came down and he rubbed my clit faster. That made me spill over that edge I needed, moaning and whimpering around Andre's staff.

Demitri groaned deeply, "Catrina, say I can bite now, woman."

I released Andre's dick long enough to grant permission, "Bite me, I give permission," I panted through my orgasm.

I took Andre back into my mouth and Demitri leaned down to my neck and bit into me, giving a final thrust as he came inside me. Andre, watching Demitri bite into my neck, made him lose it in my mouth.

Demitri pulled out of me slowly and Antonio said, "My turn," and took Demitri's place behind me. He pushed his cock into me hard and fast. He still hadn't worked out his anger; plus, he was the most dominate of the three in bed.

Andre was the one who liked to be tied up and teased or spanked from time to time. Antonio liked the slightly rougher stuff when he was mad at me. He slapped my ass harder this time then he had when Demitri was inside me. He knew Demitri wouldn't allow too much strength in my spanking, but Demitri wouldn't interfere with Antonio's time with me unless I said my safe word and Antonio ignored it.

Antonio has never done that to date, so I doubted Demitri watching over us was needed. He just wanted to watch - period.

"I know you had no control over touching yourself in front of them, but it still hurts, Catrina." Smack! Then he pumped inside of me harder. "You have bonds with them. I can see that now, and this has created a serious problem for us." Smack! SMACK! Then he began thrusting again. "I don't know if I could handle seeing another man's cock, which is not one of my brothers, inside this pussy." Down came his hand again, making me wince that time.

Andre came to rub my clit to make up for it. Demitri was biting his lower lip. Since his dick was hardening again, I thought it was because of arousal and not so much the spanking.

Whack, came another spanking to my rear. "I love this pussy. It is mine and so is this." He took his cock out and put it in my ass, quick and deep. I screamed with pleasure and pain. Demitri groaned. Andre was moving his finger in and out of me now in time to Antonio's thrusts in my ass.

One more hit to my rear. "ALL this week expect this punishment, Catrina. Every damn night; I am so pissed." And he fucked my ass harder.

I came screaming and shuddering all over. Feeling me come so hard, made Antonio spill into me. He leaned over panting, "I may fuck you every night like this for a month. Don't you dare tell me I can't."

"Ok, I won't," I said meekly.

"Move over, brother. I need her again," Demitri said and Antonio moved off of me.

"Catrina, get on your back and spread your legs for me, baby." Demitri's voice was low now, not as angry anymore.

I did as he said, and he got between my legs, easing himself inside of me.

He whispered in my ear, "I've missed you, love." He started to move in me, slow and gentle, kissing me long and deep. The Dai' Khans were quiet all the while, but I could feel their intense arousal. They liked this better. I was sure if my mates had said, 'come on in,' they wouldn't have hesitated.

I think this was a way for my mates to punish them without having to go fist-a-cuffs and hurt me, by proxy. Demitri loved me long and slow until he brought me to climax again, then he sped up, doing me harder. Every now and again, he looked up at the Dai' Khans to watch their faces. Finally, he came again and held me tight afterwards, kissing my neck.

They never bit me more than once in a single day. When he was done with his usual cuddling moments, he got up, giving me a hand to get up, as well.

"Go take a shower or whatever, but we need to talk to these guys." He patted my behind, playfully.

I looked him deep in his eyes. "Promise, no fighting?"

His brown eyes grew serious. "I will try very hard for you."

That's the best I was going to get and more than I thought I would, so I took it and walked out.

They shielded the damn room so I couldn't 'hear' what was said, but I left a thread in Ja' Kelo's mind, just in case. There was always more than one way to skin a ... 'wait a minute, I better not finish that thought'. Shit sometimes happened, even if I just thought of things and I sure as heck didn't want to wind up literally skinned, with my luck as of late.

I had showered, dressed and had eaten by the time they finally came out. Since I didn't hear any thuds against the walls, I took it things were at least half way civil, despite the grim looks on my mates faces.

"We've decided not to kill them," Andre said, as they sauntered out of the room.

Ja' Monel snorted at this, his expression daring him to try. Andre took stock in their apparent abilities. "All right, we won't try to kill each other, then."

"No?" I asked, astounded.

"No, but they can't touch you on this side of the portal. We still haven't decided if we are going to share you at all," Andre decreed.

I was stunned. "So, you're considering it, really?"

"Only considering it," Antonio said dryly, as he pulled out a bottle of brandy and poured himself a healthy glass of it. He only drank when he was too pissed to do anything else.

Ja' Callum turned a heated stare in my direction. "The decision is good enough for us for the time being, Meshama. We can be very patient men."

"I'd like to make you somebody's patient," I heard Antonio grumble under his breath. Oh, yeah, he was still pissed.

But still, this had been easier than I had thought it would be.

"So, what brought this on?" I asked.

Demitri sat down on the couch next to me. "The bonds are already half formed. If you were to cut them now, it could cause you a lot of spiritual problems, even depression or suicidal tendencies. We can't take a chance with that, so we'll give this some time to see what happens."

Ahh, I saw what did it. When my mates and I had gotten bonded spiritually, but they couldn't find me physically for so long, it messed with my head so badly that I went into a severe depression. One night, I almost took a blade to my wrist, until I remembered I still had kids who depended on me. My mates were there that night, in astral form, and it had scared the shit out of them. They didn't want to chance doing anything that might trip that kind of behavior again, especially since my pain and rage hadn't been dealt with yet.

I quickly turned my thoughts to other things. I didn't want to remember right then and cause a scene. Happy thoughts, happy thoughts, was the trick; that, and a lot of chamomile tea and St. Johns Wort. If that didn't work, I'd break out my comedies and veg in front of the TV for a while, or go for a swim. Water always helped me for many different kinds of bad moods. Worst case scenario - I'd drag my mates back into the bedroom and attempt to wear them out. Hmmm, the idea had merit. I smiled to myself.

"So, you'll be staying for a while, or going back to your world?" I wanted to know.

"We would like to stay. There are many wonders here. We trust your dragons will help keep things safe for now." Ja' Callum looked uncertain. "If that is pleasing to you, Meshama?"

"That would be great, but for a few things," I answered.

"What may those be, Meshama?" Ja' Monel inquired with a heavy look of lust in his eyes. Oh yeah, the bedroom scene had gotten to him real bad.

"Well, for one thing, while you're here, in this world, you'll need to just call me Cat or Catrina. Two, the titles of your own names will bring attention and questions we shouldn't answer at all, so can we shorten your names to just Callum, Monel and Kelo? Or chose some Earth-side-sounding names? It will help you blend in."

Ja' Kelo looked concerned. "Being Ja' or Ama is not good in this world?"

"Being *anything* out of the ordinary in this world is very, very dangerous. You must appear to be like anyone else or things could get complicated, very quickly." I stood up and moved over to him, taking his hand and making him stand as well. I turned him this way and that. "You'll also need some Earth-side clothes. This outfit will stand out. There is a shop in the lobby. Maybe we can take them down there and get them outfitted?" I turned to glance at my mates, who looked murderous at my handling of Ja' Kelo. I quickly let my hand drop off from his arm and took a step back.

Ja' Callum shook his head and sighed heavily. "I do not understand a world that doesn't revere, or at least, respect the blessings it has been given. So much so, it seems very wondrous to us, which is one of the reasons we want to stay and observe here."

"I agree with my cousin. With so many Ama's and Amu's in one generation, there might be something here we may be missing in our own world." Ja' Monel looked at me. "Though, the blessings seemed to have spilled over into our world with your visit, Meshama. I am sorry - 'Catrina'." he corrected himself, taking my suggestions to heart.

I found that a relief. I had thought they would be more stubborn about it.

I snorted, "You didn't tell them about the rest of my siblings, or the other pantheons of children did you?" I threw that question to my mates.

Demitri was the one who answered. "No. We didn't see the need for them to know, but if you insist." He arched his eyebrow at me.

I stuck my tongue out at him. "I have two sisters and three brothers." The Dai' Khans eyes grew wide. "They have three mates each, as well. There are also many other pantheons of religions that bore physical children on this plane, all to help with the Great Shift."

"So many?" Ja Callum grew alarmed. "This sounds more dire now than a blessing, if so many are needed."

I nodded my head sharply. "Exactly. So, don't go thinking Earth has anything better or more than your world. It actually may be in much worse shape to need so many of our kind here. I have been thinking of another reason while I was showering."

Andre came over with a juice for me. "What are your thoughts, Babe?"

"When I was over in their world, Ja' Callum told me they are only expecting a slight shift, not a major one like we are. Yet, as with this shift, it is connected to many other dimensional worlds which are opening up. What if this world is some sort of center piece, a cornerstone for other dimensions, and that's why they will only face a small shift compared to this one? Therefore, this world needs all the heavy guns, spiritually speaking, as opposed to those other worlds? This world's outcome will have severe consequences on all others." I looked around, waiting for some feedback for my musings.

"It tracks, Babe," Andre nodded in agreement. "I would have loved to have been able to have a reasonable discussion with those other races we fought a month ago and see if they, too, are only going to experience a minor shift."

I threw my empty juice box at him. "Who the fuck are you trying to kid? You loved every damn battle, you warmongering friggin' Conan the Barbarian."

He caught it, laughing. "Only the barbarian with you, baby."

"Yeah, right," I said.

The Dai' Khans were wide-eyed at our play, and the way we interacted together. I saw the quick glance Ja' Callum had given Ja' Monel that said 'see, I was right about us needing to be here to observe,' look.

I looked back at Andre. "For that bullshit line, you get to take them shopping; since you're as much a clothes horse as you're a barbarian. Just a well-dressed barbarian." I gave him a saucy smile, taking in his change of clothes of a silk black shirt and black designer jeans. His boots were hand-tooled by a custom boot maker. He wouldn't wear anything else but Gregio's specialty boots which cost anywhere from a grand or higher. He spoiled himself on his wardrobe, as did Demitri. Antonio had nice clothes too, mostly due to Demitri picking them out for him from time to time, but he would wear his workout clothes when around the house or working in his shop on some new gadget.

"Fine, you evil woman. I suppose if I don't do this, you'll threaten me with couch time." Looking at the Dai' Khans he said, "Come with me, if you want to live. You haven't seen her get mad, yet." He cocked his eyebrow at me with that movie line.

Ja' Kelo snorted, "Oh, yes we have. Very impressive language. What does fuck mean, by the way?"

My mates burst out laughing, while I fumed, watching them having fun at my expense. The couch is looking good tonight, oh, yeah!

And they say women shopped 'till they dropped? Sh'yeah! Whoever got that old line going obviously hadn't seen any of my mates in action when it came to men's wear. They came in with arms filled with bags of every size and description. Andre showed them to the part of the suite with rooms they could use while we were here. After they were done changing, they came back out looking like sex on a stick.

They each had on designer jeans that hugged their well-shaped asses. Buns of steel had nothing on these guys. They each had long, well muscled legs and broad chests that peeked through the finely made shirts they had on.

Demitri groaned when he saw the look of lust in my eyes. "Did you have to dress them so well, you dumb ass?" Demitri asked Andre.

Andre looked at Demitri, then at me, then to where I was looking, and said, "Shit, I guess I fucked this one up, huh?"

Demitri gave him the, 'Duh', look. "No shit, Sherlock."

The Dai' Khans were grinning smugly.

When I could get my mouth closed, I cleared my throat. "Umm, a few words of wisdom, fellas. Come here." I directed them to the bar. "See this stuff? It's alcohol." I poured a glass of whiskey, the hardest stuff that was in the bar. "Take your finger, dip it in and taste it."

They each did as I asked. Ja' Callum got a nasty look. Ja' Monel seemed to like it and Ja' Kelo kept trying to rub if off his tongue.

"Good, anything with alcohol in it can have drastic effects on your magick. Never, ever, do magick and drink this stuff at the same time," I cautioned them.

"Ahh, it's like Simoo at home, cousins." Ja' Callum caught the understanding. "We never touch the strong drink when we practice our magicks."

Ja' Kelo nodded his head. "I do not think that will be a problem. With apologies, but that drink is not good."

"Well, there are many, many flavors of alcohol and they will all do the same thing - mess up your magick," I instructed.

They all nodded sagely. "Thank you, for the warning Meshama," Ja' Monel said.

I gave him an arched look.

He made the proper name change. "Catrina."

"Ok, moving on. See this stuff here?" I pointed to wire sockets for plugging in electrical equipment. "And this here is a TV." I showed them the lamps and anything even remotely electrical. "All these things are electric. If you do magick near any of these things, you may blow up the wall or your magick can get screwy or return back on you. Electricity and magick equal *danger*. If there is an electric line under your feet and you make a power circle or a shield, the electrical line will cut through the shield, making you vulnerable there. Your circle will NOT be closed properly and negative things can ride in, understand?" I looked hard at all three of them.

"I understand that there is danger, but I do not understand why." Of course Ja' Monel didn't understand the why of it; they didn't have any electricity at home. Oh, wait, maybe they had lightening?

"Do you have storms at home where there is lightening that strikes the ground?" I queried.

Ja' Monel said, "Of course, Catrina." He looked at me like I was being silly.

"Ok, what happens if you were to do magick in the middle of that storm with no shield?" I was trying to get him to understand the connection.

"You could blast yourself apart, Catrina." Oh, he was getting good with my name, though his eyes turned a darker shade of amber every time he said it, throwing me off my lessons on Earth world safety for the major magick user.

I shook my head clear. "Right." I picked up the TV cord and showed it to them. "This cord going to this appliance has a small bolt of lightning harnessed inside of it."

Their mouths gaped at this revelation. "That is great magick, Meshama." Ja' Kelo was so struck by the wonder of it, he forgot to use my regular name.

I slapped his shoulder. "Catrina or Cat. Now, this is a very small charge in comparison to a bolt of lightning, but it is of the same essence as lightening. See how this cord goes to that plug in the wall?" They nodded. "Inside is another bigger cord that has a much larger charge of this harnessed lightning, which goes to an even larger box of harnessed lightening and so on. Once you learn electricity and power stations you'll understand better, but for right now, if you feel a buzz of electricity near you, do not do magick."

Their faces turned grim and Ja' Callum said, "Now I understand, as I am sure my cousins do. This is very dangerous. But, how can we tell if there is this electricity, as you call it, near us?"

"Open your senses and feel around. Don't harness your power, just your natural inborn senses and 'feel' around you. If you hear a buzzing sound like a low hum, then move away until you don't hear it anymore. Watch me." I dropped my shields and 'felt' out and around me with my aura, gently testing the air. "See? I feel a low hum when I move closer to the wall where the socket is; the hum gets louder and faster as I move nearer."

They used their second sight to watch me test the air and surrounding area. Then, they copied the movements. They moved this way and that, getting to know the sound and the changes it made when moving closer to it, and then moved further away. Once they felt they had a good grasp on the situation, one by one, they remade their shields and stopped to look at me.

"I think we have it now. Thank you for the warning. There is a lot of this electricity in your world?" Ja' Callum asked.

"Yes, everywhere in some places; cars, trains and airplanes. Streets outside, the shopping market you just came from to the elevator you just rose up here in. You have to be extremely careful where you let your magick out. The best case scenario, is that you get these lights to flicker around you, which draws attention to you and can out you as a magick user. The worst case scenario, is you blow yourself up or possibly kill someone else. There are many children around that can get hurt, or worse, in the crossfire, too." With that statement, I knew I had impressed upon them the seriousness of watching their magick use.

Children would be a high commodity in their world, more precious than gold or diamonds. I could tell they would be careful now.

But, just to add to the plight of open magick use, I added, "Magick is not acceptable to use in this world. We have secret government agencies that hunt our kind to trap and experiment on us; or if we are really lucky, just kill us."

Ja' Monel growled, "They would dare?"

"Yes, they would dare. They outnumber us a million to one. A few years ago, they had caught Demitri." I pointed over to where he was sitting. He nodded, confirming my charge. "They had him and Shamus, as well as more of our people. We barely got them out before they had started to cut into Demitri to find out what made him tick, because they knew he wasn't the ordinary magick user they usually got a hold of. Someone like you, they would have kittens over. Being a person not even of this world, but from another dimension. So, please believe me when I say it is for your protection that I think of when I warn you of free magick use in this world. Magick has to be the very last thing you use in defense of yourself or others when you're in a situation and not the first, as *you* would do in your world."

Ja' Monel was furious. "They would dare to defile an Ama and an Amu. This world does not deserve what has been so graciously given them."

"Oh, I agree with you there, but you have to think of the innocents that would be lost if we turn away from this world. The children, the animals and the planet itself. Should they, too, pay the price? Not to mention the overflow of evil that would stream into both of our own realms, sooner or later, from here." I sighed heavily, "It is too horrendous to even imagine."

"Ja' Monel, you have missed something, cousin." Ja' Callum was grinning from ear to ear.

Ja' Monel turned angry fiery amber eyes to him. "What have I missed?"

"She worries for us and our well being. This whole lecture and safe guards she has taught us, shows care."

Ja' Monel froze, thinking of what he said.

I groaned and sat back in my seat. Antonio growled and glared at all of them.

The three Dai' Khans then looked at each other and started laughing.

We spent some time with Rock and the team later that night to discuss everything we were going to put in our reports for General Pierce. We decided to just tell him everything and let the chips fall where they may. Things were a bit strange with a few of the men who didn't know exactly how to treat us anymore. Once we assured them that we were still the same people who fought side by side with them and would continue to do so, they relaxed a bit with only an odd stare or two every now and again. Rock had scrambled a sat-com phone to General Pierce and gave him the twenty-five cent version of events. Rock and I were ordered to stay there until he, himself, could come out and take a look at things with his own eyes.

My mates and I immediately broke the rules, and took the Dai' Khans out for a sightseeing tour, which I had been dying to do ever since we arrived. I was jealous that the Dai' Khans had an easier time than I did, since they knew the language already. And I was from this world damn it, sheesh. We agreed that I should restrain from using any more of my powers, even for an information download, until I was completely healed. It seemed that the damage that was done to my psychic centers in body and brain, magick could only heal so far. The rest had to heal the slow human way.

After doing a daily scan on me, Shamus found out that every time I used major magick, another bleeding spot was appearing in my brain and slowing down the healing process for the rest of my internal and spiritual injuries. My little temper tantrum on Kla' Din had caused a lot of spots to appear. So I agreed - no more magick until I healed.

My mates tried to console me by spoiling me rotten with every place we went to. Either that, or they were trying to piss off the Dai' Khans. I couldn't figure out which. I still enjoyed the Japanese tea gardens and a traditional Kabuki show. We went to a dance club and an authentic Japanese Karaoke bar. I had a blast there singing my favorite songs I found on the play list. I was surprised they had them in Japan and tried to do the songs justice.

The Dai' Khans thought it was great and I told them all about our family bar, The Nightwolves Lair, back home. And how we not only had the Karaoke box, but we also did our own music and played other songs ourselves with our own instruments. I told them our bar was a private family club where only family members and the military soldiers we fought with were allowed, so we could talk freely there, relax, and have a good time. I showed them our 'wolves howling at the moon' tattoos that most of our group now sported, like the tattoos some Special Forces members had. My mates weren't happy with the sharing of information, but I think it was mostly out of jealousy than anything else.

We were eating in a restaurant, showing the Dai' Khans the wonderful cuisine of Sushi, when my pager beeped. I grabbed my cell phone and punched speed dial for the number to call.

Rock answered, "Cat, General Pierce is here and he ain't happy. Get over here now with your mates and the Dai' Khans."

"Major Payne," throwing Rock the title of the movie he semi-quoted to me. "Pierce is pissed, huh? 'Wanna place a bet?"

"What's the bet?" he sounded curious.

Thinking quickly, I said, "I bet with one sentence, I can get myself out of trouble. And no telling the General, 'cause that ain't fair."

"One sentence? No friggin' way! You're on. A hundred says you can't get out of this one." He sounded sure of himself.

"A hundred it is." I had a huge smile on my face that he couldn't see. "Make the rounds with the rest of guys for a nice, big, fat win. I'm going to use the money to get a real silk handmade Kimono."

Sounding smug, Rock replied, "I know General Pierce. You are so going to lose."

"We'll see. We're on our way." Purple silk handmade Kimono, here I come.

"Good luck. I'll make the rounds on the sly." With that, Rock hung up.

"Ours didn't beep," Demitri made it a statement and a question.

"Rock knew you guys would be with me. Seems we may be called to the carpet for not hanging around in that stuffy hotel. We need to get back ASAP. Daddy General has spoken," I laughed.

"Who is Major Payne, Catrina?" Ja' Kelo asked, since I had also told them about everyone in our military unit and that name hadn't been mentioned. Good recall, I thought to myself.

"It's a movie title. Don't ask. I will take you to one someday. It's the easiest way to show you. Anyway, we play a game; well, two games, actually. We bet on the outcome of missions, and we quote movie lines or song lines to each other and the person has to guess correctly which movie or song it came from," I said, looking around for the waiter.

The Dai' Khans must have sensed our urgency, since the questions came to a halt. I saw our waiter and flagged him down. Demitri took care of the bill and we made good time back to the hotel.

Romeo was waiting for us in the lobby. He cracked a grin. "I'm in. You're done for," and took us to the room General Pierce had gotten for his stay.

When we walked into the General's room, I could tell we didn't have a happy camper - no, siree.

"Cat, you disobeyed a direct order." He didn't even say hi. Yup, the General was pissed.

Everyone else was looking around the room, trying to avoid eye contact with me. My mates and the Dai' Khans looked affronted at the treatment I was receiving.

General Pierce wasn't done raking me over the coals yet, either. "I gave strict orders for everyone to hold here, until I got here myself. Do you mind explaining yourself?" His hazel blue eyes were flashing anger at me for the very first time.

I took off my sunglasses and gave him my most innocent, wide-eyed look. "You're not going to spank me are you?" I said, in a meek little girl voice. "Because my ass still hurts." I took my hands and covered my rear like I feared a whipping from daddy.

Shocked silence erupted throughout the room. My mates and the Dai' Khans mostly had their mouths hanging open. Rock and his Special Forces team were looking at me like they couldn't quite believe I had just said what I had. The marine squad froze, in stunned disbelief. The General, himself, gaped at me, incredulous at my question.

Wizard started it first, with the muffled chortles, which slowly turned into belly rolls. That set off Romeo, and both of them wound up on the floor holding their stomachs from the hilarity. One by one, then groups at a time - soon, the whole room was pealing with laughter. Even the stoic Major Stewart, General Pierce's attaché, was trying hard not to snicker and lost it after seeing everyone in the room falling about, hitting each other on the back, slapping their knees or trying to hold themselves up with the wall.

General Pierce closed his mouth and looked about him. "Oh, for the love of Pete," turning away from me as he held his hand over his mouth, shaking his head.

I just kept up the innocent scared expression, which set the guys off even more. Seeing nineteen men lose it, and a General trying hard not to follow, was hysterical. I had a hell of a time keeping a straight face, but I really wanted that Kimono. Not that my mates would deny me; it was just a pride thing. I wanted the Kimono on my own money, and getting it from betting was fun.

After Antonio got a hold of himself, he bent to whisper in my ear, "I can't believe you just did that. Now the guys are going to tease the hell out of me."

I said through the side of my mouth, "You deserve it, you big meanie." And that got him going again.

There was a knock on the door. Babyface collected himself first to answer it. In walked my sister, Cassie, with Major Miller, one of my favorite squad leaders to work with. Even Rock liked using him and his squad when we could get them on rotation. They both looked around with eyebrows raised, wondering what it was they had missed.

Babyface, who rarely, if ever, even cracked a smile, actually wagged his finger at me in mock scolding and walked back with the rest of the Special Forces team. Rock was recovering, as were the rest of the men.

General Pierce turned back around and took a deep breath. "Cat, I know you're a Merc and have been your own leader for a long time. But, the next time you disobey a direct order from me, I will take you out of rotation, is that clear?"

"Yes, Sir. I apologize," I said seriously. Behind my back, where Rock could see, I rubbed my fingers together in our code for 'pay up'.

Any other time, with anyone else, they would have been sent back stateside, facing scud work until they could prove that they could follow orders. That would be the first time for disobeying a direct order. A second time, and you might never see the inside of a war room again. In all things magickal though, I had the say. I could disobey and get away with it, if I felt the situation needed it. But, this wasn't a magickal situation, this was purely physical, and in that area, General Pierce was top dog. But I got away with it. This time.

'*Sister, what did you do?*' Her tone in my head was curious.

I answered, '*I had fun.*'

She clucked in my head, '*You should know better.*'

I gave her a mischievous grin, totally unrepentant. '*Wait until you see my Kimono.*'

General Pierce asked, "So, are you going to introduce me?"

Ahh, yes. The Dai' Khans. A magickal situation, therefore, my bailiwick.

"General Pierce, I would like you to meet Ja' Callum, Ja' Monel and Ja' Kelo, Dai' Khans of Kla' din." I turned to the rulers of Kla' din. "Dai' Khans, this is General Pierce, the leader of our Nightwolf Force of Earth."

'I thought our titles were not a good thing to make known, Meshama?' Ja' Callum asked, but I could sense the other two listening in.

'For this man, this one time, it is proper,' I told them simply. They sent their understanding.

"Nice to me you, Dai' Khans. I hope Cat has shown you a nice time while you have visited here?" he said a tad sardonically in my direction.

"Yes, we have enjoyed many new wonders in your world, thanks to Meshama," Ja' Callum answered for them all.

I sighed, "Not that title." Then realized I had actually said that aloud.

"Yes, you have a lot to explain, Cat. But first, I thought to see these two worlds for myself. As you can see, Major Miller is here and his team will be with us for this next excursion. O'Hara has filled me in and if it were anyone else but O'Hara, I would have him back stateside, STAT." He took a deep breath to calmly add, "But, I am willing to go and see and I hope for his sake, his report is true, or I will be very disappointed, Catrina."

My whole name from General Pierce. He had never done that before. This must be my week for pissing people off.

My sister was the first to take offense, however, and she rarely ever lost her composure. "My sister has never led you astray." She walked up to him face to face. "She has never lied to you. She has put herself at great risk for you, your people and your damn planet."

"She has omitted many things," the General defended himself. "Things that would have made some of my decisions quite different."

"Exactly. And, how much worse would this situation be if you had?" With that, she walked away, too infuriated to continue.

The General looked uncertain for a moment. "Why don't we go see, then we will have a long talk about this."

"You guys ready for a quick trip home?" I asked the Dai' Khans.

"We will be able to stay with you, right?" Ja' Kelo seemed tentative.

I nodded my head and lead the way out the door. I couldn't speak. I was getting so angry, it was best to exit, stage left.

Chapter Six

Insults and Vendettas

Once we were at the park, we divided up the team again as evenly as possible. Major Miller wanted badly to go through the portal with us along with his split team members. I agreed to that plan and left this side of the portals defenses up to Andre and the men who would stay. Demitri and Antonio came with me this time, not trusting the Dai' Khans alone with me on their world. I looked archly at the General, having lost my sense of humor the more I thought about what he had said. I guess I couldn't really blame the guy, but I had been there for him and his military many times and that should have bought me *some* credit. I walked through the portal and waited patiently for the others to come through. I was happy to see two dragons guarding the gateway and gave them each a hug. General Pierce had just come through, when he saw me cuddling up to a dragon, and he stopped to gape at the sight.

I disengaged from the hug and said to the General, "This is my friend, Corves. He is the son of my dragon, Cornelia." Others had stepped through the gate and stopped as well. "Please, no alarms and no shooting or I'll kick your ass. You'll only piss them off anyway. These are my friends Corves and Gordon. They are guarding the gate on this side. I guess I should have warned you."

I had known, but I was still upset and thought this would be good payback. I was feeling a tad bitchy.

My sister gave me an evil grin. She knew exactly why I did it, and surprisingly, she agreed with my method of vendetta.

"Umm, well yes, pleased to meet you both." The General was trying hard to roll with this situation. He had done well with everything I had thrown at him before, but I could see he was going to have trouble with this one, and we hadn't even started yet. Corves, picking up my true emotion, snuffled and let out a puff of smoke which enveloped the General, making him cough. I had to hide my face so no one would see that I was highly amused.

Once I had my face arranged correctly, I turned back around, to say, "He says hello."

"He really understood me?" the General asked, between hacks of coughing.

"Yes, they are highly intelligent and telepathic," I informed him with glee. I knew how badly telepathy troubled the General and waited for the unease to come. I wasn't long in waiting.

I decided to get really bitchy. "There are more dragons coming to fly us to the portal of Trinidad, and no, there is no other way there fast enough," I said, before the General could ask which, of course, made him even more uneasy.

Demitri and Antonio came to flank me. Demitri sent me a thought, *'Sweetheart, you might want to ease up a bit.'*

I glared at him. *'Why the fuck should I?'*

Demitri's eyes were round in shock. I had never lost my temper so badly with him. He made the prudent move to give me space to cool off. Antonio was no fool; he backed up with Demitri.

I moved far away from the group. Even the Dai' Khans had stayed where they were and I watched the dragons come through the skyline towards us. Cornelia was in the lead, moving like a black shadow through the blue skies. When she landed, she picked up on my mood and blew out fire through her nose. I ran up to her to calm her and threw myself up onto her back using power, not waiting for her to shrink and bend her knee for me.

I knew Demitri and Andre would instruct the others in climbing and riding, so I just took off. Cornelia and I circled around in the skies so I had a birds-eye view of Kla' din. I saw way off to the west side the beginning of civilization and wondered which province that was. I was trying any method I could think of to cool off. None of it was working. I knew the General was going to be difficult, but it hurt that he so doubted, after all this time.

Finally, they had all mounted and were coming up towards our position in the sky and we headed for Trinidad's portal. I had no idea what good he thought that this would make. He would most likely just rationalize it somehow, as most humans tended to do when confronted with something out of the ordinary. Oh, I was in a foul mood and getting worse by the minute. We rode right though the portal and landed in the meadow, waiting for the others to make their way safely through.

Soon, the whole field was filled with dragons, with their riders dismounting from them. Some made it off their dragon gingerly, as if afraid to hurt the dragon and make them mad. Good move, I thought; a pissed off dragon is a very dangerous thing, not that riders could really hurt a dragon while dismounting. I just stood there, getting more steamed by the minute. I had no idea why I was reacting so strongly. I really should have expected this attitude and taken it in stride. For some reason, I just couldn't chill out over the insult I felt to me.

General Pierce, having no clue, obviously, that I was in a really bad mood, came up to me with his men trailing behind. My mates and The Dai' Khans, being more attuned to my mood, stayed back a bit further. They knew I wasn't over it yet.

"So, this is your world, Cat?" the General asked.

I pressed my lips together and spoke tightly through them, "Yes, this is Trinidad."

He looked closely at me. "It is very nice here."

My eyes flashed green with power, though he couldn't see it through my sunglasses. "It is perfect! I have created every plant, every rock, every bit of dirt and ocean. My castle is in the distance and I made that, also."

"You did all of this, eh?" waving to the surrounding area. His tone still didn't sound like he quite believed me. I started subtly shaking and then a loud crash rent through the air above us.

"WHO DARES?" a deep female voice echoed through the air.

The skyline darkened and the heavens above us rumbled threateningly.

I felt the power of my Mother and She wasn't happy.

I looked around to the men. Demitri and Andre had dropped to one knee and bowed their heads.

"Down," I said to everyone. "Down on your knees now and bow your heads. Both knees, if not related by blood or by marriage." The Dai' Khans were at a loss on what on to do and decided to go the safer route and dropped to both knees.

I knelt on one knee and bowed my head. The General wasn't quick enough for my taste and I hissed, "Never piss off a Goddess or a God. They are capricious at best, or your worst nightmare, otherwise. If you value your future, do as I said now."

He slowly did as I bid. When the others saw him kneel and bow his head as I was, they, too, followed suit.

The air grew thick and heavy. Lightning flashed through the now dark cloudy skies. From the middle of the forming storm came a bright blue oval light. My Mother descended from the heavens, as a bright blue oval ball of spirit at first. As She drew nearer to the meadow, you could see She was wearing blue colored robes with a hood covering her hair. Her face was hidden within the depths. I knew that to look upon Her face, one would see shifting female visages. She was one - She was all of the females who ever had been, or will be. She was The Cauldron of Life, the Cauldron of Rebirth and The Cauldron of Knowledge. And something had pissed Her off.

As Her feet touched the ground of my meadow, I asked, "Mother, what has upset You so? What can I do to make amends?" I asked humbly of Her.

"What has upset *you* so, Daughter?" She returned. "Never before have you come to your world and been unhappy. I have gifted you with the power to create, so you would have this world as a retreat. Yet, the second time you have stepped physical feet upon your lands, you are enraged."

She looked around to the group of kneeling people. "Who here has so enraged My Daughter in her world of refuge?"

Scanning the men one by one, She soon lit upon General Pierce. "Ah, you, Richard James Pierce, you have caused the anguish and anger in My Daughter here in her world."

I grabbed his hand and squeezed, giving him a warning look not to speak yet. "She sees you as a physical father figure. Someone she respects and looks up to. To protect even, as a daughter would protect those she loves. You have won a place in her heart and you have wounded it." Lightening shot through the skies causing thunder to rumble through.

"Mother, please," I implored Her.

Her attention turned to me. "Yes, My Daughter?"

"He didn't mean to hurt my feelings. The Gods and Goddess have had no direct interaction with most humans for many millennia. Is it so hard to understand their skepticism now?"

"You still wish to protect him?" I could feel Her smile in the air. "Your heart is too compassionate, Daughter. It is your greatest strength and your greatest weakness." She turned Her attention back to General Pierce. "Know this, mortal. My Daughter is protected here and ill done to her, is done as to Me. It is for her sake I will let this pass - once. Do not squander My forgiveness. Daughter Cassie, come walk with Me."

"Yes, Mother," Cassie said obediently. She rose to walk with our Mother.

"Thank you, Mother," I said to Her, as She made to stride away with Cassie.

Over her shoulder, she said, "You are most welcome, Daughter."

I waited until they had cleared the end of the meadow before I rose to my feet.

"I must apologize, General Pierce. I didn't realize She was watching over me so closely here. I would have controlled my rage better if I had known." I felt bad for putting the General in such a situation. It could have gone very badly for him.

"So, that is a Goddess?" He looked shaken.

"That is a Goddess, yes. Please watch what you say here, even though She has gone from the meadow." I scanned the group of open-mouthed soldiers.

We were going to need food and drinks, the best things for shock. I didn't think waiting until we made it to the castle would do it. I chose an area off to the side of the meadow and made appear a large purple tent with a long blue table inside it with matching chairs. I was hoping to also appease my mates in honoring their colors by choosing these shades.

"Come inside and sit down, please. I will get you food and drinks to help calm your nerves." I looked toward the direction of my castle and shouted, "Simon, I need you now, please." Though my voice wouldn't carry all that distance to my castle, the telepathy I put into the call easily would. "Demitri, Antonio, help me get these guys inside the tent." I took General Pierce gently by the arm and guided him inside.

Simon had translocated inside the tent near me. "What is your need, Princess?"

"I need food and drinks for everyone. Chamomile tea, coffee and such, if you would ask someone at the castle to bring it?"

"Immediately, Princess. We felt your Mother's anger all the way there." He hesitated, "We felt your anger first. Is all well?"

"Yes, all is well. I am sorry I didn't control myself better." I felt bad for bringing such a negative emotion to my place of peace.

"No harm, Princess. I will return, though you may be deluged in visits again," he warned as he left.

"We may be the ones to blame for this Meshama," Ja' Callum appeared guilty.

I was confused, since it was I who had been angry. "How so?"

"With three new bonds, and feeling our anger for your treatment, you could have been overwhelmed and not realized to separate our feelings, along with your mates, from your own slightly hurt feelings."

"He means, we may have added to your feeling of anger when your own was only minimal, but amplified by all six of ours," Demitri expounded.

My eyes lit up. "Oh, yes, that would explain why I couldn't release the anger quick enough, but that's not your fault, either. If we had known, we would have prepared for it."

Smiling now, feeling much less guilty myself, I went to sit down next to the General. "Well, having fun yet or what?" I said flippantly.

He looked askance at me and seeing me smile, he cracked one of his own. "Ever since I met you, you have been a constant source of amazement. I honestly don't know how to deal with this situation. There is nothing even remotely close to this in the books," he admitted.

"You've dealt with the weird from us before," I reminded him.

"Yes, but I was able to see it as more of a Stargate type of situation after Wizard and Antonio got that box together. Your PETS." He grinned at me. "Something more normal that science could explain if we had all the right equipment for it. The weird didn't seem so weird anymore. Now this?" he shrugged his shoulders. "How could anyone put the science in what happened today into a box?"

Ahh, I saw his problem. He had rationalized and gotten used to the idea of what we were as something science could explain, given enough research. Mundanes were so good at that, not wanting anything they see or hear to be something that they could not eventually control. No mundane would ever be able to control a God or a Goddess though; no matter how much science progressed.

I was disappointed in him. "You haven't seen anything yet." Raising my voice, so everyone at the table could hear me, I said, "My people are coming with food and drinks. Please, just bear with us. None will harm you as long as I am not attacked."

In came my fairies and wizards, bearing trays of food and pots of various drinks. I laughed, seeing the look of incredulity on the men's faces. Only Rock's team was taking it in stride, but they were more used to it than the rest. Especially Rock. After seeing the General served with a cup of calming chamomile tea, I explained the reasons why the Gods and Goddesses were on the move on Earth again. I also told him of our suppositions of why Earth may be a corner stone with other worlds and much hinged upon its success for future safety of their own.

"Well, this incident, if nothing else, has convinced me of your heritage. But, what I don't understand, is why your Mother's contact is so blatant here and only minimal on Earth." He looked at me.

"The Gods and Goddesses have rules even They have to abide by. I, myself, don't understand the reasons why, but I do know they have had to keep a low profile on Earth for a long time. However, recently that has changed more than you know in the last few years; it seems to me there are still some restrictions. Here, since it is my world and She is my Mother, She is also my Goddess. She has no limitations on Trinidad. I admit, I didn't know She was watching me that closely here. She had never before been so Solid here, to date."

General Pierce said, "She seems protective of you; yet, from your juvenile records, your childhood had to have been hell with your physical parents. How did that happen?"

"You can't have a strong sword that hasn't been through the fire," I told him.

"Yes, but your hospital records from your childhood show massive damage..."

I cut him off, not wanting to remember. "Yes, but now I have an understanding and compassion that few people do of what some children go through on Earth. If you have never lived through the experience, yes, *you* may feel bad for them, but at the end of the day, it really doesn't haunt you; make you feel the strong need to protect, day in and day out. One can never fully understand what it is like to know that kind of life. You have to live it, before you can really feel it deep inside the soul."

Someone who had lived through it, would have known better than to just blurt out 'hospital records' and 'trauma' like that. We wait for the other to volunteer the information. If they don't, it is never mentioned, out of respect. A survivor will talk about it when they are ready, and not before. Pushing the topic is not only extremely rude, but further traumatizes the person on a mental and spiritual level.

I forgave him anyway, knowing he honestly could never understand, since he obviously had to have had a nice childhood. Good for him. Babyface was sitting not too far away and had clearly overheard the conversation, because he looked me dead in the eyes, filled with knowledge of what it meant to be a survivor. When I saw our shared pain reflected in his gaze, I knew then, one of the bricks that was in his foundation was what made him a stone cold killer.

Most males never really adjust in adulthood without becoming part of the continuing cycle. They grew up to become an abuser to themselves, to others, or both. They usually hide from the pain with jail, drugs and alcohol. Some men made it into the military for the structure it provided them, helping them keep a lid on it and a safe outlet in war. Females, for the most part, reacted differently as they grew up, having problems with codependency and depression, or become mental or physical abusers themselves.

My mates worked overtime in our relationship to sidestep my emotional landmines and help me deal with problems as they arose. Antonio gave me a safe way to fulfill some of my needs that could never be undone, even if I had an eternity of counseling. Some things in the human psyche, once broken, can never be truly fixed again. Babyface and I were plainly prime examples of that, as I returned a nod of recognition with him. Rock had also caught the exchange. I looked in his eyes.

No, he didn't have that deep pain, but I could tell he was The Rock, as his code name labeled him, for Babyface to hold his shit together and function within the accepted norm in the military. Well, now Babyface had another person to come to if he needed someone to lean on. I let that show in my face to them both before turning my attention back to the General.

"There are many of us. We each had to learn different lessons of what it is like to be human. Sure, I seemed to have gotten the short end of the stick, but I am also sure that things could have been much worse. I am grateful for the childhood I did have." I said this in total seriousness and the General looked aghast at me.

"But, She allowed this?" He just couldn't get over the fact that my spiritual Mother allowed me to be put in such a horrendous physical environment.

"We both allowed it, though I don't consciously remember it," I admitted.

"Excuse me?" The General looked confused.

"Most, are born on the astral planes first, as I was to Her. Then, when we are ready, we choose two other lower spiritual beings to meld with and are incarnated into a physical babe, either at conception or during birth. Actually, it could be at any time. The point is, free will is on the astral planes, as well. To allow being born or reborn into a physical body, you have to agree and most know what it is they are getting into. So don't feel too badly for me; I apparently chose my own physical birth parents."

"Why would anyone deliberately chose such a life?" He wasn't getting it.

"To learn, to grow, to experience and when one is done learning that particular experience, they will move on to yet a slightly higher spiritual level and chose another life that they can learn and grow from and become more each time. It is a process much like making a sword. You throw it in the fire, let it heat up, then you take it out and pound the impurities out of the sword. You put it back into the fire, heating it up again, and take it out to pound it again. The more you pound out the impurities, the stronger the sword becomes until you have the perfect blade. Don't ask me what happens after that, for the normal human. For me, I'll get to come here and stay forever, if I chose to. That's worth any pain I may have to go through to have this until the end of time." I was gazing out to the open field through the side of the tent that had been pulled back for the view. All of my friends from here were moving around, and some of the men had decided they were brave enough to go out among them and pet a few, talk with others, and just enjoy the novelty of the event.

"Look out there, General. There is so much more to this world you haven't seen yet. I hope someday you will. Once I get to lay down my sword, my mates and I can reside here among those beautiful creatures and beings that you see. I'll be able to have more children and be immortal, living among my people. I'll get to watch them live and grow, having children of their own."

Ariel was coming toward the open flap of the tent, tossing her white mane into the wind and stomping her hooves. *'Come ride me, Princess. Please. It's been too long since we last rode together.'*

I did something I would never be able to do on Earth. I took off my leather jacket and unstrapped the wrist sheaths for the blades I had on my forearms. I took off my gun holsters, laying down all my weapons, putting my gear in front of Demitri on the table and walked outside. I launched onto her back smiling wide, showing the happiness in my heart that this beautiful creature wanted to spend time with me. I didn't bother saying goodbye. My mates would appreciate the need that drove me; the Dai' Khans would learn, and the military men? Well, they would have to try to understand, as I headed into the skies of Trinidad riding a Pegasus.

Before we headed back over to the world of Kla' din, I had a meeting with my mates, the Dai' Khans, and Shamus. I had noticed that our worlds were syncing together in time. If it was night on Kla' din, it was beginning to be night on Trinidad, as well. I wanted Simon to watch the sun declination on Kla' din and compare it to our sun here.

The Dai' Khans were amazed that Trinidad sported three moons as well, but they were all white. I also wanted guards on our side of the portal around the clock; not because of fear of the sorcerers, but the vampyres. Trinidad was now vulnerable, with access through that portal. I didn't want my people at risk, though many of the breeds here could make mince-meat out of any tribe of vampire. That's why the dragons were chosen for guard duty in shifts. I made caves nearby, so they would have a place to rest, and added another meadow close to here, filled with cows for hunting.

We named this meadow Dragons Landing Meadow. With the naming, the air sparkled for a minute and the world around me felt even a bit more solid. I took note of that, and added to the duties of my astral self (still busy naming the new babies on this world), to include naming places. This world was huge, being three times the size of Earth. She was going to busy for a while, which was a good thing, since it would also keep Trixie here and not off mooning over Rock on Earth. Right now, the flowers she left him were yellow. That was good, since yellow represented friendship and liking. If they ever turned red, I may suggest Rock run and hide. Red was love and passion. If white flowers ever showed up, he was doomed. White was for an offer of marriage among the Fae.

Back in Kla' din, the General wanted to know about the Bokaris and the vampyre problems they had there. When the General found out that there were many different types of vampire, he got that tight look in his eyes again. I didn't know how much more he could take and keep trying to roll with the situations as they popped up. Even Army Generals had their limitations, I supposed.

General Pierce had heard my plans to help the Kla' dins keep the vampyres at bay until I could find another solution for their problem. No world deserved wholesale slaughter like that. The Vampyres were treating that place like their own private free buffet. No longer, if I had anything to do about it. General Pierce was concerned with me spreading myself so thin, trying to cover three worlds now. I told him not to worry about it; I had many people and beings to help me cover these two while my family and I took guard on Earth.

Once more, we went through the portals, then it was off to the base stationed in Okinawa, Japan and then home. However, I picked up my Kimono before leaving. No way was I going to miss out on that. I had earned it, damn it!

We were at the base in Corpus Christi, trying to get permission for having the Dai' Khans out at the Nightwolves Lair after debriefing, as had become our tradition. My mates weren't happy that I was fighting so hard for their being with us. The General was leery of them being out on their own accord, with no one but us to oversee them. In between the lines, I could see the General wanted them covered at all times, because he feared what these sorcerers could do on their own. I didn't blame him. They didn't know our laws and customs here. It would be too easy for them to get into some sort of mischief, which could blow the whole operation we had going at the base.

To be fair to the General, the Dai' Khans could be extremely lethal. However, I eventually won. It may have been a peace offering from the General for the tiff between us. However, he did give me an order to never leave them completely on their own.

They came with us to the Nightwolves Lair like many of the other soldiers did. I explained the warning lights to them and showed them the exits, just in case. I explained that the lights were to help the General keep a lid on the fact that he had Mercenaries working with his Special Forces on the base. If big brass came through the door, we wouldn't be able to keep them out, so we had hidden exits for us to scram to, in case anyone who could cause grief showed up. The warning system looked like a sideways traffic light. Red, was for all Mercs to leave quickly. Yellow, was to warn us that there was someone in the bar who was not one of ours, such as repair people, electricians and so on. So, we would watch what was said when that happened and keep a lid on teeth and claws. Green, meant for all military to leave quickly, in the event something magickal was going down and they needed to exit, so we could deal with it.

My sons had heard through the grapevine what was up with the Dai' Khans and came down to get a peek at them. Craven, my youngest at sixteen, glared in his usual overprotective mode. Although he was the youngest of my three boys, it was he I worried about the most, because he was a werewolf. He had been bitten by an enemy werewolf on one of our missions and was turned into one. Now, getting angry could make him lose control and wolf out. He did not like anyone putting the moves on his mother unless it was one of my mates. Crimson, my middle son, was eighteen, and didn't seem to mind one way or the other. At least, not to where you could see it. Christoph, my eldest at twenty, just shook his head and walked away. He was usually pretty mellow, but I think he thought I was at fault for this somehow. This wasn't anyone's fault, really. Shit happens sometimes and all you can do is deal with it.

Gerard, my youngest and most favorite brother, came down, as well. He took one look at the situation with his cold blue eyes that went well with the Italian good looks he inherited from our mutual physical Mafia father and made an offer to my mates to "take care" of the Dai' Khans. Antonio's eyes lit up, until I uttered one word. Couch. Antonio sat back in his seat and fumed.

'*You hurt your mates, sister,*' Gerard berated me on our private path.

I looked at him. '*I don't mean to, but this is out of my control and I like the Dai' Khans.*'

His eyes slitted at me. '*I can make it easy for you, sister. Let me handle it before your feelings get any more involved.*'

My lips pressed tightly. '*I clean up my own messes. I love you, but stay out of this.*'

He bent his head slightly to me. '*As you wish.*' Then he moved off in his usual cool way, though you could see the anger in his steps. He liked my mates and had a lot of respect for them, much to the dismay of our physical father. He was angry I was hurting them in this fashion. I couldn't blame him for it. But, I had a feeling that if I cut the bonds that were forming between the Dai' Khans and I, it would turn out very, very badly for everyone involved. I didn't see how, exactly, at the moment, but I could just tell. I was listening to that inner voice, though I ached for my mates' pain.

I watched Cendra, my other sister, stroll into the club wearing a slinky green dress that brought out the color of her red hair and bright blue eyes. She smiled at Antonio as soon as he looked up at her and I could swear the bitch cocked her hip at him. Never mind two of her mates had walked in with her; she was still making moon eyes at one of *my* mates. Antonio and Cendra had dated before he and I did the ritual for our bonds. She had been trying to get him back ever since. She was constantly bitching about her own mates and how they didn't give her enough attention, so she was always making a play for mine. I had warned her, if she pushed too far, I would be hard pressed not to kill her.

And what did she do? She scooted right up next to Antonio in the booth, since I had taken the chair on the other side, so I could play head bouncer while I was there. There was barely an inch of space between them and for the first time, Antonio didn't move away from her. Her mates, with their usual obliviousness to her machinations, took a seat where they could get back to whatever topic was enthralling them this week. My hands closed into a fist and I counted to ten.

"Hello, Antonio. I heard you had a hard time over in Japan," she batted her eyes at him, all sympathetic to his plight.

"Things are fine, Cendra," he answered her shortly. He wouldn't play into her game too far. He knew I was close to exploding.

"Oh, really? Well, I am here if you need someone to talk to," she offered sweetly. I took a deep breath and stood up, grabbing Antonio's hand, dragging him out to the dance floor with me.

"Breathe," Antonio suggested. He was amused. He shouldn't be. I was getting pissed.

His face grew serious. "Can I ask you something, love?"

"Of course you can. What?" I snapped.

"Is this thing with the Dai' Khans payback for us not protecting you from the dark mage who cursed you? Or for not finding you for so long?" He pulled back from me so he could watch my eyes.

Shocked, I stopped dancing. "How the fuck can you say that? No, it is not."

He saw that it was the truth. "Sorry, but we have seen you wait months, sometime years to even scores with those you've felt have fucked you over, or in our case, let you down. You're usually pretty quick on your vendettas, but sometimes, if you can't even a score right away, for whatever reason, you put it in this box marked for later repayment...with interest...and you wait. Then, when they least expect it, out of the blue, you land like a ton of bricks on them." He picked up my hand again and slid his other arm around my back to continue dancing. "We've watched you over the years when we couldn't be with you physically, and had seen you pull some doozies on those that fucked you over." He looked at me. "Not that they didn't have it coming," he reassured me quickly, before I could get defensive. "But, it was still remarkable how long you could wait. And you never forget. Very un-Aries like." He frowned at me. "That's more of a Scorpio trait. Like your father."

I raised my eyebrow at him, something I was picking up from Rock. "Should I take that as an insult?"

"No, I didn't mean to insult you. It's just an observation." He pulled me close to his body as the music kept playing. "I just don't want to lose you."

"You and your brothers won't lose me. I am happy. Honestly. It's just that this thing with the Dai' Khans is a pull I can't seem to ignore. And believe me, I have tried hard to ignore it. But, the truth is, I have this gut instinct that if I do anything wrong with this, the fall-out will be bad and it won't land on just me, or I would take the hit for it. Honestly. Remember that time I got tricked into cutting my astral selves away?" He nodded.

It was a real bad time for us before they found me physically. It was the first move into being able to curse me so thoroughly. It had left me spiritually defenseless.

"Maybe, this is the Universes way of making me pay for it, or some kind of karma thing. Anyway, I don't know, but it's something. I can't put my finger on it yet. I've been racking my brain over it. I know this is hurting you and your brothers and I am sorry for that. I would change it if I could, but I can't. I won't fuck up like that again, because the ultimate cost could be losing the three of you, as well. That's a price I won't chance on paying. Not now; not ever again."

Having to wait fifteen years for them was cost enough the first time. My soul still carries the scars from that prison sentence. Yeah, prison sentence - because that's what it had felt like - having them so close, but not able to touch them with my own physical hands for so long. He pulled me closer, feeling the pain racking through my body in waves as I remembered the, 'dark time', as I called it. The worst fifteen years of my life.

The abuse my physical mother and stepfather did to me as a child for the first twelve years of my life paled in comparison. Physical torture ain't shit to the pain that was done to me spiritually and mentally, in having to wait for them for so long. I'll take the physical torture any day.

"It's ok, baby. I will try hard to make peace with this. You just need to give me some time." He was rocking me on the dance floor now, more than dancing with me. I pulled my head out of the bad place and focused on the here and now.

Smiling up into his face, I said, "You know that I love you more than life itself, right?" letting him feel the love pouring through my heart chakra.

"Yeah, I can feel it." He bent his head down so he could kiss me long and sweet.

The song ended and we walked off the dance floor to rejoin those at the table. I guided him to the seat I had used before and I sat in his vacated one.

I turned to Cendra. "So, Sis-ter, how are things on the home front since I have been gone with my sweet mates in romantic Japan?" giving her my innocently interested expression. Her gaze flicked over to where her own mates were still sitting, in deep with their discussion of what sounded like political agendas.

Her smile was fake and the look her in her eyes told me another story. "Fine, and you?" Her smile turned venomous. "I heard you've made quite a conquest with some rulers of another world." She made sure the volume of her statement would reach my own mate's ears.

"I've been presented with a challenge, true. Have you met them?" I kept my tone even and light.

"Why, no, I haven't, sister. They do look scrumptious though, and not the type to share well," she added waspishly.

"They share just fine," I dripped honey in my tone. I knew my mates would know I was exaggerating the mildness of the situation just to piss her off. It worked, too.

"How positively greedy of you. Three wasn't enough?" Her own tone dripped with sweetness.

"Yes, one would think three would be enough, wouldn't you?" I responded archly, snapping my own gaze to her mates. "Come, let me introduce you." I took her hand and gave her no choice but to follow, or risk causing a scene. That wouldn't be the impression she wanted my mates to think of her.

She wanted to come off as cool and sophisticated at all times, but she was white trash, just like me. The only difference was, it never bothered me to have been poor. In fact, I took pride in raising myself out of it alone. She, however, always tried to play her life off as some forgotten princess that the dirt of the streets had never touched; some debutant that had gotten lost, but was now found. I think she felt that people, like my mates who were born rich, would accept her better and want her more.

I thought she was stupid for caring about what anyone else thought. If someone can't like you for what you really are, then you are wasting your time with them. Maybe if she were more real, her mates would pay more attention to her. I fumed, walking across to the bar to where Rock had taken over guiding the Dai' Khans through the denizens of The Nightwolves Lair.

Rock had seen us coming and tapped Ja' Callum on his shoulder and pointed to me.

I changed my facial expression to one that was lighter. "Dai' Khans of Kla' din, I would like to introduce you to my other sister, Cendra." Turning to my sister, I dropped her hand and motioned to the Dai' Khans. "Cendra, this is Ja' Callum, Ja' Kelo and Ja' Monel." The Dai' Khans must have picked up something, even though I had thought I had presented her well enough.

However, instead of the very reverent and pleased greeting they had given my other sister, Cassie, they nodded coolly to her. "We are pleased to meet yet another one of our true mate's siblings," Ja' Callum said. The other two just bent their heads a bit in accord with Ja' Callum.

I held back my laughter. Even with Gerard, they tried hard to make a connection, and had answered him respectfully, since they could tell he was another of my siblings whom I loved to pieces.

Feeling challenged with the cool reception, she widened her smile and preened a bit. "It is lovely to meet rulers of another world. I would love to see it sometime. I'm sure it's beautiful."

Ja' Callum took a step towards me. "Meshallima Ama Ja' Catrina seemed to have enjoyed it." Wow, he used the whole title they'd given me on Kla' din. I must be slipping, on hiding my true feelings. They didn't even address her with her first name.

"Well, except the part of battling the Draugrall, cousin," Ja' Monel reminded him.

Ja' Kelo snorted. "From the way she took that Master Vampyre on her own and won, I would say differently." Oh, he was getting to know me well, already. He was also extolling my combat abilities.

Cendra's eyes narrowed. Rock was watching the exchange carefully, as if taking notes for something. I didn't pry into his mind, since I tried hard not to do that with people who couldn't shield me out. I thought it was rude. Cendra was about to say something, but was interrupted by a shout of, "NO, SHE ISN'T," on the other side of the bar. Then, a loud smack was heard like the sound of a fist hitting someone's face.

People started shouting and Rock and I waded through to do our jobs as head bouncers. We both got to the center of the action at the same time. Sergeant Miller was standing over Sergeant Pearson, his face red with anger. Sergeant Pearson stood back up with his fist at the ready and Rock stepped in-between the two combatants.

"What the fuck is this all about, men?" Rock commanded.

Sergeant Miller pointed to Pearson. "He keeps saying Cat is evil, devil spawn. That we must be lying about what we saw on Trinidad."

Sergeant Pearson had been left Earth-side with Babyface, and had missed the wild show, having heard it all second hand. Unlike Babyface, he didn't believe a word of it.

Rock turned to Pearson. "And you?" he asked shortly to get his side of the argument.

Pearson answered defensively, "It's against everything I have been brought up to believe. She drinks blood for Christ's sake. How can she be anything but evil?"

"If you two have a problem, take it the pit," Rock decreed. This was personal, not military, so it would be worked out between only those involved.

Cendra hissed in my ear, "Why is it always about you?"

"Maybe because I am not a self-absorbed bitch," I hissed back. "Now get out of my way, I've got work to do."

I muscled past her to follow the two Sergeants into the room where the pit was. In the middle of the room, was a modified boxing ring. My siblings and I, each had one in our homes as well, which gave us the idea to have one here. Even the best of relationships had its bumps, and when talking couldn't fix the problem, it was worked out in the ring, like my mates did. They were all brothers - and brothers, no matter how much love there is, sometimes still fought.

Like my mates, even my sons used the ring at home, from time to time. Though, Craven had abstained lately, due to the unfair advantage of his werewolf strength. He also didn't want to take the chance of seriously hurting one of his brothers or infecting them. My other two boys had yet to learn how to turn their power into inhuman physical strength, but they were slowly getting better at it.

Both Sergeants had gotten into the ring after disarming themselves, as were the rules here. There were four rules: no weapons, no powers, no fighting for sport, and the last was, you cheat, you get hammered. Rock and I would be the ones who did the hammering, if needed.

The combatants got into their stances and the fight started slow, with feints from one or the other, testing each other out on distance and speed. Neither were fighting stupid, letting their anger rule their moves. But, I could tell it was there, underneath their fierce glares to each other. Miller had about twenty pounds and a few inches on Pearson, but Pearson had the reach, both in arms and legs.

Rock made the suggestion first. "Sixty on Pearson." No way; he'd already gotten clocked once and was on the floor when we came into the middle of it. However, Rock had a good eye for what his men could do.

Still, I had a feeling about Miller. "You're on. I'll back Miller."

Right then, Pearson came up with a left kick to the side of Miller's face so hard, you could hear the snap, as it stung Miller's face. Miller twisted and went down with one hand holding him up off the mat. Pearson backed off, letting him get back up and came at him with a punch combination with another kick, this time to the other side of his face. I recognized the moves now. Tai Kwon Do, and Pearson was good.

Rock looked at me with his eyebrow raised. "Black belt in Tai Kwon Do. State champion last year. There is no one who can match him in the platoon." He had a cocky grin on his face.

Oh, that sneak, Rock. I tried to recall what I had seen in Miller's file. If I recalled right, he had Kenpo at a brown level and was working for his black.

He had watched me fight several times and I had an idea. "Hey, Miller," I yelled out to him. He turned to look at me and I placed my hands up close together, about an inch apart, palm to palm. He got it, because he cracked a smile. He picked himself up again, blood dripping from the corner of his mouth and went in close to fight Pearson. He gave Pearson no room to use his legs or the full power of his fists. He went to work on Pearson's torso with quick jabs in fast combinations. Then, Miller leaned back enough to give Pearson an upper cut to his jaw which threw Pearson up against the ropes of the ring. It didn't knock Pearson out, because Miller couldn't put his full force into the punch, since he had leaned back, taking some of the power out of it. When Pearson got back up, before he could clear his head, Miller shuffled into a stance and kicked Pearson hard in the gut with a strong front kick with full power. That knocked Pearson back into the ropes again. The men watching roared their approval. Out of breath now, Pearson got back up and came at Miller, who reached in close with his right elbow, knocking Pearson hard across the jaw. Pearson went down. He didn't get back up right away. Rock rang the bell. The fight was over before it got too serious and went over the edge. No one would gainsay Rock's judgment.

"I am costing you a fortune this month, aren't I, Rock?" I said, smiling widely.

"There will come a day, you'll see." Rock handed me my money, which I put into my jacket pocket. I could see money exchanging hands with the other people in the bar.

"Thanks. Now, let's get these two and bring them into the staff room for a sit down." Looking at the blood on Miller's face and his swollen eye, I added, "And some healing."

We got them into the staff room and Pearson sighed heavily. "How long will I be in the cage?"

We had two cages for those who got out of control at the Nightwolves Lair. One was a regular jail cell for the military men, the other was titanium and silver coated with this substance in a mesh form, that my youngest brother, Gerard, made to keep anyone in it from using magicks.

"No time. I just want to talk. Miller, sit here." I guided him to a chair. Rock pointed to another chair and motioned for Pearson to sit down. I rubbed my hands together to get the heat going and held my hands over Millers worst injuries.

Spinning white-blue light into the healing, I spoke to Pearson. "I, personally, could give a flying fuck how you feel about me. So long as your prejudice doesn't interfere with our missions, you can hate me all you want." I moved my hands up to Miller's eye. "The thing I want you to ask yourself, is do you hate me because of what you were taught, or do you hate me because God hates me?" I looked over to him and his face got a confused look. "The reason I ask is this - your religion says God is all merciful and love. I believe that, too. Jesus, for all the controversy of whether he really was the son of God, was a very peaceful man. He loved everybody. Not once, did he ever preach hate for anyone, even hookers." I grinned at him. I went on, "God's commandments, though they are exactly like the Egyptian Book of the Dead laws, which was written thousands of years prior, says 'thou shalt not kill'. It doesn't say 'thou shalt not kill unless they are homosexual', or 'thou shalt not kill if they don't follow my way'. No, it says simply, 'thou shalt not kill'. There are no addendums. Neither are there addendums in the Egyptian Book of the Dead." I finished healing Miller, who just sat back to listen. "If your God, who is professed to be a God of love and mercy, hates anyone, then He becomes a contradiction. A cult. My way or die. When a religion preaches my way is the only way it is, then, by definition, a cult. Like the Moonies. Jesus never preached that. He never once said, 'kill them if they don't follow my Father'. Can you recall a single verse in the Bible that says that?" I asked him seriously. He reluctantly shook his head. "The true God or Jesus isn't about hate, conversion or death. It isn't about intolerance or bigotry. It's about being the most excellent you can be, so you are rewarded when you go to your heaven. How can you be pure enough for heaven, with hate, fear and intolerance in your soul?" Pearson couldn't answer that. "If God was really like that, he would be a dark God, because those are dark emotions. That is not being a God of the light. I won't follow a dark God."

"You don't follow God at all. You worship a pagan Goddess," he accused me. Correctly, too.

"And if I am wrong, then God, not you, nor anyone else, will have the right to judge me. It will be my bad and I will pay for it. But who the hell are you to give me punishment now when you may not have all the facts?" I waited for a response. I didn't get one right away so, I continued to make my point. "You follow a lot of dogma that isn't about God. Stuff that was fed to you by some man who thinks he knows it all or knows he is feeding you bullshit and that's his plan, to keep you in the dark. Until you have actually read all the books, have actually studied the political climes of when your religion and others were made, you really can't judge me, even on thinking you're right. Because you're not. You're just spouting some bullshit intolerance crap some asswipe preached to you. I like God and I like Jesus. I reserve my right in believing whether he is actually the son of God until I see a certain paper that has been rumored to be able to prove differently." Before Pearson could say anything, I rolled on. "I don't care, other than academically, whether he was the son of God or not. I do like him, regardless. I like what he said about loving *everyone*. The only other proof I have for myself, is being with the Arch Angel Michael, many times. He has saved my ass more than once and we fought the dark forces together often. He doesn't seem to have a problem with what I am. He likes me just fine as I am and he is an Arch Angel. His opinion would hold more weight with me then yours ever will, or any TV evangelists' crap. Point is, you don't have the right to judge anything about me, because you are not God and you are not Jesus. If I messed up, I am sure I will pay for it. But, that's between Them and me. Not you or anyone else."

I sat back and waited for him to speak, but it was Miller who spoke first, his Brooklyn accent heavier than usual. "I was born and raised a Catholic. They can be the most intolerant of sects in the Christian religion, but even I don't believe she is evil or needs to be put down. If God has a problem with her style of fighting to keep this world safe from the dark-side shit, then He has a problem with me, and I'll deal with that when my time comes."

"But, what is being said about her is blasphemy. Being the daughter of a Goddess ain't right, man. It's against God," he implored to Miller.

I snorted, "Who says?"

"The church, the Bible. Lots of stuff," he said petulantly.

"A church that was built out of fear by a pagan Roman Emperor. A Bible that has been rewritten fourteen times, to date, at least, if not more, my friend - BY MAN. Man, who can be greedy, self promoting, and use the words of God and Jesus to twist them any way they can, to control you and everybody else to do and feel what they want?" I shook my head. "No. Not me. When God, Himself, or Jesus, appears on my doorstep or the Arch Angel Michael tells me personally, differently, then I'll consider it. But, intolerant, bigoted, control crap written by man? Oh, hell, no. You can kiss my white rebel pagan ass."

"You're saying the Bible is nothing but lies?" Pearson sounded offended.

"No, I am not. There are grains of truth to it, just like any other book written by MAN," I stressed the point. "You've just got to be smart enough and ambitious enough for your own soul to suss out what is true for you, personally, and go from there."

"But basically, you're saying my religion and belief isn't true," he persisted.

"Look Pearson - when a billion people pray, hope and believe, that makes it real. Millions, over a two thousand year period, have prayed to this God and Jesus and Mother Mary. Whether or not He was real before, He is now. THAT I believe. The God Yahweh and the Christian God, are two different Beings; ask any Rabbi worth his kosher. I also believe, however, that when a person kills in the name of God, he curses and brings blood to that God. A God that professes love and mercy would weep at that action, don't you think? The Holy Crusades were a bad thing, in my opinion. When a person kills a gay man - it is a very bad thing; because, what right does he have to kill another, just because they are different? Because of one comment in the Bible about homosexuals, put there by the hand of man, some poor soul has to die? Who the fuck died and made them God to judge like that? If God wants them dead, isn't He powerful enough to do the job Himself, if He wanted it done so badly? A gay who dies, will face whatever it is he faces in judgment on his own. Some asswipe doesn't have the right to speed up the process, just because he is homophobic and probably just repressing his own homosexual feelings."

Rock burst out laughing. So did Miller. "That's just my own opinion. Personally, I don't think any gay or lesbian have anything to worry about, so long as they are true to their self. You know that saying, 'to thine own self be true'?" He nodded his head. "Follow that first, be truthful with yourself first, then look around and see what you see." I slapped him lightly on the knee. "So, you gonna let me fix you up there, or do you want the pain for the time it will take you to heal?"

"But, that's witches power," Pearson said.

"Oh, really? Then, I guess Jesus was a witch." I let him stew on that. I gave him a break, because it looked like I had shattered all of his preconceptions enough for one night. "Jesus said, 'You can do everything I can do and do it better.' It's one of those seeds of truth in your Bible."

His face lit up a bit. "Yeah, yeah, he did. Ok, if you want to." He relaxed and let me take his pain away, healing the cuts and contusions. I even healed the small scrapes on his knuckles, as I had done for Miller, so there would be no sign of a fight when they got back to the base. I went to pull away when he stopped to grab me. I allowed the close contact this one time, because he was staring intently into my eyes. I let my eyes be open, showing him the whole of my soul. I knew it had scars and wasn't perfect, but it was still a good soul, and I showed him that. He may not have been a practitioner, but he still saw enough to nod his head a bit and say quietly, "All right." He squeezed my hand a bit and let go.

I turned to Miller. "You have to buy him a drink. Now, off with the two of you and play nice," I mockingly scolded.

When they walked out the door, Rock shut it completely again. I sat back into my chair and groaned. I was tired from the healing, from the mission we'd just got back from, and from the unease the Dai' Khans and my mates brought to my table, as well as a plethora of other things.

"That was a good job, Cat," Rock said quietly.

"Thanks. Not too preachy?" I queried, cracking an eyelid open.

He shrugged his shoulders. "A little preachy."

"I try not to be preachy, but 'tis one of my soapboxes," I admitted.

He chuckled, "Yeah, I know about your soapboxes. I try to avoid them."

"Smart man." I grinned at him.

His face grew serious. "You weren't supposed to use your powers, Cat."

"I know, but I owed them both the healing since the fight was over a misconception of whether I'm evil or not." I sighed, knowing I was going to get my ass chewed out for it later.

"Well, you look like something the cat dragged in. Pun intended. Do you need blood?" He was already rolling up his sleeve for me. I smiled at him and my heart swelled. I loved this man like a brother already. There was so much about him I admired. He was a steadfast friend and a rock in a storm when you needed one. And the damnedest, toughest mortal fighter I had ever seen. Of course, Special Forces didn't do anything but tough.

I shook my head at him. "Thanks, I have already called one of my mates in here to feed me. Two for one that way - a bitching out and a feeding. Saves time," I grinned at him.

"You're a glutton for punishment, aren't you? Don't you ever do things the easy way?" Rock was already exasperated with me. I had a tendency of making people feel that way about me.

I made a look of shock go over my face. "There's an easy way? Well, shit; why didn't you tell me?"

"Smart ass," he said, as he walked out the door, and Antonio walked in.

Antonio leaned in to kiss me. "What'd I miss?"

"My sparkling personality," I kissed him back.

He helped me stand up. "You look wiped. What did you do?"

"Something you can spank me for later," I smiled mischievously at him. "Right now, I need to feed." I reached up and slowly licked his neck. He groaned and shuddered in response.

Stopping my play, he whispered, "Wait, love. I want to show you something."

Curious, I followed him into the store room. He reached behind one of the stacks and pushed a secreted button and a hidden door cricked open. Beyond the door was a small bedroom. It looked like a bedroom anyway, since it had a bed and a table with a phone on it.

"Demitri had Lee get this installed. We thought it might come in handy," he leered at me.

"You guys and your concealed bedrooms. I don't think you have a single branch office in any state or country that doesn't have one." I shook my head at Antonio.

He smiled, "Like I said, they do come in handy. You need sex and blood to help with your energy levels. You are way too low. That means, Ca-Tri-Na, you have used power again." Before I could defend myself, he kissed my lips silent. "I will be spanking you later for it when we get home, but right now, I just want to love you gently." He then slowly unclothed us both, until we were naked in each other's arms on the bed. He kissed his way to my neck, then down to my chest where he spent time sucking and licking each of my nipples in turn.

I was breathing harder, as I felt his hand trail down my stomach to see how far my arousal was getting, gently touching me between my legs. He found me wet for him already and urged my arousal even higher by slowly inserting his finger inside me, sliding it in and out. He kept kissing my breasts and playing with me until I was begging him for his cock. I could feel him smile against me. Instead of giving me what I was begging for, he kissed his way down to where his hand was. Once there, he didn't stop, until I was screaming his name in release. His eyes dark with passion, he rose back up and teased me with the tip of his penis at the entrance of my pussy.

He rubbed it up and down. "How bad, baby?" he asked with his voice husky.

"Bad. Please. Fuck me." I tried to move him into me by tilting up my hips.

He arched out of my way. "You gonna come for me again if I love inside of you?"

"Please, yes. I will, just give it to me." I needed him in me now!

He pushed in with one stroke, making me moan with pleasure. "That's my girl. Let it feel good," he rumbled, as he pulled in and out of me, slowly and rhythmically.

Throughout his lovemaking, he kept telling me it was ok, and to let it feel good to me this way. When he felt my excitement get close, he said, "Bite me. Take what you need," and placed his neck within easy reach of my mouth.

I licked his neck and then bit down, taking in his blood. As his blood flowed in, the world seemed to stop and then my climax hit like a thunderclap inside of me.

He came with me and we blended into each other astrally. One part of my consciousness knew I was in a bed with him, but another part of me knew I was with him elsewhere and we were one. I could feel his love flowing through and around me; gently, unconditionally and endlessly. I let him feel the same love from me. For a brief moment, it seemed time itself stopped and stood still. There wasn't even the sound of our breathing, just peace and the energy of everything around us. We were a part of it and it was a part of us. We were nowhere and everywhere all at the same time. Then, time picked up again and we were breathing heavily, back on the bed. I licked the wounds closed and pulled back to look at him. We were so moved by the experience, we both had tears flowing gently down our cheeks. He pulled me tighter into his arms and just held me until his heartbeat slowed down to normal and matched rhythm with mine.

He kissed the side of my neck. "Forever, mine," he whispered to me.

"Until the end of time," I agreed, smiling with him.

The Dai' Khans stayed with us at our house. They got to know the boys better and marveled over the Harleys that were in the garage. 'Wheeled horses' they called them. I thought it was too cute. My mates surprised me by teaching them to ride, and several times brought them home with one or more being hurt from a spill. I would make my mates heal them up, but I would wonder if my mates were setting them up for death by accident on a Harley. Then they would be totally blameless. Nah, they couldn't be that cold blooded. That would be something I would do and they were better than me. Still, I kept a weathered eye on the situation. One day, they all rode up, their Harleys growling into the driveway and they were laughing as they came in the door.

Male bonding at its best. You gotta love the incidents that could cause male bonding. Drinking, fighting, or riding a Harley. Sheesh. I didn't worry so much about any of them coming home in a body bag after that.

I was lazing by the pool when my pager 'blew up'; a technical military term for being paged by the big man to get your ass into work, STAT, Special Forces style.

I heard everybody's pager going off in the house as well, and hustled my ass. If everyone was being called in, it was important. I grabbed my cell and hit the speed dial to report in. Then, I had to haul ass into the house, get my clothes on and my weapons strapped.

The Dai' Khans came down the stairs. "Meshama, what is wrong?"

"Oh, good, you guys are dressed enough. You should come with us. When our pagers beep, we have no choice but to go saddle up and ride," speaking euphemistically. They got the gist of it though, and were willing to head out to the base with us. Of course, since I said the word 'ride', everybody headed for a Harley. I had to stop and braid my hair, so it wouldn't tangle in the wind and grabbed a bike for myself - my favorite, a black chromed '56 Panhead. A classic never dies.

The MPs at the security gates were going to have kittens. I laughed into the wind and hauled ass down S. Padre Island Dr. with nine others; my mates, my sons and the Dai' Khans, cruising on our hogs.

Like I said, the MPs had kittens, until we showed them our stinkin' badges and the temporary passes for the Dai' Khans. They were cool. I honestly did like them, but it was just too much damn fun to mess with them every now and again. I couldn't help myself. We got to the war room in decent time I thought, but the General looked grim.

Every member of the Coven was there. Rock and his team, Babyface, Romeo and Wizard were there. The Captain and his four squad leaders were there, as well. I couldn't figure out what we had done wrong, but it looked like a firing squad being set up for us.

"What's up, General Pierce?" I asked him defensively.

"We have a blip out in Kansas. We are sending out a team there to scout the situation. What we need from you is to know how far you have taken some of these men in training them in magickal arts?" His voice was hard and clipped.

"Some have gotten a few of the basics. Those that have, can learn healing next. It's what I have planned for them anyway," I answered.

"Healing? What the hell good is that?" Captain Holland said, sneeringly.

"If you're out in the field and you have wounded, it makes it to where you can get another gun out there fighting, once that man is healed. That's what good it does. Plus, it saves lives. It saves soldiers so they can fight again," I snapped at him.

The General's eyes hardened. "Cat, I agree with the Captain. They need to learn more defensive arts now. I want you to get on it, ASAP." Captain Holland had a gloating look upon his face. For once, the General was in his corner. That pissed me off.

"Then find yourself another teacher," I replied, knowing I had them over a barrel here. There just weren't many who could or would work for the military on the levels they needed right now. "I am the one in charge of magickal training. If you skip the basics, if you skip the white magickal training, all you will do is make dark practitioners. Magick, in its purest form, isn't about throwing witch balls or hexes, curses or death spells. It's about helping, healing, urging life within the Earth and health for those around you. If your men don't learn these lessons first, they will, sooner or later, dabble in the darker side of the magickal arts and I won't set them up for that kind of fall. Yes, I will train them in defensive magicks, and yes, I will teach them about the dark arts. Not for use, but to know how to fight it. But, first and foremost they will, by the Goddess, learn that their power is to be used for good, for the growth and learning of their souls, and not to be used to cause scars and marks upon themselves by using dark magicks. I won't be responsible for that."

All of my siblings and their mates, as well as mine, stood up as one, to show support for my decision. The Dai' Khans also moved to stand behind me, showing their support, as well. None of us would be budged. There was too much at stake when you were talking about the soul of another being. You didn't hand them a gun without giving them their safety lessons first. It would be irresponsible at best, irreprehensible at worst. Besides, the Karma would be a bitch for irresponsible teaching. In what the student does, the teacher shares the Karma; so it's a wise teacher who shows her students to use their power for good and not for evil.

The General actually took a step back, feeling my righteous indignation of trying to get me to be a negligent teacher. Then, I saw the comprehension fill his eyes. No leader would ever send his men out with bad training or without the proper training they needed to complete their mission successfully. At least not the good ones, and bad leaders had short careers in the military. General Pierce was not the type to be the latter.

He sighed heavily and sat down in his seat. "You're right; it would be a careless decision."

Captain Holland looked outraged that I had once again gotten the General to bow to one of my judgments. Sergeant Miller seemed pleased and even Sergeant Pearson had a look of respect in his eyes for me, for the first time. He and the rest of the squad leaders finally understood what we were all about. If we were truly evil, we would have shown them how to cast spells for ill right off the bat. Yet, here we were fighting to show them that magick isn't supposed to be used for that. Magick, like a gun, could be used for ill or for good. It just depends on whose hand was holding the gun; a good person defending his country and home, or a bad person killing for illegal gain and murder. The gun itself wasn't evil; neither was magick.

The General rubbed his face. "I don't see how they can fulfill the objective of this mission then, since it would also be irresponsible to send any of you out in the field again."

I didn't hear that right. "Come again?"

The General leaned back in his seat, as if he was preparing for a battle. "One does not send someone who is..." he was searching for the right word, "well what you and the rest of your Coven are, into a potentially dangerous situation. It would be like sending the President of the United States onto the front lines. It's just not done."

My mouth gaped open; astonished he'd actually said those words. It went above my comprehension. The rest of my Coven and the Dai' Khans, who themselves went on the front lines often to defend their people from the Draugralls, also had the same look of stunned disbelief on their faces.

I started laughing. Hard. My stomach hurt, I laughed so hard. The military men didn't know what to do and just let me ride it out with an air of amused impatience.

When I finally collected myself enough, I wiped the tears from my eyes, taking a deep breath. "You know, if this world would make their damned leaders duke it out themselves, we would have half the wars and we would save so many lives; instead of them sending in our men to fight for their pockets in oil rights and export laws. If they had to actually fight, bleed and die for their fucking gains, not the peoples - theirs - they would quickly learn to stay at the negotiation table like grown fucking adults and quit wasting lives of people they don't even know the names of. Makes it easier for them to sleep at night, I suppose," I snorted in disgust. "I appreciate the sentiment. I really do. But, this is what we were made for. Bred for. This is our fate. Take that away from us and all we have gone through to get here will be made trivial. Don't make my past trivial, General, nor those of my people." I didn't say we would go anyway, with or without his leave. However, I'm sure he understood the subtext.

His eyes narrowed. "Fine, though it's against everything the military has taught me - but under one condition."

I waited for him to finish his ultimatum, before I would decide to agree or not and do what I wanted anyway. "You already have a tracking chip in you; I want to add a micro earpiece. The CIA uses them in their black ops. It can send, receive and make it possible for us to hear everything around you." He gave a half grin. "It makes up for you having the telepathy and we don't have a way for instant communication from you. It would ease my mind to know what is happening to you at all times."

I considered it for a moment. "I'll wear the piece. So, what's shaking in Earth's world now?" I sat back down in my chair. Everyone else took their seats as well.

The General flicked his finger to Rock, who slid a file across the table to me.

"This blip showed up after nine tornados ripped through what they call tornado alley. Kansas got hit again. This blip showed up and we'll need to send a team to find the portal and see if it's hostile or not. If it is, close it for now and if the Dai' Khan's would be so kind as to send in some Bokaris to this world, we can start setting them up to keep the portals guarded and closed, if hostile."

The Dai' Khans looked at each other. Ja' Callum spoke for the three of them. "We have two requests."

The General nodded. He knew you didn't get something for nothing. He had been expecting the negotiations for a while now, but the Dai' Khans, up until today, hadn't made any demands. I hadn't pushed, because I knew they would state their wants when they felt the time was right. It was another thing that had pissed off the Captain, because he had been urging the General to get me on the Dai' Khans backs about it. Since the portals we had closed up were safe for the time being, I didn't see the need to be pushy. The General agreed with me.

Ja' Callum started with his 'short list'. "We would like to be able to stay with Meshama Catrina and have free access to and from Kla' din to visit her here when she is needed and have her on our world when she has time."

Ja' Monel continued for them. "We understand her duties, for the time being, come first here. We would also add our magick, strength, and blades to her Coven and to the Nightwolves." They understood that the military and our coven together made the Nightwolves, each agreeing to combine their resources to help stem the tide of preopening hostile portals and keep Earth safe until the Great Shift was complete.

"We do this in return for their help in defending Kla' din from the Draugralls," Ja' Kelo finished for the trio.

Having three powerful sorcerers added to the Nightwolves would give us all an even greater advantage and the General knew it. "From the military side of this call, we don't have a problem with it and would be agreeable to this alliance. However, we can't speak for Cat's Coven or her mates." He arched his eyebrow at our side of the table.

My mate's faces were tight, but not as fiercely grim as they were before. Demitri spoke for my mates. "Since the Dai' Khans have abided by our rules on governing their behavior with Cat so far, we are agreeable."

Cassie appeared surprised by the decree from my mates. Never before, had a mated priestess added to her bond, but she recovered fast and sent telepathic thoughts to the rest of the Coven.

Soon, she turned back to face the Dai' Khans. "Their mating is their business. If her mates are agreeable, then so are we."

Relief flooded the Dai' Khans and was felt through our forming bond.

The General waited for what they would want for the Bokaris. Ja' Callum again, started the request. "We would like to also use the portal to send calling spells through for more mates for our people." Ja' Callum dropped his bomb. "We understand free will is imperative and would not want it any other way. However, if the female that is called would be amenable, we would be able to save our dying race by providing mates for those who don't have one and never would otherwise."

Ja' Kelo quickly added, "The females would want for nothing and would be treated very well. Meshama and her Coven could come and check to see we mean truth."

The General sat straight up in his chair. "This would pose a tactical problem, since we are supposed to be covert in our operations with other worlds and magick. If the woman in question, for whatever reason refuses, she would have knowledge that could end our operations here."

Not to mention end his career, I thought to myself. I had been expecting something like this for a while. Females were the only thing Kla' din lacked in. "General, if I may?"

He gave me the floor, saying, "Please, if you have a solution that would keep this a safe, secret operation and get us the Bokaris."

I looked at the Dai' Khans. "The spell you cast to call me there was the finest weave of power I have ever seen." Ja' Callum swelled with pride at my praise. "Free will is imperative, so we can't just erase memories from those who have a problem in accepting the idea of another world or those who could never overcome their conditioning of fearing anything out of the ordinary. But, if you could twist your spell, just a bit, to have the spell call only those who could be accepting and overcome their fear and conditioning, then I think we could keep a lid on the fact that we have a portal open to another world. The females, too, would have to be women who have no physical ties here, who wouldn't mind leaving this world and never coming back. If you can bend the spell that way, then I think the risk to such a condition would be minimal."

Ja' Callum rubbed his chin. "Yes, Meshama, I think it could be done as you say. We would abide by that restriction then."

"Cat, are you sure of this?" the General asked.

"I am mostly sure. Not a hundred percent," I had to be honest about it, "but if there is an incident, I will give my word I'll find a way to deal with the situation one way or another. Kla' din's future is too important."

"All right then, I will agree to this on the condition you will find a way to deal with any negative outcomes," he consented, taking me at my word. It made me feel good and I smiled warmly at him.

Ja' Monel smiled himself, which was rare. "We will show you and yours how to activate and set them for what you want them to do."

"We'll have a caravan on the way today from my province to wait for us at the oasis. It should only take them about three days to make the trip," Ja' Kelo said excitedly.

"How about on dragon's backs?" I suggested. "They could be there by tomorrow."

He gave me an impish grin. "I didn't want to assume, Meshama, your wonderful dragons being used as beasts of burdens."

"I'll ask them, but I am sure they won't mind. It's for a good cause." I smiled at his cute grin. Ughh, mushy stuff again. Antonio grumbled.

"Good, now if you could pick your team, Cat, and then head off to get them fitted with the micro ear pieces. I'll go get things set in motion for the scouting team as a whole."

"Didn't Kansas get hit with an F-5 Tornado not too long ago?" I asked, looking at the file.

"Yes, back in May, '07. I think you had made some kind of sarcastic comment about it, as well." Rock was recalling the event.

I grinned. "Yeah, how that TV evangelist wouldn't have anything to say about how God was punishing the heart of white bread Christian Bible belt, but when New Orleans got hit in August, '05 with *that* F-5 hurricane, he was claiming it was God's way of taking out the homosexuals and voodoo practitioners. He didn't say crap, but how it was traumatic that Kansas got hit, not that it was God's will, even though an F-5 tornado is called the 'finger of God'."

Andre interjected with a laugh and said softly, "Twister." I gave him a mock glare and turned my attention back to the discussion.

Rock looked interested in seeing where I was going with this. "Yes?"

I nodded to where my second son was sitting. "Crimson here, watches the news and the TV evangelists for me and tells me what they are up to. He told me that when Haiti got hit with that earthquake, the TV evangelist spouted it was God's way of getting those evil pagan voodoo practitioners."

Crimson nodded saying, "He and another big named TV evangelist got into slight trouble, because of how they said it, was pretty rude. One of them, who is known for his outlandish comments, really went overboard on it. Then a Baptists rescue aid team," he rolled his eyes, "tried to steal Haitian kids from Haiti, saying they had no living parents, which some of them did, and were survivors of the earthquakes. The plan was to take them to orphanages and sell them...oh, I'm sorry, to adopt them," he used his fingers to make quotation marks in the air, "to good Christian homes. They didn't bother telling anyone they make money for those adoptions and it's a good way to genocide a culture and their religious beliefs by brainwashing the kids with their own religious ideology. The Anglican church and Catholic church had used the same method against the American Indians and Eskimos."

Gerard's mates were vigorously nodding their heads in agreement.

Lacy, one of Gerard's mates spoke up. "They take the children, then beat them if they speak their own language or mention anything of their history or religion. They refuse the elders to teach them our oral traditions or the ways of our people. The children grow up not knowing their heritage and learning to hate their own people. To hate themselves. They have no respect after that for the elders teachings when they are older and out from under the grip of the churches or the Christian families they were raised by. A whole generation is lost to us then."

"Figures," I said sarcastically. "Then they rake in the bucks for adopting out the children at the same time. Nice scam. All in the name of God. Makes me sick. I am sure their God will have a thing or two to say about that, but that's not my problem. Right now," I added, with an evil grin. It will be, when I had time, I thought to myself. "The connection I saw is this: When that TV evangelist, who incidentally, is actually a dark-side practitioner, made a comment about New Orleans, an F-5 tornado came. He makes a comment about Haiti and nine tornados came. Both times, Kansas, which is known for its strong Christian beliefs, was the main target. Nine is a power number used by all magick users of all flavors. Children being kidnapped by church type people, plus vilifying comments by a TV evangelist and you can piss some voodoo people off, whether they are White Laos or Black Laos. Can't say as I blame them, either. I would have stuck a bolt of lightening up his ass myself if he said anything to me or had come after my boys when they were little."

The General asked, "So, what are you saying, Cat? That those tornadoes are retribution for his smart mouth by voodoo people?"

I nodded, "Yes, but what I don't get, is if a blip happened after nine tornadoes came, then why don't we see an open portal for that F-5 tornado? That one would have had enough power to create one, for sure."

Rock cocked his eye. "Something to add to our gathering Intel mission, hmm?"

Something was definitely off with this. I didn't believe in coincidences at all. "Oh, yeah."

"Meshama, since we now have permission to come and go, we will need to leave to set things in motion for the transport of the Bokaris. We hate to leave you now, but this sounds like an investigation, not fighting, yes?" Ja' Callum looked around for remarks.

"Yes, very easy. There should be no danger. We'll just go, look and close the portal if we have to. And, find out what happened to the one that should have been there after that F-5," I affirmed. No one contradicted me on the slight possibility of danger. We're on our home turf, so there really shouldn't be any danger. We've kicked butt on every hostile portal so far and I didn't expect our odds to change.

"Good, we can leave with an easy mind then. We are sure your mates will watch out for you here." Ja' Monel's tone had a slight edge, but my mates let it slide. Though, Andre did give a slight sneer in response.

"I'll be more than happy to escort you to your home world Dai' Khans, while my sister is off on her mission," Cendra said sweetly.

I frowned at her. "No, Cassie is the one who knows Kla' din and Japan best. She'll escort them back to their portal until we can get them passports and IDs for this world. They also need to learn how to navigate our world. You'll have to be the one to watch my back on this mission, along with Antonio, since Demitri has a board meeting in two days and can't come. Andre also has other plans or he would be taking his turn this time." I looked at Rock who had an odd expression on his face. "Is that all right with you, Rock? Cendra and Antonio with me as our three man team with your special forces and a squad?"

His face looked strained, but he gave his nod to me.

Confused, I looked to Gerard and his mates. "You guys could look into any operations led by any organization, church or otherwise, who may be stealing kids. Start in Haiti, then work your way around. Find out who and what they are and set some watchers on them to track their movements. I can't stand the thought of some innocent kid in the hands of those false people who say they are there to help; when they are really there to help themselves by making victims out of those kids. I know I said I would wait, but if we could at least gather the Intel needed, it will be a start and make our job easier when we are ready to move."

Gerard gave a sharp nod. "I am with you, sister, and I am sure my mates will be more than happy to help." His blue eyes were cold with anger. For all his deadliness, when it came to kids, he was as protective as I was.

All three of his mates were nodding with determined looks on their features and their eyes glinted just as coldly. Yup, that's why they're mates. I smiled.

Chapter Seven

Cat in the bag

I knew a recipe for disaster when I saw one. Taking my sister Cendra and Antonio together on the same mission was not a good idea. Sometimes, things get out of one's control and you just have to make the best of it. Besides, with me riding shot gun on the situation, I was hoping to avoid having to challenge my own sister and kicking her ass. She sure liked pushing those buttons though, and she did it with such an innocent air too, always sitting on the other side of Antonio when she could. She would jump up when Antonio would voice a want or need and offer to fulfill it herself. She seemed to be taking the place of the traditional June Cleaver wife. I think she thought she was making me look bad or not a doting enough mate. The 'see how much better she would be' routine was actually pretty funny. I also knew it wasn't going to work.

For one thing, I had played the June Cleaver wife routine with my first husband and he wound up screwing a waitress who worked at Denny's when I was three months pregnant with Crimson. Secondly, she hadn't acted this way for him when they were dating before he and I bonded. Most of all, I knew my mate. He was grinding his teeth at her actions and would never even think of it now, because I was all he needed just the way I was. Still, a nice right hook was looking really good just for the hell of it. I watched her smile sweetly at Antonio and I was clenching my fists when

I felt the AC-110 start its descent into Kings City, Kansas's Middle Army base.

Great, if I could get them off the plane and separated, I could control my anger better. We had cars waiting for us there, but the reception by everybody at the base seemed to be colder than usual. It grabbed my attention and I started scanning around for emotions, but not invading their personal thoughts. The air was guarded and a few of the soldiers were antagonistic, but not overtly, so I didn't dip into the heads of the few who seemed to have made this a bit personal for some odd reason. Maybe it was a 'pissing in someone else's pool' thing with Special Forces being here with Mercs.

Whatever the problem was, it faded when we hit the highway headed for Ford, Kansas off the 154, where the PETS showed us an active portal had been established. Antonio and Cendra cloaked the whole team, so the locals wouldn't see us in our military gear with weapons. Things like that tended to make the local authorities a tad nervous. So 'glamouring' everyone in a situation like this became part of our operations. To the mundane eye, we all looked like normally dressed people; when in fact, we were dressed in our tactical clothes and had guns, knives and swords bristling about our persons. No one would let me use magick yet, so it was up to the rest of my team to handle the magickal load.

Once we neared the place where the blip showed an active portal, we wound up trailing it into a small park with large trees all around. It had settled between two big, dark brown boulders. I scented around the portal to see if there were any tracks and smelled something dank and wet that didn't match the rest of the aroma of the park.

I showed Antonio and Rock what I'd found. Though Rock couldn't smell it himself, he took us at our word. "We should track the scent to see if anything came across the portal," I looked at Antonio.

He nodded sharply. "No telling what mischief it can cause if we close the portal and it can't get back home. It would be better to find it and send it back through first."

I had a thought. "What about a quick peek through the portal, so we can tell what it is we're hunting?"

"I'm game," Antonio smiled at me.

Rock sighed, "You guys are a glutton for punishment, I swear. Babyface and Romeo will go with you, as well as these four. We'll stay here and guard the portal. Be back quick as you can, though. And Cat?"

I glanced at him with a wide eyed stare. "What?"

He cocked his eyebrow at me. "Don't bring back anymore boyfriends."

I glared at him. "Like I planned it, sheesh," walking though the portal without so much as a 'by your leave,' with the others hustling to keep up with me.

Once we were through, we saw that there was water everywhere, except for the big rocky land point we were on. It was grayish rock, with parts of it covered in these big nests. One nest was right there by the portal door. I looked up into the sky, which was dark grey with a feeble-looking sun.

"Whatever came through the portal is a nest layer. Most likely, non-sapient. An egg layer, by the looks of it." I was scanning the broken egg shells all around mixed in with the pebbles on the rocky outcrop of land we were standing on. Every nest was empty, but there were streaks of water wetness left behind. As if they had just jumped into the water as we stepped through, most likely listening to their flight instincts.

Antonio was on the same page with my thoughts. "Most likely, non-aggressive, since the first thing they did was flee the area. Big ones, though. Look at the size of the nests."

"Yeah, I agree. So, back through again my love, so we don't disturb them anymore than we have already?" I asked him.

He nodded. "I've got a good scent for it," and started to delicately pick his way through, back to the portal.

To the others, I said, "Be careful not to step in the nests as we go out. I don't want to mess with their environment. Lady knows what kind of damage that could cause to their breeding habits."

Some animals or egg layers won't nest in an area that has been disturbed and if this was their only nesting site, it could accidentally cause the genocide of an entire species. I didn't want that on anyone's conscious.

We went back through with as little disturbance as possible, with Rock looking relieved I didn't have anyone or thing in tow.

I filled Rock and the team in. "Just a species that lay eggs. More than likely, non-sapient and scared. They don't seem the aggressive type, since they didn't defend their nesting site."

"Good, then tracking and getting it back through shouldn't be a problem." Rock looked at Babyface who shrugged. If it wasn't aggressive he didn't much care one way or the other.

Rock started ordering the team to set a perimeter around the portal, so no one else could come or go until we found the native of that wet world and got it back home to where it belonged. "So, you guys are the hunters this round?" Rock asked, grinning.

"Thanks bud, I do guess we are up. Howards and Orlans should be enough back up for us, cool?" I motioned for those two to come with us.

"Good enough, since you're on this side, this time. Shout if you need us," Rock teased.

I gave a fake sneer. "Kiss my white rebel pagan ass."

He just laughed.

We took off, scouting the native's scent and got into a good jog. We wound up in a district with warehouse buildings. Some were in a lot of disrepair, most likely from the tornado that ripped through here.

"Hon, I am going to go around the south side with Orlans. You come in from the other with your sister and Howards, ok?" Antonio suggested.

"Sure thing," kissing him before he could take off.

Cendra, Howards and I kept trailing around the side of the building, cautiously taking in everything around us.

Three minutes later Cendra made me stop. "Maybe I should go check that other building." She pointed to the side building loosely connected to this one.

"Fine, take Howards with you," I told her. If it kept her happy and away from Antonio, I didn't care.

She nodded and they took off. I kept moving along the long warehouses side, trailing the wet tracks behind the building and finally got to the other side. Cendra should have returned by now with Howards. Irritated at my sister, I carefully bent to see around the corner and felt a sting in the back of my right thigh. I looked down to see a dart with fake red feathers on it. Shit. Then, darkness descended in a heavy cloud and I passed out.

Antonio heard a mewing sound coming from behind some boxes stacked against the warehouse wall. A creature that looked like a giant lizard snapdragon was curled up around a smaller one. The big one looked to be able to stand, was five feet tall and had huge dark eyes that slitted against the bright glare of the sun. It was protectively holding a much smaller version of itself, as if to ward off any blows in the young one's stead.

Antonio slowed as it mewed louder when he approached. "Hey, there, it's ok. We won't hurt you. Shhh, it's ok." The mewling subsided a bit.

"Orlans, don't shoot or make any threatening moves," Antonio said in a low tone of voice, soft and gently. "Come on," he clucked to the lizard person. He sent calming vibes through the air, which the creature seemed to be able to scent. Slowly, it extended its head towards Antonio's hand, sniffing at it.

"That's right - see - friend. Is that your baby?" The creature, afraid again, curled back around the little one.

"No, no, it's ok. I won't hurt the baby. Everything is fine. Come on; let's get you both back home." The creature looked at him at the word home and the pictures Antonio tried to send mind to mind of the scene he had looked at through the portal.

He didn't know if the creature was telepathic and could pick up the picture, but he would bet it was at least empathic. "That's right, home. Let's go back home, come on."

He moved away slowly, beckoning it to follow him. The creature slowly came out of its huddle and held tightly to the little one across its middle.

"That's good, come on." He didn't smile at it in case it mistook the show of teeth as a threat or as being predatory.

He just kept his voice calm and gentle, urging the creature to follow him out of the warehouse district and back to the park where the portal was.

"Orlans, make sure my way is clear with this creature. I don't want anyone stumbling across us and scaring it again. Warn Rock we have a non-threatening species coming in and to give us plenty of room."

"Oh, look, you found it.' Cendra had come around the corner, totally oblivious to what Antonio was trying to do.

The creature was mewling again and went back into its huddle around the little one.

Frustrated, Antonio turned to his sister-in-law. "Damn it, Cendra you scared it. Back the fuck off, before you piss me off," Antonio snapped at her. Although he instantly regretted the tone of voice, since the creature was mewling loudly again.

"What?" she complained.

In an irritated tone, he said, "Get out of here now. And where the seven hells is Cat?"

"Back down the aisle of warehouses. She should be coming along soon. Let me help here." She moved forward and shrunk down. "Come on, it's all right." the creature only mewled louder, ending now with a honking sound, as if sending out a cry for help.

"I said back off Cendra; you never had the knack for animals. Go get Cat and leave me to this," he ordered her.

Her bottom lip pouted out. "I was only trying to help." Then she flounced off to find Cat, he hoped.

Cat would be the best at this; animals seemed to follow her anywhere, all the time.

He went back down and tried to calm the creature again. It took longer, but eventually he got the creature up and moving slowly after him, with him coaxing it every step of the way.

Rock had cleared an area for him and the creature to walk through the park, unimpeded.

They reached the portal and he pointed, "Home is there. You'll be safe now." The creature sniffed and mewled a bit and walked through to the boulders. Once it disappeared through the portal, Antonio closed it up, so no other creature could accidentally walk through again.

"We'll mark this as a non-threatening portal, but no sapience other than empathy. We need to keep anyone from going in there and fussing with the creatures. I just hope we haven't caused any harm as it was." Antonio looked worried.

"What we did couldn't be helped and we at least kept the impact to a bare minimum. I call this a win." Rock looked around, and asked, "Where is Cat?"

Antonio turned around, looking down the street where he had come from the warehouse district. "I sent Cendra off to find her a while ago. They both should be here by now."

"Anything with that telepathy you all use?" Rock's eyebrow rose in question.

Antonio had a grim look on his face, "No."

"I'm not getting anything on the receiver." Rock kept tapping on the module and calling for Cat with no response. "Just dead air."

"Cendra is on her way back with Howards." Antonio motioned down the street, where two people were walking towards them.

Rock wasn't going to wait. "Hernandez, Gibson - take the south side of the warehouses. Babyface, Gordon - take the north. Check in if you find her."

They took off to comply. "You and Romeo will go where you saw her last." Though she was Antonio's mate, the mantel now went to Rock, who wasn't going to wait for her to come back on her own.

Antonio nodded and they both moved off.

Cendra strode in with Howards. "What? Antonio said to come right away." Rock saw the sweetness was gone.

Rock frowned at her. "We haven't heard from Cat. Where did you see her last?"

"On the north side of the warehouse. She's fine," she said, with her eyes rolling.

Rock's voice went tight with frustration. "Antonio can't reach her. Can you?"

She tried or it looked like she did, but came back with a negative. She still didn't look concerned. She seemed more annoyed than anything else.

Everyone reconvened, but no one had any sign of her. The only thing Antonio could do was track her scent to two warehouses over and then it seemed the scent vanished without a trace. They had concluded she was most likely taken by some kind of transport, since the exhaust smell was still heavy in the air. They went back to the base to use the surveillance room there, but were stopped by the base commander.

Without authorization, he wouldn't let them use anything other than the runway to take off and that was it. Since their operation was covert, there wasn't any authentic authorization they could bring to the table. Rock had to scramble a call to General Pierce. Once he heard that Cat was MIA and presumed kidnapped, he told them to hold for an hour. He would be there himself to throw his weight around. Being a General had its privileges on any base.

He came a bit sheepishly with her boys and her other two mates in tow. The boys had refused to be kept away from the situation, now that they had heard their mother was missing. Her mates didn't even try to stop them. Gerard too, had come, armed to the teeth to give support to her mates and kill anyone who dared take his sister.

General Pierce won his way into the surveillance room, hoping to be able to use the tracking system here, but as at the base back home, there was no blip on the screen that marked Cat.

General Pierce turned to the men in the room. "The tracking system isn't working here either and her ear piece isn't sending or receiving. I want contingency plans, people. We aren't leaving here until we know what happened to her." His eyes grew dark and serious. "And who's responsible." Everyone had the same look as the General. No one would be leaving until they had her back.

Chapter Eight

To Skin a Cat

I woke up strapped inside a silver colored cell. They had taken off my tactile vest and boots and stripped me of all my weapons, which only left me with my Gaileyah. They had also taken off my cowl, and my face was now exposed. My hands were spread out on either side of steel and silver reinforced bars, in silver reinforced cuffs and my ankles were likewise in ankle cuffs. I was in a rectangle rack spread out in an x-shape inside it. They had black mesh over the cage, which darkened the cell inside.

There was no one else in the room. However, there were steel trays filled with what looked like medical instruments, plus the wall rack filled with whips of every description, which didn't ease my mind at all. I knew I was in deep shit and had to call for help on this one. I focused within, trying to find my bonding cords and got - nothing. I couldn't even feel my chakras.

Oh, this wasn't good. I tried connecting with any one of my mates on a telepathic private or wideband link, and again, nothing. My powers were completely cut off from me. I was getting panicky and looked around the room again to see what might be holding my powers in check. I could see some crystals here and there, but I had never heard of any crystals that could cut off all powers, magick and psychic.

The black mesh looked pretty ominous. It reminded me of the substance we used on our cell back home at the lair for when one of ours gets out of hand. Though, it wouldn't cut off their power within the cell itself; it would stop anyone from sending power out. Maybe this black mesh did the same thing, but worse. That left me with only one option. Physical means only.

Oh, I really hated doing this, because it did hurt like a bitch, but I would heal. I looked up to the wrist cuffs and started pulling my thumb into my palm, making my hand the same size as my wrist. It was a trick I had used several times when I was arrested as a juvenile - making my hands small enough to slip through cuffs. I sometimes dislocated my thumbs at the base to do it, but they never could hold me for long. I, and people like me who did it, are probably the reason why cops use those plastic tie cuffs now. Not so easy to dislocate your thumb and slip it through in those damned things. But, on this rack they had me on? Oh, yeah, piece of cake. I heard a pop on my right hand, and pulled my hand through the cuff quickly, before the swelling could get me stuck again.

I was focusing on my left hand, which always took longer, when I heard someone on the steps outside coming down towards the door to my unique room of torture. Thinking quickly, I tapped the ear piece in my ear, turning it on, since there was no way I would have enough time to get myself loose the rest of the way and escape now.

The door opened. There were three men who walked in, wearing dark black cloaks and masks over their faces. "Well, looky here, kitty cat is trying to wiggle lose. Naughty kitty." One of the men moved quickly to the cage and lifted the mesh. Unlocking the door, he moved up to me to grab my hand. I moved it away from him, and then tried punching at his jaw.

"Why you little bitch," he moved back. "Give me a whip," he growled to the other two outside the cage.

"Who the fuck are you people? Trying out for the Death eaters with those masks? Give it up, you can't compete with them. They're scarier looking." And I set myself, as he came at me with the whip his buddy had given him. He snapped out and tried to grab my hand at the same time. I tried to grab it, but missed and it hit my lower leg.

Hissing, I said, "Oh, you're going to pay for that." That is, if I could get my strength back. I had left part of myself in Trinidad, which makes me weaker, both physically and magickally. Plus, the fact that the drugs they used were still messing with my head.

"I'd like to see how, seeing since you're the one in here and I have the whip." He cracked it again and caught my hand, making me wince with the pain. I used what vampire strength I had left to not let him get my hand back into those cuffs. The drugs though, were still sapping my strength.

He swore and yelled for help. Between the three of them, they managed to wrestle my hand back inside the cuff.

One of the scary trio asked whip boy, "Should we reset her hand?"

"No, let the bitch suffer for it, for causing us so much work getting her back in," he snarled.

I laughed, "That's the best you got?"

"Oh, it'll get more interesting, I promise you that. We're just waiting for the guest of honor. Should be here shortly, so don't you worry." He and his little posse chortled over that.

"While we're waiting, why don't you tell us a few things? If you're a good kitty, we won't hurt you so bad." One of the men rolled the interesting steel tray I seen earlier with all the tricks of the trade of torture on it. "But, if you're bad, then we'll get creative," his voice sounding ominous.

"That's supposed to scare me? Dickhead, please - my mother is scarier than you. She had this look in her eye when she got pissed when I was a kid that used to make me wish for..." A fist hit me in the jaw, snapping my head back, effectively shutting me up.

"I don't want to hear about your momma, little girl. I want to hear about the man you work for," he snarled.

I glared at him. "I don't work for anybody, dickhead."

Another fist into my face had me spitting blood. "We know you work for someone. Who is it?"

"I don't play well with others," I spat at him.

He turned to the third clown. "Get me the whip with the razors in it." As the third guy went to do as he was ordered, clown number one got a knife and went behind me, cutting my tee shirt down the middle.

"You fuck nut, do you know how much it costs to have these made?" I yelled at him.

"Now it's a dish rag," he laughed.

"That's the point, dipwad," I sneered at his bohemian ignorance. He moved my hair out of the way and reached for the whip his buddy brought him. "One way or the other, it would have been skinned off of you anyway," and he laid in with his whip with a snap. I arched my back against the pain and felt the blood start to drip down my back and into the tops of my pants.

The leather whip he used had nine tails, each with a thin strip of a sharp razor glued into the ends of the tips. Oh, boy, this wasn't going to be a nice time. It was time to get nasty with this guy and make him hurt me bad enough to make me pass out or kill me. I'd be happy with either one right now.

I started with the obvious insults. "My momma hits harder than you do, wimp."

"Oh, really? I'll have you screaming for your momma soon enough. Who do you work for?"

He laid the whip to me three more times.

Each lash felt like hot shreds ripping down my back, but I still refused to scream. "I told you, I don't play well with others." I panted, "Do you know I've been hit by two year olds harder than you?" trying for the ridiculous. "Besides, I thought torture was 'you ask first, then hit when you don't get an answer'. What? Can't do this right, either? Not surprising, with those dumb ass masks."

I knew the tears in my back would heal in minutes, at least to the point that they wouldn't bleed anymore. But, it still hurt like hell to have the skin on my back sliced open each time.

He growled and laid into me some more. I think he would have kept going, if another man, also dressed in black and sporting his own clown looking mask, hadn't walked in and ordered, "Stop."

I groaned, my mouth bleeding from biting the inside of my lips to keep from screaming.

I taunted them both, "Oh, wonderful, you must be the Wizard of OZ to have enough pull to get tweedle dum here to stop with the pussy whipping he was giving me."

He didn't say anything right away, but tweedle dum was pissed and having a hard time not whipping me some more, despite being ordered not to.

The grand wizard pooh bah walked into the cage and stood right in front of me in a stance I recognized as a military one. So this guy was military, eh? That was interesting.

"Catrina Garcia. It's so nice to meet you at last. I am sure we are going to have a pleasant time getting to know each other," he said, with a menacing tone of voice.

"Oh, please, all you need now is to rub your hands together and give an evil chuckle for the full effect. Go ahead, try it out on me. See if works, oh wizard of the basement of torture devices and grey walls. Hey, what's with the grey brick walls and no windows anyways? You just have this black mesh stuff over this barred cage, but it has no skulls on it. Black mesh with skulls would be a good dramatic effect, don't you think?" I was trying to give as much detail as possible for those on the other end of the ear piece to hear about. It was my only other option if I couldn't get them to kill me right away.

"You think you're tough, don't you?" the Wizard sneered through his mask.

"Tougher than you and your three butt monkeys. At least there aren't little men singing, though. That would drive me up a wall, quick, if you started singing." I was doing my best to piss them off. "I hate that fucking movie. So, I must not be in Kansas anymore, huh? No singing." I was starting to ramble a bit from the pain. Things were going in and out of focus a bit to.

"Oh, you're still in Kansas, dear. So close, yet so far away from your people. I made sure of that." He took the whip from his homeboy and walked behind me slowly. "I know a lot about you already. I know you aren't a normal human and I know you have three children and three husbands. You also have a pass to the base at the Navy Air Station." He leaned so close to my neck that I caught a good sniff out of him and recognized his scent. The same smell that had permeated General Pierce's office some months ago, when a visiting General, a General Robertson, who was also a dark-side practitioner of the arts, was trying to get dirt on our General, and failed. The same buttwad who turned lose hellhounds on our base and freaking werewolves on our team on a mission, infecting my son, but failing to kill us. At least, up until now, I had thought he'd failed in all his plans. How else did he know about me?

"That's the part I am interested in. Why do you, a nobody, have a pass at a military base in Texas? Why did you have a military special op tracking device in your arm?" Damn, that means Rock and my guys can't track me to these coordinates. I was in deep shit. Well, at least I knew now why they hadn't busted down the door yet.

"I have no idea what the fuck you're talking about, asswipe." I gritted though my teeth, "I think you got some bogus info on me. I'm innocent. Didn't do shit. Ain't seen shit. Don't know shit. And you are a pile of shit. That's all I know."

CRACK. The whip hit across my back deeper than the other guy had done it.

"Then, why is your back healing so fast, eh, kitty, kitty?" number one clown asked.

"Hmmm, you are correct, my friend. She is healing too fast. Well, we'll have to see about that," Mr. Wizard practically gloated.

"Interesting. Mind if I try something?" asked tweedle dee.

"No permanent damage," Mr. Wizard allowed. "At least, not yet."

Tweedle dee took a gun and pointed it into my stomach. Low enough not to hit any internal organs or my kidney and pulled the trigger. The bullet went through with a blaze of hot pain. My body jerked from the shock and I started breathing hard, so as not to scream from it.

When I could talk again without moaning, I said, "You asshole. One more time and I swear I am going to take that gun, stick it up your ass and give you another asshole to shit out of." I was yelling, more to let the pain out, then anything though. At least this way, I wouldn't give them any satisfaction that they hurt me.

The fucker ignored me. "See how the wound is closing already? Sure, she is losing blood, but the wound is healing at a phenomenal rate." Oh, great, I had a mad scientist type on my hands. They were the hardest to get to lose control. Sociopathic in the extreme, their only love was causing pain and the results they got. Many of the secret government and university underground labs had these kinds of people in it.

"What are you, his pet Igor?" They both ignored me again.

"Bring me that bottle with the red stopper," Mr. Wizard ordered, sounding slightly pissed now.

Damn, I was closer than I thought in pissing these guys off past their restraint.

"What? Poison? Snow White I ain't, Mr. Dickless Wizard, or can't you see out of that mask?" I taunted some more.

He snapped the whip against my back again. "If I were you, I would learn to control my tongue."

"If I were you, I would need a dick replacement so no one would know how small it was." Nothing gets a man pissed faster than attacking his manhood.

He snapped the whip four more times until I was seeing that lovely black tunnel I knew and loved so well as a child. I let myself fall into the black hole of unconsciousness with relief.

Andre was pacing back and forth in the room, hands clenched into fist. No one wanted to get near him right now. They heard one man order another to pour the bottle into her mouth while she was unconscious. Then, there was silence for a few moments.

Then one man asked another, "Do you think this will work?"

"It should. We've used this on a few of the supernatural's we've caught and experimented on before; it's how we came up with the potion for those that heal too fast," the man she called Mr. Wizard answered.

"How long does it take?" She called this man tweedle dum.

Mr. Wizard responded, "It should be working now."

The one she called a pet Igor asked, "Mind if I?"

"Go ahead," Mr. Wizard said. "Same shot as before, though."

They heard the report of gunfire again.

"Yes, you're right. It is working now. The wound is not closing. How extraordinary." The man, Igor, was practically gushing.

"Now, let's see if we can't wake this cat up and get some answers," said the one she called Mr. Wizard. The snap of a whip came through the intercom and everyone in the room flinched for her.

Andre hit the wall hard enough to make it shatter with cracks. Demitri moved quickly to stop him from doing any other damage they couldn't explain. Demitri started talking to him low and urgently, trying to calm him down.

Antonio had tears coming down his face. Christoph and Crimson had to take Craven outside, so he couldn't hear their mom being tortured and 'wolf out' at the base.

Cendra had moved close to Antonio, eyes full of sympathy and tried to put a hand on his shoulder. "Don't - you - fucking - dare," he said to her in a low menacing voice.

"I just thought..." she started.

"If you hadn't left her alone with no back up, she wouldn't be there now," he growled at her.

She tried to defend her actions. "I just wanted to make sure you were all right."

Gerard came over and grabbed her upper arm, pulling her away from Antonio. "He had back up. Don't say anything else. I am tempted to challenge you myself, sister. Now shut up." His cold blue eyes glared at her.

Rock looked up at Antonio from his seat. "At least, we know she is still in Kansas. We will tear this state apart looking for her." He looked back down on the map, circling the place where they had been and the base itself. "Five hours, it took for us to get a signal from her ear piece. We now know she is stationary. So, if they drove in any direction at say, seventy-five miles an hour, just to be on the safe side, they would be within this radius." He drew a circle around a piece of Kansas. "It was a good thing she had her ear piece off or they would have picked up the signal from it and removed it, as well." He got up and walked over to Antonio showing him the map. "The base is also within this radius. He'd said, 'so close, but so far away from your people. I made sure of that.' He sounded gloating. Like he was teasing her with something."

Antonio nodded. "He was taunting her. Maybe he accidentally gave her a clue or maybe deliberately, to give hope, then take it away. We are close to her, but none of us can feel her. With or without using our magick. How is that possible?"

"She was talking about a black mesh over her barred cage. Maybe they're using the same kind of thing we use to stop magick from going out of a cell?" Gerard offered his opinion.

"How would they know of your potion?" Rock asked.

Gerard shook his head. "Anyone could make it, really. You just have to know how to create the opposite of your targets electrical charge. It negates it within its area."

"So, she wouldn't be able to send out for help or for us to send to her to help or track either," Antonio mused.

"No, because she and you share the same kind of electrical magickal pulse. So would I, or anyone connected with her by blood or bond."

Demitri snapped around. "What did you say?"

Gerard cocked his head. "That none of us could use our bonds or blood ties, because of the magickal negation of what they are using. We all share the same magickal pulses."

Demitri grinned evilly. "Not the Dai' Khans. Their energy signals would be different and their bond is half formed. Not enough for a true blending, but maybe enough for them to track her." Demitri turned to General Pierce. "We need them back here now General. Can you get us clearance to bring them to this base from the base in Okinawa?"

"Done. You call Cassie. Tell her to bring them back here." The General moved to a phone to start the process.

Antonio was already reaching for his cell phone to contact her since he was too upset to find his center and use telepathy. It was fortunate that Cassie had chosen to wait for the Dai' Khans to come back though the portal to guide them and the Bokaris to Texas. It would save a lot of time. Time Cat needed desperately, as they heard her awaken, screaming.

"Hello Kitty, glad to see you back with us. Now, what do you know about General Pierce, Captain O'Hara and his Special Forces team?"

"What do you know about the Wizard of Oz? There are supposed to be midgets, small people and a yellow brick road. I don't see a yellow brick road, you fucking Neanderthal," I growled at him.

He responded by hitting me repeatedly with that damned whip.

"They took you out of New York away from an FBI agent. Why?" he growled.

"Do you know which dweebie town we are in? This has to be a dweebie town if you're in it. Is it the same one Dorothy flew off in her house?" Anything to piss him off some more or anything to get more information. Either one will work for me.

He jeered, "This is my home town. I admit it isn't New York, but it's the perfect place to seem completely harmless. I eat at the pastor's house once a month. He comes to play here in my basement with other younger delights. We hide what we are better than you do. Wolves in sheep's clothing, if you will. Singing Gods praises in the day and practicing our arts in the night." And he showed me one of those arts with his whip.

Gasping, I told him off, "Hey, don't diss wolves; you're not even in their league, you sycophantic piece of shit."

"Is that what you are? But you can't be. You haven't shifted yet and you would have at this level of pain. So, what do you know of werewolves? I happen to know of a pack that was quite amenable to my direction until you and that Special Forces team went and closed the portal." Snap went the whip. "How did you close a portal? Once opened, they were supposed to stay opened." The whip cracked again. "Why do you think we put you inside the Moiré Net?" I didn't care what I was in at that point. I was seeing that black tunnel again.

"Damn it to hell, the witch passed out again," Mr. Wizard had growled over the intercom.

"Shall I wake her?" Igor asked him.

Mr. Wizard sounded disgusted, "No, I need to think. She isn't breaking very easily. We must get more creative with her. We'll come back later; we have all night. Let's let her bleed for a while. It will weaken her."

Antonio turned to Rock. "They're about 7 hours away with using the C-37A Gulf Stream opened up," informing them of Cassie's and Ja' Monel's progress to the base.

Rock nodded. The C-37A Gulf was the fastest airplane the military had and was used often for special ops that needed speed. He just hoped for Cat's sake that those assholes will leave her alone and for the plane to make it here before they got more imaginative with her. Even Babyface was getting pushed beyond his capability of maintaining his cool. Usually, he was cold blooded and methodical when on a mission, but he seemed to be taking this one personally, which worried Rock. Rock looked at the rest of the team and the squad of marines who were waiting for orders, any orders, to do something about this. He knew they were all feeling pretty helpless during this situation and that wasn't good for morale.

Hours later, sound come from the intercom again. They tried to wake her up and fearing they might have killed her, dressed the wound to her stomach to stop the blood flow.

"She isn't rousing. Maybe some water might wake her up along with some food?" Tweedle dum suggested.

Mr. Wizard agreed, "Yes, that might be a good idea. The tranq and loss of blood could have been detrimental and I haven't gotten any answers from her yet, so we can't afford to lose her at this time."

There were sounds of movement over the speaker. Several moments later they heard, "Holy shit."

They couldn't hear who said it, but it got Mr. Wizard's attention. "What is the problem, Hector?"

With a shaky voice tweedle dum said, "Look at her teeth."

"How extraordinary," Igor declared.

"This can't be. She couldn't be one of the Prince's clans. His portal just opened in '07. She has a juvenile record and a college record, so she must have been here long before the opening of any portals," Mr. Wizard exclaimed.

"But she is a vamp. He is the Prince of the vamps, so she has to be one of his," Tweedle dum stated.

Mr. Wizard sounded unsure of himself now, saying, "But then, either he is working against us, using her as a cats paw, or he doesn't know about her. She could be a lost progeny of his from millennia ago. She can't be a new made. She hasn't been anywhere near that particular portal. We've hidden it well. So no, not a cats paw or a spy." They heard Mr. Wizard pacing back and forth trying to figure her origins out. "No, she could be a blood line of his that got trapped on this side when the portals were closed long ago. If she is his get by blood, then hurting her could cost us much. He wouldn't be pleased. Though, if we don't tell him, he won't find out either, since he obviously doesn't know about her."

"But, bringing in a lost blood line could win us much from him. To date, he has been loath to work with us, no matter the sweets we've tossed him. This could be a strong bargaining chip," Igor advised. "Think of the possibilities. He might turn one of us and that's all we need to turn the rest of the Coven."

They heard Mr. Wizard stop pacing. "You're right; we can't afford not to try to see if they have lost a bloodline. A breeding female vampire would be worth much to them, regardless. With three children, she has already proven herself capable. Those children of hers could also be worth much to The Prince. No, don't touch her anymore until I get back from the portal. I must have an audience with the Prince first and see where this could lead. We'll deal with the situation at that point. Maybe lay down some contingency plans for capturing her children next."

"What about her wounds?" Igor sounded worried. Whoever this Prince was, obviously scared the little rat, Rock thought.

"No, leave them for now. We'll tell the Prince we had to, in order to keep her, since she proved herself too strong. Yes, that would appeal to him, a very strong breeding female that took such extraordinary efforts to contain. He'll forgive the injuries, I would think. Come, we haven't much time."

Footsteps echoed, then were gone and silence took over the intercom again.

Chapter Nine

To Find a Lost Cat

Well, we have a first name, 'Hector'. And we now know they are hiding the other portal that the F-5 tornado opened up." Rock was writing down all the information that could help them narrow the search for Cat. "He also knows about the New York incident and had a talk with Special Agent Williams." He cocked his eye at Gerard. "How hard would it be to nab the FBI agent and pump him for information?" Knowing Gerard had mob connections with the five Mafia families in New York, things could be arranged in a hurry.

"A phone call could have that agent in our hands and singing in less than three hours," Gerard responded to Rock's question.

Rock nodded. "If the Dai' Khans can't do anything, we'll have to break a few laws then, fuck it."

Antonio was rubbing his chin thoughtfully. "Another race of vampires that has a prince. It also sounds like he doesn't like working with this 'wizard of oz' either. How could we find this portal and have a talk with him ourselves? Maybe he could tell us who this Mr. Wizard is."

Wizard looked up from his laptop. "That F-5, which went through Greensburg, Kansas in August of '07, also happens to be within the radius Rock has sketched out. I'm betting the portal is within the city or the immediate surrounding area. Every portal we have caught on the tracking system was opened near the place the natural disaster struck, so far."

"But, over ninety percent of the city was wiped out," Rock said, looking over Wizard's shoulder at the information he had brought up on his screen. "That's still a lot of area to poke around in."

General Pierce grunted, "Let's make that a Plan B; Plan A, is having the Dai' Khans being able to trace her."

Babyface barked, "Incoming."

Ja' Monel and Cassie were escorted by two of the bases MPs into the room.

One of the guards asked, "Do you need us to stay, General?" giving Ja' Monel an uneasy sideways glance. The General couldn't blame them, since he came in with his swords and head wrap on. Cassie was dressed for action, as well, and looked like a small dark black blade. The look in her eyes was glittering with anger, as was Ja' Monel's.

General Pierce waved them away. "No, thank you, we've got them from here."

The other MP didn't move away. "Are you sure, General?"

The General assured them, "Yes, they are fine with us here. You're free to go."

Seeing there were others in the room dressed as Cassie and Ja' Monel, they decided to let it go. Both of them saluted and marched out the door.

Cassie was the first to speak, in a low angry hiss, "What has been done so far?" Her furious gaze settled on Cendra, who had chosen a corner of the room to hide in. No one wanted to stand with her at the moment. Still unrepentant, she sniffed with her lips pursed.

"Shhh, wait," Demitri silenced them.

"De-Demitri," they heard her whisper.

236

"Come on, baby. Tell me," he whispered back.

They could barely hear her. "Know him."

"Know who? Him?" He was getting frustrated.

"Hurts," they heard her whimper.

Demitri hung his head. "I know, baby. I am so sorry."

Andre was pacing near the intercom. "Come on, tell us and we'll kill him. I swear we'll kill him."

They heard her trying to speak, then, "Gen..ner..al." She took a deep sigh and was silent again.

"General? But he's here. Been here the whole time or does she want him to come get her?" Andre was asking anyone in the room for clarification.

"Maybe she thinks he can help?" Demitri answered.

Antonio shook his head. "He's here, helping already."

"But she doesn't know that." Even Romeo was at his edge.

Ja' Monel's heated stare fell on Antonio. "Do you have any idea where our Meshallima is?" his voice low and coldly infuriated.

Antonio slowly shook his head and gave him the few clues they did have. "She said 'Know him', then 'General', but he is here, so I don't think she was accusing him. Maybe, that he knows how to find her or has a chance of finding her?"

Demitri interrupted, "We called you here to see if you could locate her with your bonds. Where are the others?"

Ja' Monel turned to Demitri. "On Kla' din. There was an invasion from Draugrall; larger than they had ever sent before. They stayed with our Meshallima's dragons to fight them off and I came."

Cassie stepped forward. "It was bad. Ja' Kelo's province was hit harder than ever in their history. I was about to step over into Kla' din to give aid, when we got the red alert on Cat."

"Will just one of them be able to hone in on Cat, though?" Andre asked.

Ja' Monel closed his eyes and focused for a long time. "There is something black wavering between our bond. Her unconsciousness isn't helping, but it seems she is in that direction." He pointed to the Northwest.

Andre brightened. "How far?"

Ja' Monel admitted, "I don't know how to tell male, female bonding distance. I have never had a female bond with me before."

Demitri, desperate to try anything, suggested, "We could just go driving and see if he can hone in on it?"

"It beats fucking sitting here and listening to her torture." Andre was ready to move.

Antonio pulled himself together. "Who is going?"

"The General can't stay here alone. Things have been decidedly hostile since we've been here." Rock didn't trust the feelings he was getting from those on this base.

Rock organized the teams as best he could. "Wizard will stay, since he is tech and Antonio will have to go." He knew there was no way Antonio was going to stay behind. "Babyface can stay, as well. I'll take Romeo with us and half the squad."

"Cassie and I are coming, as well." Gerard's eyes dared anyone to refute him.

"I will, too," Cendra piped up.

Everyone turned to look at her, but it was Antonio who made the decision. "No, you will stay here. I think you've done enough damage for one day," Antonio said coldly.

Ja' Monel's eyes narrowed at her. No one had told him her part in Cat's capture. They weren't too sure what exactly he might do about it. He seemed to have picked up everyone's anger at her though, and put it together with Cat's kidnapping.

When everyone was settled into their groups, the rescue team headed out with Cat's boys tagging along. They refused to be left behind and threatened to cause a scene if not allowed to go.

Since they didn't want to try to explain having a werewolf on base, they caved in and allowed them to go.

Rock, Cassie, Ja' Monel and Cat's mates took the lead car.

"Damned kids of hers are just as fucking stubborn as she is," Rock grumbled.

"You expected anything different from Meshallima's get?" Ja' Monel said sardonically.

Rock eye did his eyebrow trick. "If they're going to be a part of my team some day, they'll have to learn to follow orders, sooner or later."

Cassie stated simply, "They'll never be Special Forces."

"Why not? They're skilled enough." Rock sounded a bit put off.

"Skilled, yes. But, the hard structured military discipline would never take with one of our children. Their spirits are too free and would suffocate under such a demand. They will always be Mercenary," Cassie explained.

Rock disagreed with her. "The military isn't as harsh as you make it sound, Cassie."

"It is to one of us, where we would be pulled into two different directions at the same time. Follow our instincts or follow orders. Eventually, such a strain would make us snap." She turned to look at Rock. "Could you see Cat flourishing in the military life?"

He thought about it, and then shook his head. "No, she would wind up court-martialed, sooner or later, dishonorably discharged, at best," he admitted.

"The same would happen to her sons. Eventually." And with that statement, she turned her attention back out the window, trying to focus in on Cat's energy signal.

"The General is going to be disappointed. He was hoping to recruit them someday." Rock laughed, trying to imagine Craven not wolfing out with a drill instructor in his face. No, she was right, they wouldn't submit to the discipline of the military. They'd hit somebody some day or kill them.

They drove for ten miles, when Ja' Monel said to turn to the left. They went through to an upper residential neighborhood with names like MacArthur, Sheridan, Custer and Patton. They arrived at a three story house with a strong colonial architect. Getting out of the car, Ja' Monel nodded that this was the place.

Rock wanted to establish a perimeter before tossing down the doors and windows, but Craven apparently had other ideas, wolfing out in front of God and everyone. What came out of the full shift wasn't the normal werewolf they had seen before, but a full-sized Dire Wolf transformation. He stood on his hind legs, which looked more like heavily muscled tree trunks, and at a full height of well over six and half feet. Craven was huge and more humanoid in this form than his werewolf shift. Cassie's sharp intake of breath slowed Rock's pursuit of Craven to try to calm him down.

"What the fuck is going on, Cassie? He's never shifted looking like that before," Rock demanded to know.

"We were afraid his Fae astral blood would have repercussions to being Were. This is a Dire Wolf form.

Highly dangerous." Cassie was trying to slow Craven down with soothing hand gestures.

"What do we do then, Cassie? Cat isn't in any condition to deal with this." Rock didn't know whether to point the silver loaded P-90 at Craven, or not.

"Stay out of his way and don't piss him off. I don't think silver will work, especially now," Christoph volunteered, as he placed his own body between Craven's Dire Wolf form and Rock's gun.

Craven was howling and sniffing the air, trying to move around Cassie to the front door of the house. Craven towered over her small dominative form, but for some reason, didn't get aggressive about his wanting to move forward. That gave Rock hope that Craven was in some control in this form, as well.

Rock lowered his gun, but kept his finger on the trigger. "If he keeps making that racket, we could have one hell of a situation here, Christoph." Craven scented something and went still for a moment, then moved around Cassie so fast, she didn't have time to try to intercept him. Rock glared at Craven's brothers, who looked slightly apologetic.

Christoph shrugged his shoulders. "He smells our mother," and went running after Craven, who had blown right through the front door of the house. Everyone else ran after them, trying to get them to show some self perseveration. None of the boys were listening. They moved, en mass, to the living room and since they didn't see anyone there, made their way through the dining room. Then, they heard movement in the kitchen and one of the men who had tortured Cat came out from that area. Craven smelled her blood on his clothing and ripped his head off with one swipe of his clawed paw, howling with rage. The man's head bounced off the walls of the dining room and landed underneath the dining room table. Rock knew there was no way he could calm him, now that his blood lust had been set loose and he worried how they were going to contain him with Cat not conscious.

Ja' Monel seemed to be watching Cat's son with pride and had his scimitars out, covering the Dire Wolfs back from any attacks. Her mates took note and flanked around Craven as his Dire Wolf shape went through doors and men, most of whom were convened in the kitchen for an apparent lunch break, with the single minded purpose of getting to his mother.

All the rest of them could do was watch his back, so no one could disrupt his search and maybe turn his rage on anyone else within range. They had no idea how much of his consciousness was in control. Rock saw through the kitchen's side door that a few men were running down the stairs, also in black robes, from the upper floor, with guns firing toward the Dire Wolf. Rock and Romeo took aim with their P-90's and killed them before they could even get halfway down the stairs.

Craven would wound or kill anyone in his path. Those that were only wounded would be swiftly dispatched by Ja' Monel or Cat's mates. They weren't leaving anyone behind alive today. They made it to the basement without too much difficulty and again Craven ripped off the door and waded in. There was only one man on his knees pleading, but there was blood on his clothes, as well. He was killed quickly, ruthlessly and without any mercy. They hadn't shown Cat any, so they would receive the same treatment.

The black mesh burned Craven's clawed paws, but he ignored it and ripped it off the cage. He then tore the cell door off in one huge strain of muscles. He crouched to enter the cage and sniffed at his mother.

Rock was worried about what he might do with the blood smell so heavy in the air; even the humans could smell the coppery tinted scent. "Ah, someone want to get a hold of Craven in case the blood smell is too much for him?"

Cassie fearlessly walked over to her nephew, cooing, "We need to help your mother now. We can't do that if you don't get out of the way and change, Craven." The Dire Wolf turned his massive head towards her voice and his muzzle drew back in a half snarl.

Andre, who had the closest relationship to him, called out, "Craven, my man, you need to back up so we can get to your mom. She needs blood, son. You did your job; she is safe now. Let us help her."

Craven turned to Andre's voice and blew out a cough with a snap of his massive jaw, but he began to back out slowly. Cassie eased around him and went to Cat's back to heal her.

Her gasp was quickly silenced when she saw Craven stop his retreat. "Go ahead Craven, we'll take care of this," but they could tell she was crushed inside by what she saw.

Ja' Monel strode in quickly, as did her mates and tried not to show their anger at what they were viewing. Ja' Monel just slashed at his wrist and put it to Cat's mouth, urging her to drink. Her mates allowed him the first feeding, since it was because of him, they were able to find her in the first place.

Cassie scanned for Rock in the crowd, now with their weapons aiming outwardly to keep them safe while they tried to get Cat to recover. "We need a gurney. She won't be able to sit or lie down in the back of that car. I do not want to move her too much, until we can lay her down on her stomach or side." Tears were spilling over from her eyes, though her voice was clear and in control. Rock could imagine how bad the damage was.

She kept pouring power into Cat's injuries, but it didn't seem to heal any of the wounds from the side view he had. He radioed for an ambulance from the base, so they could try to contain the situation from local law enforcement. He was surprised they hadn't shown up yet.

Ja' Monel glanced over at him, as if sensing his thoughts. "I threw a spell of silence and blindness over the house when Craven lost control. Cat said no one outside of the Nightwolves could know about his condition. She said it would be dangerous to him?" as if looking for confirmation from Rock.

He nodded, "Yeah, it would be bad. Quick thinking, there. You saved me a lot of paperwork, too."

"It is amazing how much this world fears the blessings that come upon them," Ja' Monel shook his head in disbelief.

Gerard came into the room and told them there was no one else in the house to worry about. Rock took that to mean he'd dispatched everyone he came across without prejudice. He ordered the men to clear the house, just in case, and then set a perimeter until the ambulance arrived. The room seemed bigger and more threatening, now that most of the men had cleared out to secure the house. Craven was huddled in the corner trying to breathe through the blood scent enough to calm down so he could shift. He was having a hard time of it, though. Antonio waited with a blanket, talking to him soothingly the whole time, while they waited for Craven to get control. One by one, they offered blood for Cat, which had her coming around to where she was more conscious of her surroundings.

"Demitri," she whispered, in a pain filled voice.

"Yeah, sweetheart. I'm here. We got you. They won't hurt you anymore. We've got them all," he reassured her over and over.

She was trying to shake her head. "No, General; didn't get General."

Demitri crooned to her, wanting to touch her, but not knowing where she wasn't hurt for a safe touch. "He is at the base, sweet love. He came as soon as he knew you were in trouble. He helped get Ja' Monel here so you could be rescued. He's the one who found you for us."

She kept shaking her head groaning, "No. No, not him, other one."

"What other General, sister?" Gerard seemed to know what she was trying to say.

"Evil. Black. General." She passed out again on them.

Gerard rounded on Demitri. "She means General Robertson. It was him that grabbed her. Look among the dead and see if he is here, but she is trying to tell us we didn't get him."

Demitri snarled, "That son of a bitch." They went racing upstairs, to really look around the house. Mr. Wizard had said, 'it's my home'. Then, they saw the photos on the mantel in the living room. There were pictures of a happy joyful family sitting in the bright sun with General Robertson in the middle, smiling as if the proud patriarch of a fine, upstanding American family. Gerard broke the frame and took out the picture. "Take the rest of them; we can use the pictures later for other things," his voice was cold and calculating. "I'm going to get a sample of that black mesh they used." Andre and Antonio did as he said. They, too, weren't going to let this rest until each and every one of this black coven was dead.

Romeo looked around. "I wonder where the family is? They weren't in the house."

"Good thing, too. They may be a part of his family, but they may not be a part of the black coven. Until we know for sure, we'll treat them as innocent civilians," Demitri explained.

"Sounds good," Romeo's hazel eyes flashed anger, contrary to their usual light heartedness. He, like everyone else, was livid and needed this avenged for Cat - for the Nightwolves.

They got Cat down out of the rack and onto a gurney on her left side. Getting her past base security took some threats from General Pierce, but they eventually got her loaded onto their plane and headed back to Truax Field where she, as well as all of them, would be safer, until the situation at the Kansas base could be ascertained better. They all knew that something was happening there. There had been just too damn much interference and a few of those men they had killed at General Robertson's house had been military men.

The Nightwolves wing at the bases' hospital was once again filled with Mercs of every age. More than half the platoon turned out, as well, to give blood or support when needed. Yet, with all their giving of blood and healing powers of the main Coven, nothing seemed to heal the wounds that were inflicted on her. In desperation, they even had the Doctor come in with strict guidelines of what he could or could not do. However, the best he could do, was to clean her wounds with iodine, stitching together a few of the deeper ones along her back, and suturing the bullet wound closed.

"I'm sorry I can't do more," Doctor Major Kent said to Cassie, then to Cat's mates. "If, however, there is anything else you need of me, even if it's out of the ordinary, please don't be afraid to ask."

"Thank you, Doctor, we'll be sure to keep that in mind." Cassie smiled graciously at him. He had won some serious brownie points with her with that remark. It let her know he wasn't oblivious to what they have been doing and was willing to help, as a return for their efforts.

Doctor Major Kent gave Ja' Monel's scimitars a sideways glance, then practicing his air of feigned ignorance, he walked out the door without comment or uncomfortable questions.

With her voice weak, but still cocky, Cat said, "Is there any way I can con a cup of coffee out of anyone here?"

"Hey, hon, you're awake." Demitri's relief could be heard in his tone.

"Yeah, and I really hate being talked about when I am in the room, people." She tried to sit up and winced, giving up the movement. "Ok, not a hundred percent yet, I take it."

"No, not even close. The injuries refuse to heal, Cat." Andre moved up on the bed, carefully taking her hand in his.

"Well, at least I didn't give anyone up, that's the main thing." She sounded relieved.

"No, you didn't Cat, and I am sorry you had to go through that." General Pierce, Rock and Pearson walked in.

"Hey, guys, how's it hanging?" she gave them a half grin. "Besides, its part of the hazard of the job isn't it? Military or Merc? Could have been any one of us in there."

"They wanted you. The trap was set especially for you," Rock told her.

"I know. They knew too much about who the main players are in this unit. They knew about my sons somehow and my mates. We'll have to arrange for security for them now. Twenty four-seven, I don't want any one of them alone from here on out," she ordered. Even from her bed, she was still leading her Coven despite her wounds.

"It'll be done," Demitri promised.

Cat dropped her next order, which landed like a bomb shell. "We have a leak somewhere. We have to find it and plug it up. Permanently."

General Pierce exclaimed, "What? How is that possible? No one would leak information about this company or your Coven."

"Easy there, General." She assured him, "I wasn't accusing anyone specifically, but they knew too much about the players in our program. The leak could be a watcher, much like the one I sent after General Robertson, months ago. Though, his actions haven't given me much to go on, other than that meeting he had with Special Agent Williams, and the people he sees are people I don't know. Not much to go on with that, but he is somehow getting better Intel then I am. We need to fix that."

"I'll make some inquiries; find out who his friends are. He wasn't found among the dead, so we'll have to watch ourselves." The General looked disgruntled that someone in the service could be so evil. General Pierce knew, like the rest of us, there were good and bad in all walks of life. Just because you wear a uniform, doesn't automatically make you a good guy. Although some die-hards thought it should.

"So, is there nothing further that can be done about the damage to you?" His expression turned saddened for her state.

"We've tried everything. Nothing seems to help," Demitri told him, easing next to the bed.

Ja' Monel stepped forward then to ask, "Is there no other healing that can be done *here* for her?"

Shaking her head, Cassie frowned. "That potion they used on her is stopping everything we do. Her own body is not helping, either. All of her natural abilities in healing have been blocked, it seems."

"From what I can see, on a spiritual level, there is an odd green glow coming from the edges of the wounds, tinged with a black aura. There may be something from our world that may help?" Ja' Monel offered.

Demitri looked up. "Anything you think might help, we'll try at this point."

"If Meshallima would get word back to Kla' din, using Shamus, and inform Ja' Callum of the situation, he'll know that I am thinking of - the Keria din lah' Sholas. It is what we use to counteract the magicks the Draugrall will use on their victims." Ja' Monel's gaze hardened. "The few that we have been able to recover in battle. This green glow coming from the wounds is very similar, though not as black edged. It might work for this kind of magick."

Cat nodded, glad to have the rest of her powers back, at least. "It's done. Shamus will pop over there. That will save time in sending someone physically there, but Ja' Callum will need an escort back to the States from Okinawa."

Rock offered a suggestion. "I have an old buddy stationed there, Captain Mark Russell. We went through boot camp together. I trust him. He can bring him the rest of the way, which will cut nine to twelve hours from the time."

"I'll send out the orders?" General Pierce looked to Cat for confirmation. It was one of those circumstances that their ponds overlapped one another, since anything military was General Pierce's bailiwick, yet Shamus and Ja' Callum were hers. It was a delicate dance they were scrupulous not to tread upon.

"Yes, Shamus will tell Ja' Callum to ask for Captain Mark Russell, once he makes his way to the base from the portal. Shamus can guide him that far, if necessary. The Dai' Khan's telepathic communication is getting stronger with my astral familiars all the time," she added, with a pleased tone. Her mates, however, looked a bit peeved over what had previously been their private privilege.

Though, they all looked relieved that there might be something that could help, even if they would have to wait for it.

"Did anyone find the other portal from the F-5 tornado?" She looked around for confirmation.

General Pierce was the one who answered. "No one even looked, Cat. We were busy trying to find your location and retrieve you."

Cassie softly touched her shoulder. "Greensburg is a big area and they most likely have that mesh net over the portal to hide it.

"What do you mean a net to hide it?" she looked confused.

Demitri supplied the information to her. "General Robertson was talking about how they have a portal hidden. We are assuming he is using the black mesh net to cover it, since it isn't showing up on the tracker."

"Shit, how else can we find it then?" Cat asked.

"He went there earlier last night. If your watcher was following him, maybe it can trace the location for you?" Cassie's eyes looked bright at the prospect. "Especially, since it seems to be a portal to another vampire tribe."

"Friggin' vamps?" Cat was shocked. "What kind of vamps? Not the Draugrall?"

Cassie and Demitri shrugged. Demitri was the one who answered. "It could be, but the one you called Igor, said they have been loath to work with them to date. I am assuming the Draugrall wouldn't be so picky. Most likely, we may have another completely different tribe of vampire."

Cassie nodded, agreeing with Demitri's speculations.

Cat's eyes narrowed in anger. "Fine, let me see through my watcher then, and I might be able to give you a smaller area to recon."

Cassie reminded her, "Do you really think you should do that now? You're not supposed to use any power until you heal from your injuries, Cat."

"If we don't find that portal and negate Robertson's use of it, we may face more shit than we can handle later. I want this sucker nailed. I owe him big," she growled at Cassie. "And, if they have that portal, which had to have opened in 2007, then how many more does Robertson's Coven control?"

Demitri touched her hand. "Sweetheart, it can wait 'till later; just make sure it's recording and you can access it when you're healed."

"Damn it, I hate being hurt like this." Everyone could tell she was agitated. Her mate knew she needed something else to think about or she would worry at this all night.

To sidetrack her, Demitri said, "Ja' Kelo's Province got hit pretty badly, worse than ever before. They have never tried to hit more than one town before at a time. It's the first time they have tried to strike at more. Luckily, they did not succeed."

"What happened and when was this?" She looked over to Ja' Monel who had been sitting quietly in the corner of the room, watching their interactions with one another.

"Three cities within his province were raided the day you got abducted. Your dragons did a fine job of protecting the townsfolk, however, and none have been reported missing. There were quite a few injuries, bites and such. Your wizard helped with the cleansings of wounds and healing." He bowed his head to her.

Relieved she asked, "And my dragons? Any injuries there?"

"A few, but all are healed. They are quiet revered on our world now, Meshama. The townsfolk have been spoiling them with fresh meat and treats," he smiled at her.

She laughed, "Oh, wonderful, I'll get back egotistical, fat dragons. Thanks a lot, Ja' Monel." Her expression grew serious. "Three cities, though. That's not a good sign. It shows they are getting desperate and things could soon go to FUBAR city real quick."

"What is FUBAR?" Ja' Monel asked.

"Fucked up beyond all recognition," O'Hara answered for her.

"Tango and Cash." Demitri smiled at O'Hara, who nodded back.

"Yeah, what they both said. Not a good thing, Ja' Monel." She sighed and settled into her pillow. "What we need, is more of a ground force. Dragons are great in a fight from the air, but with so many injuries," she stopped Ja' Monel's refute, "although yes, they were taken care of this time, it will only get worse, if we don't find a way to cover the ground, as well."

Demitri agreed with her. "Your cousin got lucky. Next time might not be so easy, now that the Draugrall know about the dragons. They'll be better prepared."

"I have to agree with them, Ja' Monel," Cassie said. "And Trinidad never had much of a ground force to boast about."

Cat nodded. "I have predators for air, for the sea; for the land, I have Fairies and Pixies. Gnomes too, and brownies. I have a single panther and a single wolf, not enough for a fighting ground force."

O'Hara asked, "I thought Pixies were very nasty when not in a good mood?"

Cat snorted, "Yeah, they could pixy with the best of them and fairies, too can fight. But, against Vampires? I wouldn't want to risk their lives in a fight with vampires. Those Draugralls are fast, real fast. They might be able to pace with a fairy and that would be a bad thing for my wee Fae."

General Pierce interjected, "We don't have enough man power to cover both Kla' din and Earth."

Cat sighed, "No, we don't, and they would have to move very fast to get to where the attack is happening. Humans don't move as fast as paranormal creatures do. You'd need more people like us or Craven for that. We barely have enough in our Coven to cover Earth, as it is."

Cassie added her thoughts. "We seem to have several problems here. One, we need to find out when and where the first portal opened. Second, how many does General Robertson have in control? Next, how many are in his coven and who are they? What is his objective? How did he open the portal in Saudi Arabia that led to that werewolf dimension? There were no reports of any natural disasters in that whole country going back for the last fifteen years. I know - I checked. And finally, we need to find a way to cover the ground on Kla' din."

"That's a big list, sister. Antonio and Wizard can find out the portal angles. My watcher, hopefully, can give us leads to the vampire portal and others, if the General has them. And next, maybe we can spy on General Robertson for awhile, to find out how big his coven is and who is in it. Also, find out what they are after? Kla' din though; I am stumped on that one, for now. But, I will think on it and hope for a nice, big light bulb."

"We all will, hon." Demitri caressed her hand.

Ja' Monel looked perplexed. "A light bulb? How will this help Kla' din?"

"It's an expression. It means I need an idea. I just wish I could figure a way to keep the Draugrall from even coming in, but until that happens, we need a nice, big ground force for all of your provinces."

"Ahh, I see. Not to worry, Meshama, I am sure something will come up. You are our Meshallima; we will find a way together." His amber eyes grew darker gazing at her.

Demitri started to growl at him.

O'Hara saw that it was time for them to leave, before any fights broke out. "Things can wait, until you are healed. We have time for discussing all this later; right now, we need to get you back in fighting form before we plan our next attack."

Cassie nodded. "He is right; we need you healed before we do anything else, so rest for now, sister."

"Fine, I'll drop it for now. But, once I am healed we will finish this," Cat huffed in frustration.

The General made to leave. "Good, I'll get things in motion then, and O'Hara will make a call to the Captain. Take it easy until then, Cat." He nodded to her and walked out the door. O'Hara trailed behind, with a smile of encouragement to her.

Pearson, however, lingered behind, seeming to want to speak with her about something. The others in the room caught the vibes and made their excuses to leave them with some privacy.

As Ja' Monel made for the door, Cat stopped him. "Ja' Monel." He turned to look at her. She smiled up at him. "Thanks for finding me. I owe you one."

"It was not only my duty, Meshallima, but my pleasure." He shuffled a bit, as if he wanted to add something, but seemed to have thought better of it and continued through the door.

Pearson and Cat were left alone in the room.

"What's on your mind, Pearson?" Cat asked him gently.

He peered at her face. "Can't you tell?"

Giving a small easy shake of her head, "I don't go poking around in another's head if I can help it. We consider it very rude. Bad form, if you will."

His face was full of embarrassment. "Oh, well it's about what you said earlier and how your Goddess is the one you follow because it is right for you." He came and sat next to her bed, pulling the chair close. "I've seen too much evil done by people who say they represent God and Jesus lately. I've read a lot about the history of how the religion got started and now I don't think it is right for me, especially with all the evil connected to it."

She sighed, "So, what you are saying, is because of all the bad things that seems to be directly connected to the church and church-type people, you want to stop believing in God and Jesus, right?"

He had a confused look, but nodded his head.

"Don't give up on God or Jesus just because of a few bad apples, Pearson," she sighed a bit. "OK, a lot of bad apples lately. But, your perception of what God and Jesus is, is what shines the light for that religion. Without people like you, who truly believe there is a God, that there is a Jesus, whatever light that religion has will go out and the bad guys will win." She took his hand and squeezed it. "The only time you should abandon the religion you believe in, is when you are truly called to another path. It may be Buddha, it may be Taoist or many other kinds of religions, but don't leave God and Jesus just because some dipwads use it to hide what they do in the night. That's not a good reason to abandon your faith. Do it only when, and if, you are called to another path. In the meantime, be the light God and Jesus needs you to be to keep the religion good. If you are called to another path, tell God and Jesus 'thank you for being there for me this far. Another calls me right now, but I will always respect you', and then follow your new path. If you are not called to a new path, then you should stay and ask your God for help in seeing how to be not like those others, but a true Christian who loves everyone like Jesus wanted. That's the best thing you could do for you own soul, Pearson." She let go of his hand and nestled back into her covers and waited for Pearson to think of what she said.

"You really don't convert others do you?" he asked.

She shook her head. "No. If a person is meant for a pagan path, they will be called. We have nothing to do with callings; that is up to the Goddess."

His hazel eyes were racked with confusion. "How do you know if you are being called?"

She simply asked, "What does your heart say?" Again, she waited for him to think it though.

"My heart is saying God and Jesus is the right choice for me, for now," his voice filled with feeling.

"Then, that's what you should do." She smiled at him, happy he found his faith again.

"But, there is so much controversy, so many contradictions. You were right about that." He sounded unsure again.

"True, but that is because of man, not God. Man, had free will to give the right message or the wrong one and they will pay for their crimes, I can guarantee that. But, for those who know there is controversy, all you can do is ask God what is true and what isn't. What feels right to you and what doesn't." Her gaze pierced his. "Don't let a third person get in the way of you and God. That's where the mistakes and confusion come into play. You have the one simple basic rule to start with - love everyone. From that, when someone says, 'Oh, homosexuals are evil and against God; ask yourself, is that loving everyone? If the answer is no, then that's your answer. You can apply that one simple rule to everything that is taught. Rarely, will you be steered wrong then, in whatever path you follow."

His face cleared and he gave her a small grin. "Do you love everyone?"

She smiled back at him. "Why, do you want to follow me?" she laughed. "Just kidding." Then, her face grew serious and she answered with mixed emotions of anger and sadness. "No, I don't love everyone. I hate people who hurt kids, I hate people who would make slaves of others and I hate people who hurt other people out of greed or because they are control freaks. The list goes on, but those are the big ones." She looked back up at him. "I don't think I would ever be a very good Goddess. I should stay just as I am."

Pearson laughed at her. "Maybe you should; being all Holy, I just can't picture it of you."

They both laughed together, until the movement caused her to wince.

Seeing she was hurting and surmising she was most likely tired as well, he said, "I should go. Thanks for the advice. You may make a lousy Goddess, but you are good as a High Priestess."

That made her smile. "Thanks."

General Robertson slowed, as he approached his house, seeing the front door wide open and splinters hanging off the side, where the door should have been. The Vampire Prince slowed, too, as he smelled not only blood scent, but the scent of another race he hadn't thought he would ever smell again. Werewolf.

Lowering his dark eyes to the General's furious ones, he said, "My General, it looks as if your sanctuary has been invaded. I wonder what could have happened."

The Prince didn't even try to keep the mockery out of his tone, as he gave another sideways glance to the General. The General's face hardened with anger and he strode forward to see what other damage had been done to his home. Thank the dark God he'd sent his family off on a vacation to The Hampshire's, so they hadn't been home to be caught in the crossfire. He noticed the door had been blown inward, not outwardly. So, she hadn't escaped; someone had rescued her. The question now, was how did they know she was here? The Commander at the base had told him of the arrival of a Special Forces unit that was usually run by General Pierce. Their visit to his base of operations had sparked him into calling together a small force to kidnap Cat. It gave him concrete evidence of what his spy in Saudi Arabia had told him; though his operator there couldn't give him a decent description because of the masks worn by three people in O'Hara's unit. The informant did tell him one of them had to be a woman because of the body outline. Cat had been that woman; Rock and his team had come to get her from his grasp. How the hells they knew where to find her though, was the question. It should have been impossible to trace her to his home. However, they had done it. He swore by his dark God that this wouldn't go unanswered.

The Prince noticed the blood smell getting stronger and saw, as the General did, the bodies of his men he had left behind to guard his prisoner. Prince Barreiro watched the General's every expression, to gather clues to what may have happened here. He didn't like having to deal with this human, who stank of evil blood. But, what choice did him or his people have, when this man held the key to the portal that could give him access to more resources of another world? His people needed too much and soon, for him to be too fastidious about his business partner. He saw salt spread all over the floors in every room; a sure sign of cleansing evil and breaking negative boundaries. He lifted his long dark cloak that covered his 6'4 large frame, to avoid the blood and salt on the floors.

The General continued on his way down a flight of stairs leading to a basement of sorts. Prince Barreiro saw the silver cage with that hated black mesh draped over one side of it. The same kind that covered the portal to his world. Part of the meshing had been ripped, as if by claws. Again, the scent of werewolf was strong here. A whip lay on the floor inside the cage and Prince Barreiro picked it up. The scent of blood was strong on the whip, edged with sharpened metal. He closed his eyes, hiding his fury. He focused, instead, on the scent of the blood on the whip, trying to place its bloodline. He couldn't place the scent with any of the bloodlines he knew of. He tasted the end of one of the strips letting the dried blood melt on his tongue. Even with it dried, it made him shiver in recognition of what this blood did contain. She may not be of any of his bloodlines, but she was vampire and more. This Cat had access to magicks, Prince Barreiro mused; very strong magicks. That was a rare breed, indeed. Magicks in any of his people's bloodline had died out millennia ago. She could be of a descendant so far removed, that only tasting from her neck would give him the family of where she comes from. He looked up and saw the manacles that had held her for a time. Silver, and coated with that black substance used in the meshing, so strong that she couldn't break out by herself. She needed the help of a werewolf and other humans. Hmmm, interesting, she trusts some humans, but obviously not this one. She also runs with werewolves who were willing to aid her. That tidbit was very interesting. He ran his hand through his thick black hair. There must be a way to find this female.

"Well?" came a gruff voice from the corner. The General was standing next to the decapitated corpse of one of his men.

"She may be one of ours after all; but to be sure, I'll need to take blood from her neck, myself. It is the only way to be hundred percent sure. I won't accept anything less." The Prince hated setting this female up for yet another trap, but this human mage was the only one who could remove that cursed mesh from the portal. The Prince needed some way of getting to her. His people had no hope, if this human wizard found out his people held no true magick. Fear of what he and his tribe of vampires might possibly be able to do, was the only thing that kept them free from this dark adept and his black coven, so far.

If that threat ever lost its hold, The Prince feared what might happen afterwards. "I have her scent now, as well as her blood in my body. Give me leave to search your world and I will find her." His dark eyes pierced the gaze of the General, willing him to let him go search for her by himself, without this dark adept hounding his heels. If it wasn't for the fact General Robertson had demanded the possession of his young niece in return for allowing him to come see this female vampire Robertson had claimed he had, The Prince would have just simply killed him and searched for her, regardless. Unfortunately, his niece guaranteed his behavior for the time being.

"Not yet. I have one more ace up my sleeve. She may be gone from here, but I still have a way of getting to her. Thanks to my informant who is close to where she lives, I've been able to gather a lot of information on her," he was boasting again. "I'll make a call and have another trap set for her by tomorrow evening."

The Prince gave the General a half mocking grin. "And if this, too, doesn't capture our Cat?"

The General's eyes turned hateful. "Then, with certain guarantees, I may just give you that leave to find her and see if you can live up to your boast."

The Prince hoped the General failed. Then, maybe the plan he had, would have a good chance of working and this human will receive the wish he had been hoping for - the bite of vampire teeth in his neck. Though, the Prince didn't think this human would like the outcome.

Clarissa Lee Moon

Chapter Ten

Rocking at the Nightwolves Lair

The door to Cat's hospital room opened again sometime later with Rock walking in quietly. "Is she asleep?" he asked Demitri, who was nearest to her.

I opened my eyes and looked up at Rock's face. "No, she isn't, and yes, she can answer her own questions, sheesh. What's up?"

"Oh, well, I just wanted to check on you and let you know that I spoke to my buddy in Okinawa a few hours ago and he set things up for us. They left shortly after the conversation. They should be here in five hours or so."

His face still looked concerned, so I pressed, "Anything else?"

I had never seen him shuffle the way he did, but something must be up; he kept looking over to Demitri, as if asking him a silent question. Demitri just ignored him with a slightly guilty look.

I warned them both, "Ok, spit it out you guys. Something is up. Spill it, or I'll get cranky."

Demitri gave Rock a threatening glare. "Don't. She's been through enough."

Lowering my voice to show I meant business, I replied, "Too late. I know there is something and if I have to get out of this bed, I am going to kick some ass."

Demitri glowered at Rock as if to say 'see what you did.'

Demitri moved off the bed and started to pace. Demitri wasn't a pacer; that was Andre's habit, so it must be big.

"Well, are you gonna tell her or leave it to me?" Rock gave Demitri the chance to explain things. "She ought to know."

My mate sighed and stopped pacing, placing his hands behind his back. "Fine, since she won't let go of it now, anyway." He seemed to be really uneasy. "Craven has another form. It's a Dire Wolf. He let it loose earlier and busted through the house getting to you." Turning his gaze and narrowing his eyes at Rock, "I didn't want to say anything until you were cured of this new curse, damn it. It could have waited."

Shell shocked, I looked to Demitri. "He did what? He's a what?"

"Dire Wolf. He has another form, apparently, when he is really fucking pissed. He changed into a Dire Wolf." Demitri sat down heavily and waited for the fireworks.

I closed my eyes tightly. "Sweet Mother Goddess, please tell me he didn't kill any innocents?"

"No, only the bad guys. In fact, I saw him seem reluctant to go through Cassie when she was trying to block his way into the house. If he lacked full control, he would have mowed right over her. It would have been too easy; he is fucking huge as a Dire Wolf," Rock was quick to assure me.

"A Dire Wolf? It's in the legends. We talked about it, but it's been months. We thought, since he never shifted into that form before now, it wouldn't be a problem. Dire Wolves are fucking notorious for losing control and going on rampages." I tried sitting up and hissed in pain. "Fuck, I hate being hurt. A Dire Wolf? Are you sure there was no mistake? Is he ok? Where is he?"

I moved, as if to get off the bed and go check for myself, when Demitri stopped me. "No, you can't get out of bed. Craven is fine and down at the Lair eating rare steaks like they're going out of style. He's all right. We have guards on all the boys and we're keeping a close watch. It did take him longer to shift back from Dire Wolf form than it did with his normal werewolf form." He pushed me back in bed and tried to settle me in.

"What happened to debriefing, Rock?" I asked, as Demitri fussed over me.

Rock sighed and looked like he was wishing he was anywhere else but here. "Debriefing got put on hold and everyone was given leave early."

Demitri growled, "Goddamn it Rock, can't this shit wait?"

"No, it fucking can't." Raising his voice, he said, "She is a leader, as am I, and if it were me in that bed, I would still want to fucking know what the hell is going on with my men. Your people are hurting too, and she ought to know about it."

Alarmed, I asked, "What the fuck are you two talking about? What's wrong with our people? Whose people?"

"The Nightwolves - period," Rock rubbed his face as if he was already tired. "They are demoralized and kicking their own asses. I was about to head down to the Lair to make sure no extra fights break out."

"That's it. Demitri, go get Cassie. I need her now." I pushed him away.

"You can't be serious. Tell me you are not going?" Demitri pleaded.

My expression was resolute. "Oh, yes, I am going. I need that doctor guy in here, too. Snap to it babe, or I'll just get bitchy about it."

Demitri saw the look in my face and knew a lost battle when he saw it. "Fine, but damn it, don't do anything stupid, ok?"

"I won't," I reassured him, "but, they do really need us down there. This isn't good for our people, hon, neither military, nor Merc. The Nightwolves as a whole could fracture if we don't put a Band-Aid on this before it festers. Trust me."

Demitri still didn't get how serious this was. "How could waiting five more hours be such a problem?"

Exasperated, I tried to explain. "Hon, this is a fighting family and if we let this go for too long, it could have some long acting repercussions mentally and in the field. They could lose confidence. They could lose their faith in our ability to fight and win, even when things look bleak. No, this has to be fixed right now." I swung my eyes over at Rock and frowned at him. "YOU should have told me earlier." I sighed, "I understand why you didn't, but help me get ready now. Move it, both of you," I snapped. For once, they just went and did what I wanted.

Demitri went to get Cassie, while Rock went to fetch the doctor.

An hour later, I was ready to go to the bar, oh joy. I moved stiffly under my leather jacket. I had Cassie rush to my house and bring me certain clothes to wear. This one shirt I had was black silk with just two tie straps for the back, which was otherwise open. The doctor put a big, huge gauze pad on my back with antibiotic ointment smeared in it. That way, the gauze wouldn't become glued to the drying blood that would seep from the wounds. Between the backless shirt and the gauze pad, my jacket shouldn't rub open my wounds and it should hide the fact that I was wounded. I had to wear hip huggers though, because some of the cuts went all the way down to the small of my back. I had looked hard in finding a belt that could hold my blades on a pair of hip huggers, when shopping with Cassie months ago. I had to reach a bit deeper in my stance to draw the knives, but it worked. My boots weren't a problem, but, if I had to bend to get a knife from my boot tops tonight, I was going to seriously consider screaming. Cassie had to put my boot knives in for me. It was a bit embarrassing, but I could live with it. A little make- up hid the black and blue on my jaw and ice had reduced the swelling inside my mouth. Through the whole thing, I kept wishing something good would happen, to help me get the Nightwolves' optimism back. A unit that has lost its heart, made for The Reapers target practice and we couldn't leave things as they were. I turned to Cassie and handed her my brush. There was no way I could brush my own hair and not tear out stitches.

She gently brushed out my hair, while Demitri was busy fuming in the corner. Ja' Monel even came in, after feeling that Demitri was pissed off, to see what was wrong. I think Demitri had a hope that Ja' Monel would be able to talk me out of it. But, as I explained the situation to him, he narrowed his eyes and just took off his head wrap and announced he was coming along, as well.

Demitri snorted, saying under his breath something to the effect of kissing ass. Ja' Monel just turned to look at him with his amber colored eyes and said, "If you think about it, you'll understand what Meshallima has to do. It is only her pain you are upset about. But, we both can make this easier for her, in doing what we can to shoulder as much of her responsibilities as possible." He ran his fingers through his blond hair, smoothing it out. He was gorgeous with his amber eyes flashing.

Demitri sighed and I could tell from his stance he was giving in. "I really think you could've waited for another four hours, but if you must do it now, at least he'll be there for you. I will wait and bring Ja' Callum to you. I don't want to wait one extra unnecessary minute in curing you of this."

I smiled at him, gazing into his deep brown eyes. My heart stopped beating for a moment; this man really loved me. "That would really help me out, love."

The Nightwolves Lair did have an air of despondency when we walked in. There was hardly anyone laughing or joking around. No one moved from table to table to visit each other, sharing some story or joke they had just heard. What conversations that were going on were quiet and subdued. Oh, this wasn't good. When I was seen, I would carefully wave to people and smile a greeting. A few made their way over to ask how I was and I told them I was fine. This seemed to cheer them up a bit. I kept moving through to the back room where the dancing was done and the family get-together table was located. I made my way to where Christoph and his brothers were seated in the families' favorite corner-benched table. It could seat thirteen or more people, depending on how we arranged the chairs on the outside of the table.

There was another booth set up like this one on the opposite side of the room, but we preferred the one in the east corner. It was right in front of the dance floor, where beyond that, was the stage for anyone who wanted to entertain. The stage had plenty of instruments and a lighting system, as well as a karaoke box off to the side. There was also a DJ booth on the other side for those that wanted that kind of atmosphere. The place was tricked out and no one was playing anything.

Rock and I looked at each other with grim expressions on our faces.

Rock nodded towards the table, where my boys were sitting. "I'll take the troops; you take the kids and work your way up." Once they saw their mom strolling over, they jumped up in shocked surprise.

"Mom, are you ok? They fixed you already?" Christoph asked me, about ready to give me a hug. I stopped his movement and held him off with a slight shake of my head. He got the idea and a glum look came over his face. "Mom, what the fuck are you doing out of the Nightwolves Wing then?"

I gave him a tight smile. "Doing my job, as I need you to do yours. Help me get your brothers and cousins up there on that stage and turn it out."

His jaw dropped open for a moment. "You've got to be kidding."

"No, I am not. These guys need a good feeling boost. Look around. It's a Goddamn funeral parlor here. We've got to fix this for the Nightwolves." I gripped his arms as he shook his head. "Ok, I'll do what I can." He walked off to find the rest of the cousins who'd shown up tonight.

I picked my voice up, "Craven, front and center." He came over to me. "Go get your 'cuz. Get the system up and running. I want my favorite songs playing, ok?"

"You got it, Mom." His eyes grew serious. "Are you all right? I still smell blood."

"I heard you're a Dire Wolf, too." I switched the topic. "How's your control in that form?"

"Pretty good, so long as I am not too mad. Things go red, if I am overly pissed and it's harder not to bite anyone in my way, but other than that, it's cool." His face got bright with excitement. "The freedom in that form is awesome. The power flowing through me is immense."

Oh, joy, he found a new toy. And the silver cage won't hold him either. I inwardly sighed, 'We be fucked'. I shook my head and put that problem off for another time. Right now, we needed to regain the Nightwolves' morale.

"Go get people to sing son and do your thing up there, too." He almost hugged me and then he remembered my wounds. He just pecked my cheek as he went to find more people to play on stage.

"Crimson." He moved up in front of me, his eyes searching my face for something.

Whatever he saw reassured him, because he then focused on what I was saying. "Please go help get the lighting and mics set up for play." He didn't say anything, just moved off to what I'd asked.

One of the bouncers came up and whispered in my ear, "We have a situation outside that I think you ought to handle." I gave him a concerned look, but his face only showed an amused secret type of grin.

Well, this was odd. "Fine, let's go," I told him and let him lead the way to the door. It was dark outside and there were three long customized buses parked out front that I could see. One of the drivers, I had presumed, was casually lounging against the side of one of the buses. He spotted me, straightened up and walked over to me.

He outstretched his hand for a shake. "Hi, I'm Dusty Grover, manager for Silverback. We were wondering if we could come in and hang out until the repair truck can come out and fix one of our buses that broke down not too far from here."

I nodded my head to him and he put down his hand with an unsure smile on his face. Did he say Silverback?

They were my all time favorite rock band. The ultimate feel good party band rocking today. They'd named themselves after the Silverback Wolves that are on the endangered species list. They even had the wolf emblem on their albums. It was one of my favorite charities to give to, to help that particular breed of wolves recover.

To ease the rejection of not shaking his hand, I smiled, and said, "This is a private club for the Nightwolves. You might want to reconsider hanging out here if you really represent Silverback. Things get a bit rowdy from time to time in there. I won't lie." Although, inside I was going, 'Oh boy, Silverback, WOW!', I had to put our secrets and the safety of the band first, before anything else.

With Craven now having to learn to control a new form, things could get dicey real quick. I knew he shifted when angry, but would he shift when excited? He would get excited over this rock group coming in. Anyone would, but would it trigger his shift? If it did, having a famous rock band witness the transformation could expose us in ways we would never be able to cover up.

Two guys came off the bus and I recognized Todd Castle, lead singer for Silverback and his brother Dave, the lead guitarist. Yup, this guy Dusty wasn't lying; he really did represent the band.

Our bouncer for the night leaned in and whispered, "See why I thought you should handle this?" The bugger knew I loved the group and would play their songs all the time in the box, or dance to my favorite ones.

Rock came out of the club and stood next to me. "I thought you might need some backup, but what's this?"

He was worried about me fighting with my wounds, but that wasn't necessary with this group; they just wanted to hang. Under a normal situation, that would be cool but...I filled him in and he had a thoughtful look on his face.

Todd was walking over with his brother and saw Rock's uniform. "Special Forces?" he queried.

Rock nodded an affirmation for him.

Dusty cut in, "And you're a Nightwolf? She said this place was for the Nightwolves. Is that like some Special Forces squad or something?"

"We're all Nightwolves here," Rock's gravel voice grew firm.

"Even her?" Todd's brother asked, looking at my street clothes and black leather jacket.

Rock got a hard look on his face. "Yes, even her. She is also a team leader and one of the best fighters I have ever served with."

Rock was a bit touchy tonight. I put my hand on his shoulder and gave him a gentle squeeze thinking, 'over protective big brother much?'

"Cool, nice to meet you," Todd said. "What's your name?" The question may have been for both of us, but I answered. "Cat, and this is Rock. It's great to meet you, but like I was trying to tell your manager, Dusty there, things can get rough and we would be responsible if anything happened to your guys in there."

"I'm sure we can handle anything in there. We really just want some food and some beer. Just to kick back and relax; none of us will start any trouble," Todd's brother, Dave, assured us and Dusty was nodding in agreement. "It's been a long trip and we would like to get off those buses for a while."

I sighed heavily and went to run my hand through my hair and tugged some stitches.

I winced and let down my arm slowly. "Listen, we would love to have you, but we just got off a mission that was rough. Some of the men are running on edge and anything can set these guys off right now. And, I'm talking about, in a real bad way." Like Dire Wolf bad, but I couldn't tell them that.

"Sorry to hear that," Todd said. "We have an uncle that's a vet. We know how bad it can get. Maybe a song would cheer them up and they wouldn't be so cagey?"

I smiled, "Singing for your supper, eh?"

He grinned, "That's what singers used to do in the old days." I was impressed. He was smart and talented.

I looked at Rock, who shrugged his shoulder. "It could be good for morale...?" he suggested.

I was thinking that, too. I turned to our bouncer and said, "Go see if Craven can handle it."

He took off inside to track my son down and prepare him, so he'd have a better chance of holding it together. He was the main one I was worried about.

"Give us a sec and we'll see if we can accommodate you all," I said to the three of them. I knew more would be on the bus. These guys had an entourage like most of the elite did. The bouncer came back out with a grin on his face.

"OK, if you guys are sure about this, there are a few rules we have here that must be obeyed for your safety and others." I looked them all the eyes. "Make sure you pass it around to the rest of those who'll be coming in. Number one - any females in there, do not touch. They have mates that will rip your heads off for trying." Dusty was about to say something and I held up my hand. "Two - we'll be posting a guard for your section, so we can keep our rowdies away from you and you can eat in peace. Three - any problems with our people in there, and Rock and I will take care of it.

If you guys can live with that, then come on in. We have great steaks."

"Are the other women in there Nightwolves, too?" Dusty looked curious.

"Yes, as are their mates. Everyone in there is a Nightwolf. Try not to piss anybody off." I grinned evilly. I looked to the bouncer. "Yellow Alert and keep it on 'till every one of them has left."

He nodded and Dusty looked even more curious, as he watched the bouncer hit a yellow colored button on our alert panel. I led their group to the tables we usually used. It would give me the advantage of keeping anyone else from bugging them and a watchful eye on the floor.

As they all sat down, I told them, "What you are about to see, I know, is pretty amateur night for you all, but we have fun and it might help raise the guys spirits in here. Once you've eaten and relaxed for a while, if you want to do a song or two, fine. If not, don't worry about it. Just make my job easy and stay within this range here, so I can be saved on paperwork."

Actually, Rock did the paperwork, but they didn't have to know that. They were really nice about agreeing to the rules. A waitress come over and nervously took their orders.

Craven took the mic first, and being a bit nervous, he had a rocky start. Once he and his cousin got into it, they did pretty damn good, I thought. The band members clapped and hollered their appreciation. Whether they really liked it or were just being nice, I couldn't tell, but it was cool. The time went by and Craven dragged me up for my turn, but gently, in mind of my wounds. I did a few of my favorites with Cassie. The men paid attention tonight, more so then any other night, and I poured my heart into my songs for them. So they would know this didn't beat me. I was still standing and we were together as a family. We were Nightwolves. It seemed to help, as more smiles broke out among them. When I was done, I turned the mic over to the next person.

I walked back down to take over as guard for the rock group, though it looked like they did have a few of their own bouncers with them. They clapped as I walked near them and I did a very careful bow. A small fight broke out as I got close to their table. I could see Rock barreling from the bar where he was keeping an eye on Dusty, who had ambled over to get himself a drink.

"Wolves APART," I ordered. They were past listening, so I got in the middle, grabbing each by their collars and physically pulled them apart, using vamp strength to hold them. I felt stitches rip and start to bleed, but I was too pissed to care.

"What the fuck do you think you two are doing fighting so near this section? What did I say?" shaking them both.

"Not to fight with them here; but he said we were fucked, if they could take you and do what they did to you," one of the soldiers started to explain.

"Silence," I said quietly. Rock had come with Dusty trailing behind him.

"What happened?" Rock asked me.

I let go of the men with a warning look. "These two fought in this section with the yellow light on."

All the signal lights in the bar were still flashing yellow. That meant the utmost caution was to be taken, because we had people in the bar for whatever reason that were not Nightwolves. No one was supposed to talk about things, nor act out of line, until they had left and the light went off.

Rock turned to the other soldier. "Want to explain yourself, Ensign?"

"They got her. HER. I heard what they did, we all did. She has never been taken before and not kicked ass. If they can do that, then what chance ..." he looked nervously over to the table where they were definitely listening "if they could...Fuck, Rock, they hurt her bad this time."

I stopped him before he could say anymore. "Listen, you came and got me out. I am alive. It will heal. Next time, we'll be better prepared and we will kick some major ass in payback. Now, both of you to the staffroom with Rock. Rock, shrink them if you have to."

"That's what this group is missing, you know. I've been thinking about that," he admitted and walked off with the two men.

"Me too," I sighed heavily. How can any of these guys go to counseling on the base when they wouldn't be able to talk about half of the shit they've been through? Kind of hard to get any real help, when most of what's in your head has to be kept secret. Maybe there was a shrink in the family? I'd have to ask Demitri to check around.

"Hey, Cat," Dusty looked nervous.

I gave him my attention. "Yes, how can I help you?"

He pointed to my waist. "You're bleeding pretty badly."

I looked down on my right side, and sure enough, blood was dripping down onto the floor from the edge of the bandage under my jacket. "Shit."

Todd looked concerned. "What can we do to help?"

I scanned the room and saw Ja' Monel. I gave him a mental SOS and he quickly made his way over.

"Not to worry Todd, I've got someone coming to help. Thanks, though," keeping my tone even and pleasant.

Ja' Monel did not seem pleased. "Meshallima, you've torn your stitching."

"We're in public; call me Cat," I corrected him.

He snorted and examined the damage as best he could, without exposing too much to the public eye.

The waitress was walking by and I stopped her. "Get me some towels. We have a problem."

She glanced down and left quickly when she saw it was blood. We couldn't leave the blood unattended, in case someone grabbed a sample or something. I didn't think these guys would, but still, security demanded I cover my traces first, then patch myself up, in this type of scenario.

The wound I'd received on the airplane was different, in that I had to stop the blood from leaking anywhere else, before I could go clean up what had gotten spilled. Here, if I moved, I would leave a blood trail, and run the risk of letting someone get a sample or even someone stepping in it, trailing it to other places where I would have no control in getting it cleaned up.

She came back fast enough and took a towel to the floor and Ja' Monel placed a folded one over my leak, so no more blood would spill out. Dusty was watching the whole thing with an interested air about him, but I couldn't worry about it right then. I needed the blood replaced, and fast.

Once the blood was wiped up and my blood loss staunched, we headed for the staffroom.

"Man, I am telling you, something is weird about this place," Dusty said, as he bent close to the group at the table.

"How do you figure?" Dave asked him, bending closer to keep their voices from being overheard.

"Things just feel 'off', you know. Conversations stop when I get near the others. They are definitely soldiers though, but like none I have ever seen before," Dusty told them.

Todd threw in his opinion. "If I hadn't seen that little lady pick the two soldiers up off the ground that were fighting, like they were nothing, I wouldn't have believed it myself."

Dusty nodded. "Yeah, and did you see how they treated her when she was wounded? They were more concerned over the blood then the wound itself. That's weird."

Todd looked at him. "Can you find out more?"

Dusty had a plan. "Maybe, if you guys go play. It will distract them and give me a chance to chat someone up. Right now, they always have someone trailing me wherever I go, but if you guys are playing, I might be able to find out what's what around here."

"Cool. We said we would play anyway." They got up from the table and moved over to the stage.

Dusty moved towards the bar, where a likely young lad who might not be so closed-mouth might give him some information.

Rock found one of the medics in the bar and brought him in to reclose my wounds. Then, one by one, men came in to feed me, since I seemed to be needing a lot more blood than usual. Ja' Monel was upset that I wouldn't feed from him again, since he had already donated just yesterday when they came and rescued me. He may not be of Earth, and his stamina may be more than regular humans, but I figured to err on the side of caution, when taking blood from someone from Kla' din; same as I do with humans. I could hear the band playing a few of their songs and I was missing it, damn it. Figures, I would miss my favorite band because of some stupid darksiders, I grumbled to myself, biting into another wrist for more blood. I was so thirsty. It took a long time for me to feel even half way decent, and by then, the band had stopped playing. Well, at least I'd gotten to hear it second hand, in a way. That was cool; I tried to perk myself up.

"So, what did you find out?" Todd could see Dusty was practically jumping in his seat.

"You won't believe it." The three of them huddled in. "Vampires, werewolves and Special Forces, oh, my," Dusty whispered to them.

"What the fuck you talking about, man?" Dave sounded surprised. Dusty always got the dirt for them wherever they went. That was part of his job, but this shit couldn't be true.

"She is vampire, one of her sons is a werewolf, a few of the others are extraordinary, as well, and then you mix Special Forces and an alpha recon platoon and you've got some serious twilight zone shit." Dusty looked fit to burst with his news.

"There aren't any real vampires," Todd told him. "Only fuckin' lawyers with lawsuits are vampires."

Dusty had a smug look. "Oh, yeah? See that soldier right there? Look at his wrist." They looked, and saw two puncture holes on the side.

Todd dismissed it. "So, what? He might have gotten that fighting or something."

"He just came from the staffroom where they took her to treat her." Dusty pointed to another soldier. "Look - that other guy who just came out. Try to catch a look at his wrist."

They did, and for just a split second, they saw that he, too, sported two puncture marks on his wrist.

"Whoa, this is some weird shit," Todd had to admit.

Dave just sat back and said in a low voice, "Ok, I'm convinced, but if she were bad, they wouldn't be coming out all right. It looks like she just needs a bit and it's all right. I don't think Special Forces would support some rampaging vamp...or werewolf, for that matter."

"Oh, it gets better." Dusty still had more to tell them. "This bar is owned by a family of Mercenaries and they are the ones who work with the Special Forces and marines at a base near here. Apparently, they take out terrorists and other bad paranormal shit together. Jointly, they all are called Nightwolves. Get it...wolves."

They looked at him like he might have gotten too stoned or something, but he shook his head. "Nope, I only had two drinks, chatting up that young kid, who is brand spanking new tonight. Some distant cousin of the mercenary family, hoping to find his way in earning his own Nightwolves tattoo. He thought we were also part of the family from some other branch and spilled everything to me, not knowing he ain't supposed to talk," he said, shrugging his shoulders. "At least, that's the feeling I got, 'cause when I asked his uncle questions, who does have a tattoo, by the way, he just said, 'Can't answer that one. Go ask Cat,' and what would I like to drink. That's was all I could get out of him."

Todd was shaking his head back and forth like he couldn't believe it. "This is some extreme assed shit. You sure about this?" Dusty had never steered them wrong before, but this was hard to take.

Dusty just nodded his head. "Man, straight up, no shit. Word for fucking word, that's what the kid told me."

Dave whistled. "Terrorists and shit. More paranormal stuff? Like they are the good ones and they fight the bad ones? Whoa, that's...shit. What do we do?" They knew that finding out top secret military stuff like this could get everyone involved killed. The government or military never messed around when it came to this shit. Their uncle warned them about that kind of thing, many, many times during his old war stories from his tour in 'Nam.

Dave got their attention. "Heads up, man. She's coming back."

Clarrissa Lee Moon

Chapter Eleven

Rock 'n Roll and Hide

𝕴 moved over to the table, waving at the ones who'd helped and mouthing a thank you at them, as I passed by. As I got near the band's table, things felt a bit off. A few of them were looking at me with a now uneasy gaze, whereas before, they'd looked more open and friendly. Maybe they were upset or thought I'd dissed them, because I wasn't present for their playing.

"Hi. I am really sorry I missed your set, but things had to be seen to. I heard it though, and it sounded great, as you guys always do." I wasn't bullshitting them either; they always did sound great.

Todd smiled uneasily. "Thanks. Are you all right?"

I smiled back warmly. "Yes, thanks for asking. Nothing major; it's all cool now." I made like it was just a scratch.

Dusty looked up at me. "Did you get wounded on your last mission?" Dave hit him on the shoulder.

My gaze narrowed a bit. "Just a stupid fall, nothing really." I again smiled at him. He was making me lie and I didn't like that much. I was about to scan him when I realized there was movement going fast and furious all around the bar.

"Hey, what's with the red lights?" Todd asked.

I looked up, and sure enough, the red lights were flashing. Red light meant all mercenaries had to scram out of the club. I could see the front door and that fucking General Robertson was there with soldiers at his back, bullying his way in through the door. I went cold inside and froze for several precious seconds that I should have been using to vanish. But like a deer caught in the headlights, I just couldn't move for some reason. Cold sweat was pouring down my face and neck, stinging the wounds on my upper back.

Todd, who was sitting the closest to me, reached over and touched my hand. "Hey, are you all right?"

I started babbling, "No, I am dead. If that man finds me, I am dead. I have to go. He's the bad guy."

I made to move and Todd stopped me. "Hey, look at me." I looked down at him and seeing his calm, cool blue eyes, I took a deep breath to stop from hyperventilating any further. I was able to think again. If I moved now, to one of the escape hatches, the General would see me.

I felt that instinct of mine kick in again and saw I only had one other choice in front of me. "Look, I know this is going to seem really fucking weird, but can you guys pretend I am a groupie or something and never mind the magick."

Dusty and the rest had a shocked look on their faces, as I used glamour to make myself look like a big busted pretty girl with blond hair and big green eyes.

I smiled at Todd. "Is this seat taken?" He was too shocked at the change to answer. I just sat down in his lap and wrapped my arms around his neck.

I bent near his ear to whisper, "This isn't our General. If this particular General finds me, he will finish what he started on me and I will die. A lot of us will die tonight. We need you all to be stand up guys and help us out. Can you do that?" The other two heard what I asked him and gave Todd a nod. Todd swallowed, and said, "Man, this is going to make for some cool songs."

"You guys won't ever be able to tell anyone about us for at least a year and half anyway. If we're all still alive, then it won't matter. If we're dead, it still won't matter. But for now, we need silence. Can you all give us that?"

They looked around at each other, then at me. Dusty spoke for them. "Are you really a vamp?"

Shocked that he knew that much, I just answered him, "Sort of."

Dusty looked confused. "How can you be, 'sort of'?"

I looked towards the door. "No time. Can you give us your word?"

Todd hugged me to him. "Yes, we can."

"Good; know this - making an oath to one of my kind, and then reneging, has a way of making the magick really mess you up. So, keep your word, please. I would hate for anything to happen to any of you."

Then, we were out of time.

"Who are you people?" General Robertson barked at the group.

Shaking like a leaf, I pasted a big smile on my face. "Rock stars, baby. Don't you know anything?"

He grunted, "What are you doing in a military bar?"

"What does it look like?" I rolled my eyes at him. "Eating and playing here, big daddy. Who are you?"

General Robertson looked at me with a bit of anger in his eyes. "That's none of your business, little lady. You will all need to leave now."

"Well fine, if that's what you want." I did my best Barbie look and huffed out the door, dragging Todd along behind me. I knew the rest of his people would follow right along.

We got outside and I was feeling really dizzy, with trying to hold the glamour for so long. I remembered Shamus telling me I wasn't supposed to do any magick for a long time and I had created even more wounds in my brain when I'd fought so hard to get loose magickally from the silver cage the General had me in.

We got inside the bus and the driver started it up and got us moving right along. I was reeling, by the time we got to the end of the block and I dropped my glamour.

"Shit", Todd was taken by surprise again. "How do you do that?"

"Magick," I answered simply. I was so tired. "How much do you know about us?"

"Not everything, but a bit. Things seemed off in there. Why'd that General dude want you dead?" Todd looked curious.

"He, and black covens like his, are trying to take over the world," I giggled, then shook my head to clear it.

"You're not making any sense," Todd reached up and touched my face, "and you're not looking so hot there, babe."

"Funny, I am burning up." I stood up to remove my jacket, when the floor rushed up to meet my face.

"Shit, Cat passed out," Todd said, and was worried, since she'd just keeled right over.

Dave moved over and tried to help move her to the couch.

"Let's get this jacket off her so she can breathe easier. Maybe that will help."

Dave went to unzip the jacket the rest of the way.

Together, they carefully wrestled the jacket off, knowing she was hurt, but wanting to get some cool air on her body.

"Oh, fuck, man!" Dave exclaimed. Then they saw the huge blood-soaked gauze covering her whole back.

Todd's lips went tight with rage. He hated to see any woman hurt like this. Now he didn't care if she was vamp, or what; she was hurt and that was all that mattered to him right now.

"Check her jacket for I.D., numbers or something. We can't take her back to the bar, but we need to get her help," Todd ordered his brother and he lifted off the top of the bandage and saw the wounds. He sat back down, taking deep breaths.

Dave saw Todd breathing heavily. "Bro, what's wrong?"

"Someone carved her fucking back." He couldn't finish, it was just too horrid.

Dave took a look. "Fucking eh, man. How the fuck could she move like it didn't bother her?" He lifted the bottom. "Shit, look at this."

Todd looked. "Someone shot her right through. That's what bled so badly on the dance floor."

They both knew what a gunshot wound looked like. Their uncle taught them much. They, themselves, had seen too much, as well.

"Hey, here's a cell phone." Dave handed it to Todd.

Todd looked at it, then hit speed dial one; always a good place to start on a cell phone of someone you didn't know.

A man's voice answered, "Hey, sweetheart, how you doing?"

"I'm not your sweetheart, but if her name is Cat, she needs someone she can trust right now," Todd informed him.

"Why, what happened and how did you get her phone?" The voice went deadly cold to Todd's ear.

"She passed out in our bus. How do we know you are a friend of hers?" Todd was getting cautious and protective over Cat. He didn't want her to wind up in worse condition then she already was.

"I am her mate. Why isn't she at the bar and how did she wind up on your... bus, you said?" He sounded worried now for Cat.

Todd nodded to himself, this is better. "Some General dude came in and she froze up real bad. Like she was scared. She asked us to help get her out of there and then she did something kind of weird, then we got her out. When we got on the bus, she passed out." He was unwilling to say she did magick and made herself look like another woman. He was still trying to wrap his head around that one.

"Not General Pierce, another General?" the man who called himself her mate asked.

"I don't know, she just said he would finish what he'd started with her. Is that General the one who did that shit to her back?"

"Shit. You can't let him find her. Please, don't let that psycho find Cat," her mate begged.

Todd could hear the fear in his voice now. Fear for Cat. Yeah, this dude will help her. He may not understand everything that was going on, but he'd be damn if he'd stand by and let a woman get hurt.

"It's cool, but she looks like she is in a bad way." He told her mate. It sounded like he and someone else were moving through halls at a fast pace.

"Where are you now?" the man asked Todd.

"We're going West on S. Padre Island Dr. from the bar, about ten miles from the 286."

"Good, keep going until you hit the 286. There's a gas station on the South side corner. Stop only if there is no one on your tail. That General may have you followed for awhile. We're on our way. This is going to sound weird, but in the meantime, there is only one thing you can do to keep her alive until we reach her." It sounded, to Todd's ear, like he was now running.

"What's that?" Todd was all for keeping her alive.

Todd heard the guy sigh. "You need to feed her blood. Make a small cut on your wrist and put it to her mouth."

"You're kidding me?" But, he sort-of knew that was coming.

"No. If you don't, we may not reach her in time." The dude's tone was dead serious.

"Ok, man, we'll do it; just get here soon." Todd hung up. "Bro, get the guns out."

"Sure, but why?" His brother always had his back no matter what, but he still needed to know.

Todd was looking at her tattoo and remembered the Special Forces dude who was protective of her. Todd made up his mind. "Because, that fucking General isn't going to get her back if we can help it."

He took his out blade from his pocket and cleaned off the edge on his pants. He made a small cut, and put the now bleeding wrist to Cat's mouth. Her teeth came down and bit into him.

"Whoa, does it hurt?" Dave asked him, as he rifled through the back of the compartments, getting out the guns and ammo for them.

"Not bad; kind of kinky, actually." Todd smiled a bit.

Dusty moved in to help Dave. "Dudes, I hope you know what you're doing. They may just kill us for knowing too much after we help them."

Todd shook his head. "Nah, I don't think it will go down like that. We just need to keep her safe, until they can come get her. We should never talk about this to anyone, though. Ever. Uncle Marcus taught us that much."

Dave was nodding his agreement and loading ammo into a shot gun.

Dusty shook his head. "Man, we could make a fortune, though. But, you're right. It ain't worth our lives," adding ammo to another gun.

Todd started to feel a bit light headed and removed his wrist from her mouth. "Dave, I think she needs more and I'm getting dizzy." Todd shook his head to clear it.

Dave moved up and sat down next to her. Since her teeth were down, he just put his wrist to her mouth and she bit down automatically.

He winced at the sharp pain, but then relaxed into it. "You're right; kind of kinky."

Todd snorted and took another gun to load it up.

Sometime later, they were at the spot her mate told them to wait. Seeing on how no one was behind them, they pulled over and waited for whoever these people were.

Both of them used the first aid kit to wrap their wrists and then they heard the sounds of motorcycles coming toward them from the road. They both picked up their guns, placing themselves between Cat and the door, taking aim if anyone hostile came through. Dusty and a few trusted security guys were already outside, waiting by the door. They, too, had their guns out and aimed at the riders.

The brothers heard the Harleys stop and Dusty yelling at them to prove who they were. It must have convinced him, because Dusty let them through without a shot. The door opened up and two men, with their hands in the air, moved inside slowly.

One had dark hair and the other was blond. "Which of you guys is her mate?" Todd asked.

Looking at each other, the dark one shrugged, "Both of us are, actually."

Todd was taken by surprise again. "Both?"

"Please, we're running out of time. Let us get to her," the dark one asked him.

The brothers could hear the desperation in his tone and allowed him through to Cat.

The blond one lifted the bandage on her back and growled, "The one who did this, dies at my hand."

The dark one responded, "You'll have to beat me to it, Ja' Callum." They both, very carefully, lifted her bandages off. Then, they took a sharp pair of scissors and started cutting her stitches out.

"Man, why are you doing that? She ain't healed enough for that, yet," Dave asked them, shocked they were doing this so early. Usually stitches came out after seven days and those looked like they had just been put in.

"Trust us. We know what we're doing," the dark one assured the brothers. "My name is Demitri, by the way, and this is Ja' Callum."

They all nodded at each other and Demitri went back to work.

Once they were done removing her stitches, the one called Ja' Callum took a blue bottle out of his jacket and started to chant.

The bottle began to glow, and both Todd and Dave looked at each other, eyes wide at the sight. Dusty was watching from the door, amazed at the light show, himself. When Ja' Callum was done chanting, he poured the liquid out onto her back in drips all along the deeper cuts. Then, he took a bit of it and put it in her mouth, making her swallow.

She started to convulse a bit, then settled down. "Ah, look my brother Demitri, she heals now."

Demitri peered at the wounds and saw they were indeed closing. The blood loss had stopped. He clapped Ja' Callum's shoulder in salute, grinning from ear to ear. Todd and Dave peered over their shoulders and witnessed it for themselves, as well.

"Hey, that's too cool," Todd remarked in awe.

Demitri looked over at them, seeming to be a bit uncomfortable. "We need to give her blood and ....nurturing. It is the only way she'll be strong enough to be able to ride home."

Chuckling, Todd knew that look. He pointed down the aisle of the bus to where the back bedroom was. Ja' Callum picked her up carefully and strode down the aisle with her. Demitri grinned his thanks and followed them.

Dave chortled, "That is some weird family, man."

"No doubt. I wonder if we'll ever get the whole story?" He would love the whole low-down some day. It could make a good song.

Dave shrugged his shoulders. "Don't know, but let's pass the time playing PS3."

"Cool," Todd was still quietly laughing.

I heard Demitri saying my name over and over, pulling me out of the black pit I'd fallen into.

"Hey, there's my girl," I heard him say, as I tried hard to open my eyes.

"Hey, baby, how'd you get here?" I was surprised to see him over me and I was topless, as well. I could tell he'd just gotten done feeding me again.

"Todd called from your cell and got us here to you in time. Ja' Callum is here," Demitri nodded towards him, over to the other side.

"Hey, Ja' Callum. I bet I have you to thank for my back feeling so much better already." I didn't feel any tight burning all up and down my back anymore. Just a slight stiffness, like I had worked out my back muscles for too long.

"It was my duty and pleasure Meshallima," he smiled sweetly at me.

I saw the wounds on his wrist, and knew that he'd also fed me.

Demitri was lightly caressing my stomach up and down, making my skin tingle. He leaned over to kiss me and Ja' Callum made to move as if to leave. Demitri grabbed his wrist and pulled him back down where he had been on my other side.

I didn't say anything; this was between them.

"You need more than just blood this time, Catrina." And he moved his mouth to my nipple and stopped any protest I would have made, when every thought flew out of my head.

As he suckled, he took Ja' Callum's hand and put it to my other breast. Ja' Callum groaned and started to gently rub the tip, getting my nipple hardened for him to suck, as well. With the both of them licking and sucking at my breasts, I grew wet and hot for them.

Demitri stopped long enough to pull my boots and pants off. He then returned to my neck and kissed me all up and down the side of it, hitting all of my erogenous points. I was moaning long before Demitri's hand slid down to my wetness and eased his finger inside of me.

Ja' Callum's hands were busy as well, slowly and leisurely caressing where he could, like he wanted to savor each touch of my skin. Demitri obviously wanted to be the first to taste me, as when his mouth kept moving down my stomach, using his hands to gently move my legs apart, so he could ease his body between my thighs and kiss my pussy.

Long sure strokes of his tongue just made me hotter and wetter for him before he eased his tongue inside of me and made love to me with it. Ja' Callum made good use of his mouth on my breasts, gently tasting and sucking at each nipple in turn. Demitri had moved up to my clitoris and sucked it into his mouth, teasing it with his tongue.

The dual feel of their mouths on my body had me screaming my orgasm, with my body beading in sweat from the intensity.

Demitri gave me his pleased grin and moved up until he could slide himself inside of me. Ja' Callum moved back a bit, to give Demitri room to move within me. Demitri held me close, as he thrust into my body over and over again, whispering words of love into my ear, letting me know how much he'd missed me. Finally, he begged me to come for him again, while he moved inside of me. I climaxed, soaring with him, as he spilled himself inside me.

Panting hard, we grinned at each other and he kissed the tip of my nose as he moved off of me.

"Love her; she needs us both tonight," giving permission to Ja' Callum.

Smiling, he moved in between my legs and bent down to kiss me. "My love for yours; My body for yours; let us complete our bond for all time." He slid inside and I moaned at feeling him fill me. He moved gently and slowly, enjoying the feeling of being inside me after waiting so long. I felt his muscles bunch under my caress, as he held himself in check, waiting for my pleasure to hit first.

"Please, Meshallima, show me your bliss with me. Let your spirit fly with mine." He sped up his movements, and with power, he sent me over the edge with him. I felt us meld with our spirits as our bond completed itself. He shouted with joy as he felt my soul open to his and take him within myself. The air had a blue glow with white sparkles flashing all around us. Then, we came back to ourselves.

He was breathing heavily, as he held me tight against him. "Never, Meshallima, has loving been so right. May it always be so, between us."

"It will be." I smiled up at him, kissing him back.

They both had a lot of fun redressing me. Pink faced, I walked out of the room and saw Todd and the rest of his immediate group playing video games.

"Hey, she's alive," Dave announced.

Todd started chuckling.

"I would like to thank all of you for keeping our Meshallima safe for us. We are in your debt," Ja' Callum nodded to the group.

Dusty grinned, "Then you aren't going to kill us?"

Demitri looked and sounded affronted, "No, we don't kill innocents."

"Hey, it's cool man." Todd turned to his brother, saying, "See? Told you."

Dusty, ever curious, asked, "Are you guys ever going to tell us exactly what's up?"

Demitri looked at me and I stared back. "Well, we do owe them and they have already taken an oath to keep our secret." I glanced over to Ja' Callum with a question in my eyes.

He shrugged, "This is your world, Meshallima. Your decision."

"Whoa," Dave exclaimed. He'd obviously caught the subtext of that remark.

I sat down next to Todd and patted his leg. "You aren't going to believe us, but here goes."

Ja' Callum moved quickly, in removing my hand from Todd's knee. "Meshallima belongs to us," holding my hand in his big one.

I chuckled. So like my other three mates, I thought to myself.

He and his cousins will fit right in.

I, again, started to tell those that were in the bus with us the whole story. After seeing me drink their blood and the glowing blue lights when Ja' Callum had healed me, they were inclined to believe me.

We made them honorary Nightwolves that night, since they did pick up guns and were ready to protect me, putting their own lives at risk to do it. We exchanged numbers, so they could call us, if ever they ran across something out of the ordinary and if it looked like a situation we needed to deal with.

Since they were on the road so much, they would see a lot more then we could and be in a position to alert us to any trouble of the paranormal kind. They promised me backstage passes the next time they were playing near us and I thought that was pretty cool. I could see the wheels turning in Todd's mind about a new song.

I smiled to myself and wondered if he would make one about the Nightwolves now. Soon, our extended Nightwolves rock band took off into the night, and I rode behind Demitri to our home.

Things have more power if done in threes. So, the next two nights were spent not only healing, but tying the bonds between the other two Dai' Khans, my mates and myself.

Andre shared me with Ja' Monel and Antonio shared me with Ja' Kelo; even going to the lengths of flying us back to Japan and across the portal, so that we could make the three day mark. It made the bonds between us stronger and tighter.

Love really knows no limits and life can be full of surprises. The world could be full of hope and wishes can come true. The thing was with wishes was - be careful of what you wish for, because, sometimes you get more than what you asked for.

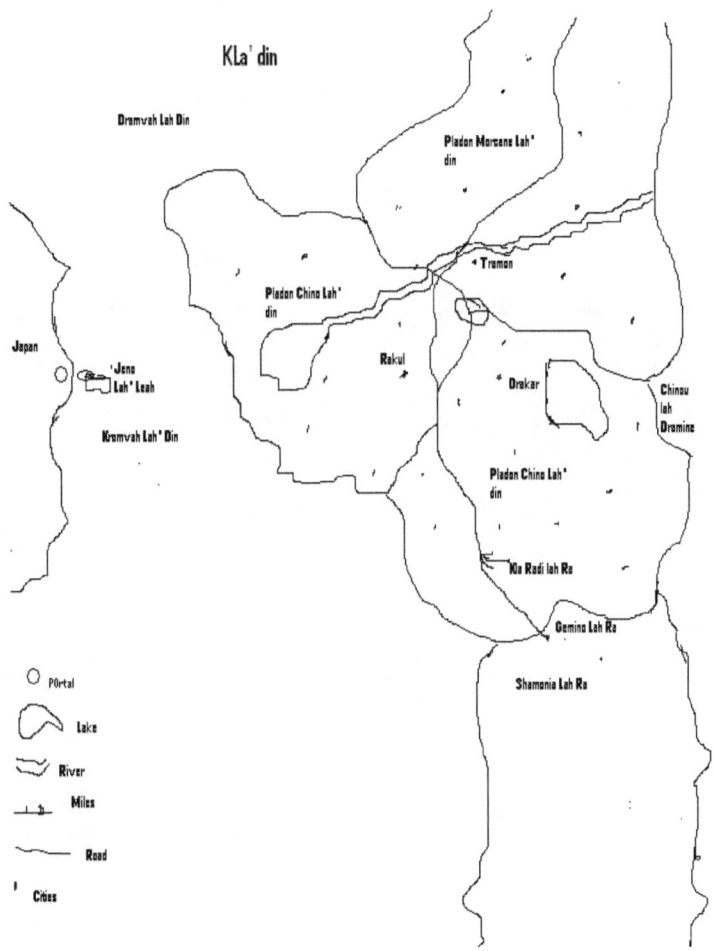

KLa' din

Dramvah Lah Din

Piadon Marcana Lah' din

Pladon China Lah' din

Traman

Japan

Jena Lah' Leah

Rakul

Drakar

Chinau lah Dramina

Kramvah Lah' Din

Pladon China Lah' din

Kla Radi lah Ra

Gemina Lah Ra

Shamania Lah Ra

○ POrtal

Lake

River

Miles

Road

Cities

Clarrissa Lee Moon

Bibliography

(The books that Rock was directed to read, to get himself and his team started in properly training in the arts.)

Scott Cunningham, "Earth Power"
Scott Cunningham, "Encyclopedia of Magical Herbs"
Scott Cunningham, "Living Wicca"
Denning and Phillips, "The Practical guide to Astral Projection"
David Krieg, "Modern Magick"
Ted Andrews, "How to See the Aura"
Ted Andrews, "How to Heal with Color"
Ted Andrews, "How to Speak with Animals"
Silver RavenWolf, "To Stir a Magick Cauldron"
Silver RavenWolf, "To Ride a Silver Broomstick"
Gaston and Yvette Frost, "Astral Travel"
Raven Grimassi, "Ways of The Strega"
Raven Grimassi, "Wicca Magick"
D.J. Conway, "Celtic Magic"
D.J. Conway, "Astral Love"
Charles Fielding, "The Practical Qabalah"
Sayed Idries Shah, "Oriental Magic"
Dael Walker, "The Crystal Healing Book"
Phyllis Krystal, "Cutting"
Lynn Pickett, "Mary Magdalene"

Published Now:
Nightwolves Coalition

Coming soon:
Nightwolves Siren's Song (TBA)
Nightwolves Dawn to Dusk (Semi Prequel) (TBA)

Nightwolves Battle for Kla' din (TBA)
Nightwolves Union on Trinidad (TBA)
Nightwolves Twilight- The Last Battle (TBA)
Nightwolves Companion - What was Real, Mundane and Magick (TBA)

Paranormal Erotica by Clarrissa Lee Moon
Celeste's Nites Novelettes First Trilogy (short stories-Claiming Celeste, Hunting Celeste and Sharing Celeste) Published Now

Celeste's Nites Novelettes Second Trilogy (Short Stories-Protecting Celeste, Contemplating Celeste and Loving Celeste)
   TBA
Celtic Circle + Pyramid 770

Connect with me at the Nightwolves Lair at:
http://clarrissamoon.blogspot.com/
http://clarrissaleemoonauthor.webs.com/

Author Bio

Clarrissa Moon would like to live like a tumbleweed, going from different states often, but her home base is in Tucson, Arizona. She's an avid reader and owner of more books and DVD's then any used book shop; she also enjoys Martial arts, swimming and raising pure bred Japanese Chins. She has written as a journalist for two E-magazines. She is also, the author of 'Celeste's Nites' Novelettes. She considers herself unique, unusual and unconquerable.

http://clarrissamoon.blogspot.com/

In Honor of our Planet's wild animals:

Please help these Organizations that save our Endangered Species such as the Wolves and Silverback gorillas.

http://www.defenders.org/

http://www.bigoakwolfsanctuary.org/

http://gorillafund.org/

Look for Nightwolves Siren's Song
Available July 1st 2011

www.ingramcontent.com/pod-product-compliance
Lightning Source LLC
Chambersburg PA
CBHW020914200626
46814CB00001BA/332